Be My Prince

JULIANNE MacLEAN

St. Martin's Paperbacks

This is a work of fiction. All of the characters, organizations, and events portrayed in this novel are either products of the author's imagination or are used fictitiously.

BE MY PRINCE

Copyright © 2012 by Julianne MacLean.
Excerpt from *Princess in Love* copyright © 2012 by Julianne MacLean.

For information address St. Martin's Press, 175 Fifth Avenue, New York, NY 10010.

ISBN: 978-0-312-55277-0

Printed in the United States of America

St. Martin's Paperbacks edition / May 2012

St. Martin's Paperbacks are published by St. Martin's Press, 175 Fifth Avenue, New York, NY 10010.

10 9 8 7 6 5 4 3 2 1

Also by
Julianne MacLean

Captured by the Highlander

Claimed by the Highlander

Seduced by the Highlander

Dedicated to Michelle Whitney.

Thank you for the beautiful cross-stitch that not only hangs in my dining room but has made an appearance in this story as well.

Prologue

From the London Ballroom Society Pages
May 12, 1814

ROYAL VISIT CONFIRMED

Attention one and all. The editors of this paper are delighted to report upon a most auspicious event. His Royal Highness Prince Randolph of Petersbourg will set sail for London in early June and reside at St. James's Palace for one full month.

The handsome heir to the Petersbourg throne will discuss with the regent a political and military alliance that may result in the amalgamation of our two great and powerful naval fleets.

This favorable military alliance is not, however, the fuel that has fired the ambitions of the great matriarchs of the ton—*for some say the true motive for the prince's visit to our fair country is to seek and marry his future queen.*

I will therefore pose the question to our devoted and reflective readers: Who among us will be the chosen one?

PART I
Secrets

Chapter One

Carlton House, London
June 16, 1814

There were certain days of her life when Lady Alexandra Monroe wished she had been born a man.

This, perhaps, was the most noteworthy of those days, for here she stood in the regent's overcrowded London reception room, glancing about at all the other impeccably dressed young ladies, each vying for a chance to meet a handsome foreign prince and win from him a proposal of marriage.

It was quite sickening, really, and she was half-tempted to walk out—for surely, she was above all this—but she could not do as she wished, for she had a duty to fulfill. She had been waiting a very long time for this moment.

"Upon my word, look at the jewels on that one," her stepmother, Lucille, said as she snapped open her ivory-handled fan. "How frightfully vulgar. Just behind me in the blue gown. Do you see?"

Alexandra leaned to the left to peer over her stepmother's shoulder. "Indeed I do."

She, too, opened her fan with a smooth flick of her wrist and took note of an older woman by the mantelpiece, studying her with boiling menace. The woman leaned closer to her own charge and whispered something that caused the girl to swing her head around and sneer.

Honestly. This whole evening was nothing short of a bloodthirsty, cutthroat competition. All the ladies were trussed up in their best gowns and jewels, eyeing each other with icy rancor.

If only we had swords and muskets, then the portrait would be complete.

She cheered herself, however, with the notion that it would all be over soon, for she had every intention of charging ahead in the next few minutes and tramping them all down into the dust. Every last one of them. Quickly and without mercy, because no one in this room deserved to sit on the throne of Petersbourg more than she did, and she was not going to surrender without a fight.

* * *

"They say he wishes to marry for love," the Duchess of Pembroke said as she picked up a glass of champagne from a passing footman. "It's quite charming, do you not agree?"

"I think it's a silly batch of nonsense," Lord Brimley replied. "The man is a future king. He must choose a bride who will serve some political purpose. He is responsible for the welfare of his kingdom. Such romantic notions are pure folly, and it arouses great doubt in me that we should even *desire* a naval alliance with Petersbourg, if this is what we will be subjected to in years to come. Kings must be sensible, and sometimes, when necessary, they must be ruthless. Romance and sentimentality have nothing to do with it."

"Well, that's the problem, right there," Baron Westley added. "The man wasn't born a royal. He has no understanding of such things. They say his grandfather was a blacksmith."

"*Hush,*" someone hissed, from outside their circle.

Alexandra glanced over her shoulder at the daring offender—another mother of a marriageable young daughter who, in all honesty, had very little hope of catching the eye of any prince, for she was wide-eyed and fretful, like a mouse trapped in a corner by cats.

"His father has been king for ten years," the duchess said, "and that will not change. The people of Petersbourg adore Prince Randolph. Make no mistake about it, Lord Westley, we are about to bow and curtsy to the future King of Petersbourg, and I, for one, find his sizable naval fleet immensely desirable."

The others, most of them red-nosed and brandy-faced, threw their heads back and laughed.

"I do not understand," the young lady whispered to Alexandra. "I thought Prince Randolph was a *real* prince."

Alexandra leaned close to whisper in her ear, "He is, but without royal blood. His father was general of the military and leader of the Petersbourg Revolution. Do you not know of it?"

The girl quickly shook her head.

Alexandra struggled not to let out a weary sigh and instead searched for a way to explain. "Twenty years ago, the true King of Petersbourg was deposed by the military. The general—Randolph's father—seized power for himself and formed a democratic government. He was such a compelling leader that they crowned him king a decade later. They now have a constitutional monarchy."

Eyes as wide as saucers, the young lady nodded, but Alexandra was quite certain she was more confused than ever.

"Do not fret," Alex whispered. "He's a real prince and very handsome. That's all you need to know."

"But what happened to the old king?" the young woman asked.

Alexandra bent close again, for she did not wish to be

overheard speaking of events that were best left in the past—at least while in the company of all these powerful Whigs and Tories. "He was exiled to Switzerland and died there. The official story is that it was a brief illness, but some say he was murdered by the New Regime. The queen, unfortunately, passed away a few months later after giving birth to a stillborn child."

"My word. How tragic."

"Indeed."

Just then the doors to the reception room flew open. A hush fell over the crowd, which split in two and formed a wide corridor down the center of the red carpet.

"His Royal Highness, Prince Randolph of Petersbourg!" the majordomo announced. "And Her Royal Highness, Princess Rose of Petersbourg!"

The guests curtsied and bowed as the young royals stepped into view and progressed elegantly down the long red carpet to meet the regent, who stood waiting to greet them at the opposite end. With keen eyes, Alexandra took in their appearance—the prince's especially.

It had been widely reported from many informed sources that he was a handsome man, and Alexandra had no choice but to concur. Only a fool would argue that point, and she was no fool.

Dressed in his impressive royal regalia—a scarlet double-breasted tunic with brass buttons and gold tassled epaulets upon his shoulders, and a jeweled saber sheathed in a shiny black casing—he was a striking figure to be sure. He was tall and dark. His hips were slim, his legs muscular beneath tight knee breeches, his eyes an uncommon shade of blue.

His sister, Rose, the young princess on his arm, was equally handsome in both appearance and stature. She carried herself with confidence and bright, smiling charm. Her hair, styled in the latest fashion, was a shiny golden hue, and she was blessed with a tiny upturned nose, deep green eyes set wide apart, high cheekbones, and full lips.

Alexandra fought to crush the resentment she felt upon seeing the princess's exquisite white gown and stunning headdress while she herself had been forced to wear rags up until a month ago.

The royal couple approached the regent, who welcomed them with a smile, and the crowd closed the corridor and resumed chattering.

"What do you think?" Lucille asked. "Is he everything you imagined him to be?"

"Handsome, at least."

Which would remove a certain degree of unpleasantness on the wedding night.

She turned to smile at the Countess of Risley, who approached with her son, a future earl. The gentleman bowed, and Alexandra curtsied.

For the next few moments they exchanged pleasantries and demonstrated the immaculate manners and wit expected of their rank and station. He was a future peer of the realm, she the beautiful eldest daughter of one of the highest-ranking dukes in England.

She, however, like the prince, was the subject of much interest and fascination, for she'd been concealed from society since the death of her father, the Duke of St. George, six years ago and, though impoverished since that day, had recently been dubbed the Hidden Jewel by her generous benefactor, who had come for her at last. According to many, she was the woman most likely to win this race for the prince's heart.

For that reason, handsome though he may be, she had no interest in this future Earl of Risley. All that mattered was the fulfillment of her duty. To that end she must be true.

As soon as the young man and his mother took their leave, Alex turned her attention back to the prince. By some stroke of luck their eyes met, and she permitted him to look at her for a long, lingering, and very satisfying moment before she gave him a cheeky smile—as if they were secret paramours—then averted her gaze and strolled off in the other direction.

Twenty minutes later, while she stood with her step-mother near a potted tree fern, fanning herself leisurely in the heat of the crowded reception room, His Royal Highness approached her with curious interest.

Just as she suspected he would.

* * *

The regent gestured toward Lucille with a white-gloved hand. "Prince Randolph, may I present to you Her Grace, the Dowager Duchess of St. George, and Lady Alexandra Monroe, eldest daughter of the late and greatly beloved Duke of St. George."

Alex and Lucille each performed a deep curtsy. "It is an honor, Your Royal Highness," Alex said as she rose to her full height.

The prince took in the details of her gown while she took note of the large emerald ring upon his right forefinger—one of the many crown jewels she knew he was entitled to as heir to the throne.

He smiled, displaying fine white teeth. "The honor is all mine."

Many eyes watched them, curious ears listened, and Alex felt more determined than ever to beguile him straightaway.

"I trust your journey was smooth and uneventful?" she said. "Not too arduous, I hope."

He inclined his head politely. "Not in the least. It was a smooth and pleasant voyage. You hail from Yorkshire, I understand? It's beautiful country there, from what I hear of it. I was also told that your father's palace is an architectural masterpiece, one of the greatest estates in England."

"How kind of you to say so," Alexandra replied. "Perhaps you might travel to the north while you are visiting our fair country and see it for yourself?"

He narrowed his gaze flirtatiously. "Is that an invitation, Lady Alexandra?"

She gave him a warm smile mixed with a hint of desire that went no deeper than the powder upon her skin. But he would not know that. He would see only what she wished him to see. "If it would please you, sir, you would be most welcome."

Though she had no right to extend such an invitation, for she'd not set foot in St. George Palace for seven years. Others resided there now.

The dinner gong rang out, and he bowed to her. "It has been a pleasure, Lady Alexandra. I trust you will honor me with a dance later this evening?"

"Most certainly."

He bowed to her stepmother as well. Then he turned to offer his arm to his sister, Rose, who waited a distance away.

Together with the regent, they led the guests into the large banqueting hall.

"If he only knew," Lucille sighed with casual triumph as she watched him disappear.

Alexandra exhaled sharply and fought to steady her breathing. "I am relieved he does not."

For if he or anyone else in the room knew that she was the true blood heir to the throne of Petersbourg, she might very well end up dead.

Chapter Two

After dinner was served and speeches were delivered, the guests filed into the ballroom, where the orchestra had already begun to play.

Alexandra glanced about at the lavishness of the room, adorned with sheets of white muslin draped across the walls. Fragrant batches of white roses were set out in every direction, while hundreds of flickering candles provided a brilliant illumination for the regent and his regal guests to mingle through the crowd.

Part of her wondered if this was all a dream and she would soon wake to find herself back in her tiny cottage in Wales with her sisters, arguing over how to scrape together enough coin to pay the butcher.

Her gaze fell upon a liveried footman. He was moving slowly through the crowd and carrying a tray of champagne. The crystal glasses sparkled almost blindingly in the candlelight, and for some reason it made her heart beat uncomfortably fast. A heavy shadow of apprehension settled over her, and she felt terribly displaced as memory transported her back to the cold chill of winter when there was not enough coal in the grate. And the dreadful fear that came at night when a sound outside the cottage woke her from her slumber. Who was it? Friend or assassin?

She had been forced to keep secrets from her sisters, who were not really her true sisters. Not by blood. She cared for them deeply and would do anything for them, but she had never been able to confide in them. She had been able to confide in no one.

A cheerful waltz began, and the prince escorted his sister onto the floor, set his hand at the small of her back, and began to dance around the room.

It was the first time Alexandra had ever seen a waltz performed, for it was very new.

How happy and carefree the young royals looked. Did they ever think of the ancient bloodline they had toppled? Of the family they'd destroyed? Did they ever feel guilty for the wealth and luxury that was now theirs to enjoy while the true king and queen lay rotting in their graves?

Alexandra shut her eyes for a moment to purge such thoughts from her head. This was not the time for morbid reflection. She must smile and be merry.

She turned to her stepmother. "I apologize, but I require a moment to myself." Lucille frowned at her, but she would not be daunted. "I must take some air and gather my wits about me, or I will never make it through this night."

Lucille tried to stop her, but Alexandra turned away and passed through the open French doors that led onto the stone terrace, which was dimly lit by two flaming torches, one at each corner.

She rushed to the balustrade and sucked in the cool, fresh scents of the night. A light breeze blew across her cheeks, but nothing seemed to ease the knot of anxiety in her belly. She had not imagined it would be this difficult. So much depended upon this one night and the performance she must deliver.

At last, the chaos in her mind began to subside. She sat down on the balustrade and looked up at the stars in the sky. "That's better. Breathe, Alex. He's only a prince, and not even a real one."

A throat cleared unexpectedly from somewhere in the shadows, and she quickly stood. "Who's there?"

No one replied, so she took an unflinching step away from the balustrade. "This is highly improper, whoever you are. Reveal yourself to me now, sir, if you please."

It was dark in the far corner of the terrace, but not so murky that she could not make out a pair of long booted legs swinging down from a horizontal position on a bench.

Evidently, a gentleman—completely unknown to her— had been using it to take a nap.

She should have darted inside straightaway, but something held her fixed to the flagstone upon which she stood. Perhaps it was the sight of the man's upper body coming into view as he leaned into the torchlight. Or maybe it was the finer details of his face—for it was a beautiful one, with strong, masculine lines and flawless proportions, capped off with an unfashionably wild mane of wavy black hair.

He held a silver flask in a leather-gloved hand, and Alexandra surmised that he could not possibly be a guest at the ball, for he wore a black riding coat and one did not wear muddy boots to a banquet.

His voice was deep and low and strangely exotic as he began to chuckle in the dark. "Not a real prince, you say. That's not very polite, Miss Whoever You Are. I ought to report you to someone."

"Like whom?" she countered, fearing suddenly that her identity and treasonous plot were about to be discovered.

"Like . . . Oh, I don't know. I can't think straight. All that music and laughter is clouding my brain. What about you? Why are you out here when all the other ladies are inside scrambling for a chance to dance with the distinguished guest of honor?" He raised the flask to his lips and took a long, slow swig as he awaited her reply.

"I don't need to *scramble* for anything," she said. "All I need to do is wait patiently, for His Royal Highness has already invited me to join him in a dance. I simply required a bit of air, that is all."

"Air?" The stranger stood and approached. He was an imposing figure to be sure, and she was strangely spellbound by each step he took across the terrace. "We have something in common, then."

The torchlight danced in a sudden gust of wind. "And what, pray tell, is that?"

He halted before her. "We both like to breathe."

Alexandra watched him for a moment, then narrowed her guarded, suspicious gaze. "You smell like a distillery. Are you drunk?"

"Only a little, but let us keep that to ourselves, shall we?"

As it happened, she was very good at keeping secrets. Nevertheless, there were rules of etiquette to consider. "If you are drunk, sir, then a royal ball is no place for you. You ought to go home. I have no doubt you'll feel much better in the morning."

He chuckled. "I doubt that."

She glanced down at his boots, then let her eyes wander with interest up the impressive length of his body. He was strong and well proportioned and possessed the firm, muscled thighs of an active horseman.

"I suppose I wouldn't know about such things," she replied. "I've never had more than a few sips of anything. Not that it's any business of yours." She gave a quick curtsy. "Good evening, sir."

She tried to leave, but he blocked her way.

"Don't go yet." He leaned close to speak softly in her ear—so close that she could smell the brandy on his breath and feel the moist heat of his words on her lobe. "I need someone to talk to, and I like the sound of your voice. It reminds me of . . ."

He paused, and her breath caught in her throat.

He was unbelievably attractive.

"Of what?" she cautiously asked.

Those dark eyebrows pulled together. "I'm afraid I can't quite recall, but I am certain it will come to me."

Alexandra felt a heated stirring of arousal in her core. She worked hard to quell it, however, for she was here on a mission, and this was not it.

Thankfully, he backed away and gave her some space to collect herself—though it was not easy to do.

"This is not appropriate," she said, realizing with more than a little displeasure that she was stalling, for this mysterious horseman from the shadows was an overwhelming distraction—and heaven knew she needed one. "We have not been properly introduced."

"You are quite correct," he replied. "Where is your chaperone? Shall I call for her?"

"No!" She looked inside, then spoke in a quieter tone. "Please do not."

For she knew exactly what her stepmother would say. Lucille would demand to know why Alex had taken her eyes off the prize.

The horseman glanced toward the open doors. "Fine, then. We'll take care of the introductions ourselves. I'll tell you my name if you promise to tell me yours."

"Agreed," she replied, "but then you must let me pass."

He bowed to indicate his agreement. "Very well then. And your name is . . . ?"

"I am Lady Alexandra Monroe, honored to make your acquaintance. Good evening, sir."

She curtsied again, made another attempt to return to the ballroom, but he stopped her again—this time with a gloved fingertip upon the bare skin of her upper arm, just below her puffed sleeve, which caused a flash of heat to rush from the point of contact straight down to her toes.

His blue eyes narrowed. "Lady Alexandra . . . Are you the daughter of the Duke of St. George?"

So he knew of her.

"Yes, but not the current duke. My father died six years ago."

Though my real father was put to death by greedy insurgents before I was born.

"Ah, yes." He lowered his hand to his side and removed his gloves. "I have heard of you. You are quite notorious in fact. They say you have been living in Wales with your sisters, and that you have been . . ." He paused. "Unjustly impoverished."

Alexandra detected a hint of compassion in his voice and had to work hard not to immerse herself in it. She had learned a long time ago that one cannot wallow in self-pity and stand strong and mighty at the same time. "Evidently I am quite the spectacle this evening," she said.

"Indeed. This is your first Season, correct?"

"Yes."

He leaned close and spoke in a husky voice that feathered across her skin. "At least the gentlemen at White's were right about one thing."

Alexandra quirked a brow. "And what was that?"

"They said you were the most beautiful woman in England, hidden away and guarded like a priceless jewel." He drew back and regarded her intently for a moment. "Beautiful to be certain, but why have they kept you hidden away, may I ask? You are the daughter of a duke. Why have you been residing in Wales? Why not at the estate where you were raised?"

She wet her lips and concealed the more pertinent question: *Why not with my real family, in the country where my ancestors had been born, and where they had ruled for centuries?*

"I am surprised you don't know the answer to that

question," she said, "when you seem to know everything else about me."

The blue of his eyes shone in the torchlight. "Indulge me."

"Why should I?"

Again he leaned close. "Because you want to."

An intoxicating shiver of arousal ran through her as she comprehended the truth in his words, spoken so provocatively.

She had never met a man quite like this one before. He was very confident and exuded a distinguishable air of sexuality. All the little hairs on the back of her neck were standing on end. Her heart was beating wildly with exhilaration, and she could not deny that she wanted to revel a little longer in this feeling of excitement.

"My father the duke died without an heir," she explained, "so the title passed to his estranged younger brother, who arrived at the palace with four daughters of his own, roughly the same age as my sisters and me. He took one look at us and decided that we would be an obstacle to the marriage prospects of his own daughters, so he sent us away, banished us to a place well beyond the reaches of polite society."

The gentleman frowned. "Because the four of you were prettier?"

"I suppose that would be an accurate conclusion to derive from the circumstances."

He inclined his head with curiosity. "Tell me more."

"His Grace provided us with a very meager allowance, barely enough to live on and certainly not enough to provide a dowry or even gowns for a proper Season. That is why we have never been to London."

He studied her with some concern. "That is most unfortunate. It sounds as if you and your sisters were greatly wronged."

Alexandra swallowed uneasily. There it was again—the compassion. But she had not told him of her situation to seek his pity and wished for a moment that she had not revealed any of it.

Another part of her, however—the deeper, more honest place that had been profoundly hurt and wounded by all the lies and betrayals from those she trusted most—cracked just a little, and she found herself opening up even further to this stranger before she realized what she was saying.

"Indeed, and here I am, dressed in a borrowed gown and jewels, hoping to win a proposal from a prince, along with dozens of other young women, each with her own story, I suppose." She paused and looked up at the stars, listened to the crickets chirping in the grass. "It's strange. There was once a time, long ago, when I imagined I would marry for love. I would have settled quite happily for a simple life with a mere clerk or merchant for a husband, but others insist that such a common existence is beneath me."

She dragged her gaze down from the stars and spoke in more practical terms. "More importantly, my stepmother controls our allowance from my uncle, so it seems I must choose a husband in a more mercenary fashion if I am to help my sisters improve their situation. I am the eldest. It falls upon me to lift us out of the trenches. That is the world we live in, I suppose. Duty must come first."

The gentleman said nothing. He seemed rather taken aback, and Alexandra wanted to sink through the ground. What had she been thinking? It was unseemly to reveal such intimate details to a complete stranger in the dark when she was duty bound to be inside seducing a prince—not only to secure a better future for herself and her sisters but also to avenge her true family and embrace her destiny as the rightful sovereign of Petersbourg.

"What happened to your real mother?" the man asked, proving himself to be a very bad influence, continuing to ask such personal questions.

My real mother died tragically in exile, shortly after giving birth to me.

"The duchess died when my youngest sister was born. Our father remarried my stepmother a year later, but there were no children from that union. I am sorry, but I must go. Good night, sir." She hurried past him to return to the ballroom.

"Wait." He turned to follow. "Will you dance with me?"

She glanced down at his muddy boots. "You're not dressed."

"I can be," he replied. "Just say yes and I will arrange a proper introduction."

Alexandra hesitated. "I am here to dance with the prince."

"So you've already said."

A spark of heady anticipation seeped into her blood as she imagined waltzing with this man . . . setting her gloved hand upon his shoulder . . . following his movements across the floor. . . .

"You're going to get in my way, aren't you?" she asked.

"In the way of your mercenary ambitions to marry a royal?" His eyes burned into hers. "I thought you said you'd settle for a clerk or a merchant if it meant you could marry for love."

Alexandra lifted her chin. "I did say that, but I must think of my sisters. As much as I would like to, I cannot settle for less, so please do not upset things."

He spread his arms wide as if to profess his innocence. "A dance. That is all I ask."

She should have taken more time to weigh the particulars, but an answer spilled past her lips before she could think it through. "Fine, but please say nothing to anyone about our conversation here. I've stayed too long as it is."

The instant she reentered the ballroom, her stepmother came quickly to her side.

"Where were you, Alexandra? The Duke of Wentworth has been engaging me in conversation. I could not break away, and I was consumed with worry that you had been abducted by some imperial spy in the garden."

"Oh, don't be silly. I only required a bit of fresh air. That is all."

But in all honesty she *had* been abducted—in the proverbial sense at least—by a handsome horseman in the shadows with a quiet, husky voice and a very dangerous sensual appeal.

It was not until that moment that she realized he had not told her his name.

She hoped he would not come to the ball.

It would not be wise to see him again.

Chapter Three

Later that evening, Alexandra watched the prince lead another young lady through a country dance. Dressed in his striking scarlet regalia, he was a stunningly handsome man. A skilled dancer as well. There was no denying it.

The lady upon his arm at present, moving with him through the steps of the dance, appeared to be foolish with awe and infatuation. Clearly, the prince knew it. He was aware of his effect on women. He had a way of teasing them with his eyes. Alexandra would be next, she supposed.

Though in her case there was no danger of becoming infatuated, for her wounds ran deep, as did her scorn for this seditious family of usurpers.

Alexandra watched him escort his partner off the floor and prepared herself for her own encounter with him. She would not giggle and gape at him as all the others had. She knew the part she had to play, and she would play it well.

"Who is that man?" her stepmother asked the Duchess of Pembroke, who had been very kind to them that night while many of the other women had given Alexandra cold looks of disdain for daring to enter the race on such short notice.

"That is Prince Nicholas, Randolph's younger brother," the duchess replied.

Like a force of magic, Alex's gaze swept to the door at

the precise instant the name passed the duchess's lips. It was *him*.

He was dressed differently now, no longer windblown from a ride in the park, no longer muddied or in need of a shave. He was now elegantly attired in a dark green silk coat, cream knee breeches, and polished shoes, and his hair was combed and styled fashionably.

Alex watched him approach his brother and speak in a manner that revealed an intimate familiarity between them.

The duchess leaned a little closer. "He is Randolph's private secretary as well, but I've heard rumors that he is a terrible royal."

"How do you mean?" Lucille asked.

"He has a reputation with the ladies. And no wonder. With that face, not to mention everything else from the neck down, a woman could mislay her virtue simply by *looking* at him."

Alexandra felt as if her breath had been cut off. The mysterious stranger from the terrace was Prince Randolph's younger brother and private secretary? And a scoundrel on top of it all?

Good God! She had stood in the shadows and carried on an intimate conversation with him. She had allowed him to flirt with her—surely that's what he was doing when he touched her arm and told her he liked the sound of her voice.

Had he been testing her or attempting to weed out the women who only wished to better their circumstances? A woman such as she, who believed Randolph was "not a real prince." A woman who had sisters to think of . . .

How could he not have revealed his status and position? What sort of bad character would entrap a lady in such a devious manner?

This was all a game to them, she realized. Nothing more. The very thought of it infuriated her.

At that precise moment, Randolph and Nicholas turned in her direction.

Randolph laid a hand on his brother's shoulder and squeezed, as if to thank him for something, and together they moved through the crowd.

"My word, they are coming this way," Lucille whispered. "And what a pair they make."

Lucille was referring of course to their extraordinary good looks. Together, side by side, they were a breathtaking force of elegance and charisma no other men in the room could rival.

Though she was anything but, Alex strove to maintain an appearance of calm as they came to stand before her. Prince Randolph was the first to speak.

"Duchess." He bowed to the Duchess of Pembroke, then addressed Lucille. "Your Grace, if you would permit me to formally present my brother, Nicholas."

There it was. The proper introduction, as promised.

Alex's stepmother curtsied and turned to the other royal. "We are delighted to make your acquaintance, Your Royal Highness. This is my eldest stepdaughter, Lady Alexandra Monroe."

He bowed to her. "It is an honor, my lady."

Alexandra curtsied as well and felt a spark of furious heat flare through her. What was he playing at? Had the brothers already discussed and deciphered every word she had spoken on the terrace? Had Nicholas repeated everything?

The orchestra began a new piece, and Randolph held out a white-gloved hand. "If I do recall, Lady Alexandra, you were kind enough to promise me a dance. Shall we proceed to the floor?"

Maintaining a cool expression of confidence, she slipped her gloved hand into his. "Indeed we shall."

Without a single glance back at his brother, she brushed

past him and focused all her attention on the man who held the key to her future. The one who would wear the crown.

* * *

"Nicholas tells me this is your first London Season," the prince said as they moved through the steps of a country dance.

"That is correct, and it has been a marvelous experience thus far. Tonight especially."

He studied her with knowing eyes. "How so? Is it the food that has met with your approval? Or the music? The adornments perhaps."

She took three steps toward him, keeping her eyes trained intensely on his the entire time. "It is the company that has held me captivated, sir, for I have lived too long away from society."

"Ah. You are enjoying the conversation and the pleasure of meeting new people."

"Yes, you have captured it exactly. New people."

They performed a number of steps to and fro as they moved through the dance.

"Anyone in particular?"

He watched her steadily. His eyes were no longer playful but serious.

"Why *you*, of course," she flirtatiously replied.

The prince took three steps back. "What a perfect answer. You flatter me."

She studied his expression and realized that she had gone too far. This man had women throwing themselves at him from all angles, all night long, and here she was, doing the very same thing and not feeling the slightest bit genuine about it.

They moved around each other, and she took a moment

to reorganize her line of attack, for she could not blunder this, or retreat in failure.

"I apologize," she finally said. "That is what I was instructed to say to you. You must find this very difficult. There are many women here, behaving just so, competing for your attention."

He took her hand and supported her in a turn. "Yes, there are, but apparently none quite as honest as you. They are either falling over themselves with giddiness or blatantly seducing me with their eyes. No one has yet confessed to having been *told* what to say."

"Would you prefer that I seduce you?"

"No. I would prefer that you be yourself."

"Honesty is always best," she said.

"My sentiments exactly."

They began another set of steps that repeated the opening.

"Since we are being honest . . . ," he said with a curious look in his eye, "tell me something."

"Anything."

He supported her through a turn. "What did you think of my brother, Nicholas? Now, now, let there be no secrets between us. He mentioned he met you on the terrace earlier and neglected to reveal his identity, which doesn't surprise me in the least."

Alexandra chose her words carefully. "That is true. I confess I felt somewhat . . . *deceived* just now when I saw him at your side."

The prince spoke candidly. "Do not fault him, Lady Alexandra. He is my most trusted ally. And it wasn't his intention to deceive you. He was only acting on my behalf, attempting to learn something about one of the ladies with whom I was to dance this evening."

"Are you implying it was a test?"

He chuckled. "I suppose you could call it that."

She took his hand and allowed him to lead her through another turn. "Did I pass?"

"With flying colors."

Alexandra shot him a flirtatious glance. "I can't imagine why."

He smiled. "I'd wager it was your honesty."

Though it was meant as a compliment, it cut her to the quick, for *honest* was the very last thing she was tonight.

She resolved, however, to feel no shame. Her true family had had far worse things done to them by others. It was her turn now to begin her own private revolution, and in doing so she would take no prisoners.

The dance came to an end, and the prince escorted her back to her stepmother. "Thank you," he said to Lucille, "for the honor of the young lady's company. Good evening to you all."

With that, he turned and whispered something to his brother, then strode across the room to escort another partner onto the floor.

Evidently, Alex was a mere spark in a very bright line of would-be queens, which knocked her confidence down a notch.

Then suddenly that quiet, husky voice spoke close in her ear. "You look flushed, my lady," Prince Nicholas said. "Is there anything I can do to relieve your distress? A glass of champagne perhaps?"

A flash of heat flared in her blood while Lucille gestured frantically behind his back to remind Alex that this incredibly desirable man was the future king's key advisor in his pursuit of a wife, and she could not afford to refuse.

* * *

He is not the one I want, she reminded herself over and over as she crossed the crowded ballroom on Prince Nicholas's arm. It did little good, however, for no amount of rationalizing seemed powerful enough to douse the flames of agitation in her blood, kindled by the mere act of touching him.

Everything about him—his looks, his voice, the intensity of his presence—ignited a full-blown battle between her frustration with him and her true purpose here.

As soon as they arrived at the dessert table, he reached for a small plate. "What may I offer you, my lady? There is much to choose from. Cherries, nuts, apples, cream . . ."

Alex cleared her throat. "A glass of punch please."

He moved to pick up two crystal glasses from a shiny silver tray and handed her one.

"You do realize," he said, watching her carefully as she sipped, "that I am Randolph's closest advisor. His first line of defense, if you will. His protector in all ways. He trusts me with every detail of his life."

"What is your point, sir?"

His striking blue eyes narrowed. "I only wish to inform you that if you desire access to the future king, you will have to work very hard to win my favor."

"And how should I accomplish that?"

"I'm sure you'll think of something."

Struggling not to appear scandalized by his suggestive tone of voice, Alex asked, "Is it true then? Is he here to seek a wife? Why not someone from his own country?"

Nicholas plucked a grape from the fruit bowl and popped it into his mouth. "He attempted such a thing in the past but was ultimately disappointed. As you can see, he has a way with women. His rank and political power attract them like moths to a flame. There was a time he was easily swayed by romanticism and believed in it with all his heart, but unfortunately, he chose the wrong woman."

She considered how best to reply. "I did hear something about that. He was engaged once before, was he not?"

"Correct. For a full year he believed himself to be in love, but a week before the wedding he found his future bride in the arms of another man. It turned out she was in love with him, but her parents pushed her to marry Randolph regardless, in order to better their own prospects. It was nothing but a game of power to them, and she was a pawn in many ways. Not that it mattered. Randolph was deceived, and he has not yet recovered from it. I am not certain he ever *will* recover."

She turned her attention to Randolph, who was waltzing around the room. In her eyes, he looked quite adequately recovered, but she was not about to say so.

"Then why does he wish to wed again so soon?"

"He requires an heir. Or rather, the country requires one. There are still far too many Royalists in Petersbourg who long for that sort of tradition."

It had occurred to her more than once to simply reveal herself to Randolph and suggest a political marriage to restore her family's bloodline to the throne—alongside of his—but her benefactor had warned against it, for Randolph wanted to marry for love.

Besides, her safety could not be assured. Not while Randolph's father still lived. King Frederick was the one who had led the revolution against her family's rule in the first place. Her identity must, at all costs, remain secret until her place on the throne was secure.

Nicholas picked up a glass of champagne from a passing footman and downed it in a single gulp.

"I thought the people of Petersbourg adored the new royal family," she said cynically, then spoke under her breath: "They must have, or they wouldn't have stuck a crown on the head of a soldier."

Nicholas caught her remark and chuckled. "Randolph was right. You *are* daring, aren't you?"

Oh, heaven help her. She really needed to learn how

to control her tongue. Yet she found it a challenge in this man's presence. "My apologies. I spoke out of turn."

"Not at all. I find it refreshing, as does Randolph. You see, we meet so many young women who fumble to say all the right things. They are like shallow pools of rainwater that will disappear when the sun comes out. You, however, seem to have some depth and spirit. At least that's what Randolph thinks after a very brief first impression. Which was why he asked me to escort you to the dessert table."

"To interrogate me further?" she demanded.

"Yes. Later, he will ask my opinion of you."

"And what will you tell him?"

"I'm not sure. I have not yet made up my mind."

She breathed deeply. "Will you interrogate many other women this evening?"

Alex resisted the urge to look up at him, for she was experiencing a heated flash of displeasure at the idea of him escorting other ladies to the dessert table and doing what he must to draw them out of their shells. Would he whisper close in their ears and make them think they stood a chance with his brother if they behaved a certain way?

Not that it mattered. It did not. She would not let it. He could do whatever he damn well pleased with those other women.

"Only a few," he replied. "Though I haven't spotted any other potential queens yet. None have caught Randolph's eye as you have."

She should have felt triumphant in that moment but felt something else entirely. She wasn't quite sure what it was, but it resembled anger, which made no sense.

Perhaps it was frustration. She felt rather powerless at the moment and did not like the sensation. "I am flattered, sir." And her heart was thrashing about like a wild thing in her chest. "I must admit, however, that I was concerned after our encounter on the terrace. I feared you might strike me off his list."

"Why?"

"Because I told you about my unfortunate circumstances—that I was here to improve upon them, which is exactly what the prince does not want in a wife. He desires true love, is that not correct?"

Nicholas faced her squarely. "Isn't that what you want, too, Lady Alexandra?"

His voice was soft and intimate, and his eyes burned into hers.

"Perhaps," she replied, "but there were other things I revealed to you as well—things I would not have said if I had known you were Randolph's guardian. Now I am completely at your mercy. I hope you will not use any of that against me, as you could easily do."

His blue eyes narrowed. "I suppose I do have you at a disadvantage, but neither you, nor I, can do anything about it now, so we must make the best of it."

"And how do you propose we do that?"

He held out a gloved hand. "Prove that your word can be trusted by honoring me with a dance, as you promised on the terrace."

Alexandra hesitated briefly, then set down her glass, for she had no choice in the matter. If she wanted access to the future King of Petersbourg, she was going to have to dance with the devil.

And his name was Prince Nicholas.

Chapter Four

On the way home from the ball, Lucille questioned Alexandra tirelessly. "Did Prince Nicholas indicate when his brother might be available for another social engagement? Will we be forced to wait until the ball at Almack's, or do you think he was taken with you? Is there any chance he might pay a call?"

"I don't know, Mama."

"I've heard he will be visiting the park. If we knew exactly when, we could arrange to be there at the same time, driving or strolling. What is his schedule?"

"I don't know that either."

"You don't know? Why did you not think to ask? Mr. Carmichael has been very generous in supporting us for the Season. He has provided us with this fine coach and a prestigious address, and a stunning set of gowns for you, not to mention wielding his influence to obtain our subscriptions to Almack's. We cannot disappoint him. He is a very powerful man."

"Not as powerful as Prince Randolph or his father," Alexandra reminded her, "who is the current reigning monarch of Petersbourg. Mr. Carmichael has not held a position of power there for many years. For the duration of my life, to be exact. We are nowhere yet."

Lucille gathered her cloak more snugly around her

shoulders. "Nevertheless, he has been most patient, biding his time until you came of age. You should be grateful to him. You *were* a few days ago, but tonight you seem hesitant. Have you lost your courage?"

Alexandra regarded her stepmother steadily in the dim lamplight inside the coach. "No. I am weary, that is all."

They were both quiet while the coach wheels clattered over the cobblestones.

"Do you think you made a satisfactory impression?" Lucille asked.

"Upon whom?" Alexandra replied.

"Upon the future king, of course! Who else matters?"

Alexandra slowly removed her gloves. "I believe you are forgetting his brother, Nicholas, who told me quite plainly that anyone who desires access to Randolph must gain *his* approval first. So I must insist that you leave it to *me* to secure my throne. Do not tell me how to behave or how to strategize, and certainly do not make me feel beholden to Mr. Carmichael, for he has his own ambitions."

Lucille regarded Alex with some concern. "That may be true, but we cannot secure the throne without his support. He has maintained many connections with the old monarchists, and you may discover you require their help when you arrive. If King Frederick discovers who you are, he may not permit Randolph to marry you and we may have to seek an alternate route to the throne."

Alexandra shook her head. "The king will not discover the truth. Not until after I provide an heir."

"You seem very confident about winning a proposal from Randolph," Lucille said. "I am impressed."

Alexandra watched the dark city pass by outside the window. "I am confident because I learned a great deal about him tonight, thanks to Nicholas. I know what he needs."

"And what is that?"

She leaned back in the seat. "Randolph is looking for true love. Something rather rare for a man in his position. I am quite sure I can satisfy his needs."

Lucille scoffed. "Well. Do not be surprised if every other young lady in London is declaring the very same thing tonight while driving home from the ball."

"But they don't know what I know," Alexandra insisted. "And besides, I have Nicholas in my corner."

"You are certain?"

"Yes," she replied, but was she really? Based on her body's response to him earlier in the evening, veering around him could prove to be a very tricky maneuver. Nevertheless, she maintained an air of confidence. "I saw it in his eyes tonight. I believe I can win his full endorsement."

Alexandra returned her attention to the view outside the window and remembered those first moments on the terrace when he approached her from the shadows. She recalled how her body had flared with heat when he touched her.

"You will need to be very cunning if you intend to manipulate that man," Lucille said. "From what I hear, he has considerable experience with a certain type of woman, and he may not be easily manipulated."

Alexandra looked down at her hands on her lap and felt a renewed rush of heat in her belly. "Don't worry, Mama. I will waste no time in establishing how best to influence him."

* * *

The following day, Alexandra's eyes lifted at the sound of a coach pulling up in front of the house. Rising from her chair in the drawing room, she crossed to the window and looked down at the street below.

"Who is it?" Lucille asked with an anxious little gasp. "Anyone of consequence?"

Since their noteworthy entrance into London society, they'd had no shortage of afternoon callers and invitations, mostly due to the fact that Mr. Carmichael had spread news far and wide about Alexandra's unparalleled beauty and tragic circumstances. She had become somewhat of a novelty.

"I cannot make anyone out," she replied, "but it is an impressive vehicle with four horses and a postilion. Wait . . . someone is getting out. . . ."

Would it be Prince Randolph?

Her heart began to beat wildly in her chest.

No, it was Nicholas.

He stepped out of the coach and looked up at the front of the house.

"It is only the brother," she casually mentioned, hiding the fact that her body was reeling with alarm, for she had lain awake all night thinking about Nicholas's flirtatious manner and impossible good looks and had grown increasingly worried about the general impediment of his position as his brother's gatekeeper. In the coach, she had assured her stepmother that she knew exactly how to handle him, but suddenly she was not the least bit sure of it.

"Is Randolph with him?" Lucille asked, leaping from her chair and practically tripping over the tea table in order to reach the window.

"No, I do not believe so," Alexandra replied. "He appears to be alone. Perhaps he is conveying a message."

She truly hoped he was, and that he would deliver it without coming inside.

They heard the door open and close below. He did not return to his coach. The butler must have let him in.

Lucille tapped Alex on the shoulder. "Quickly now, go

back to your seat and try to look surprised when he is announced!"

They returned to their chairs and waited while the clock ticked sternly on the mantelpiece.

A moment later, footsteps tapped up the stairs and the butler announced their gentleman caller. With unshakable confidence, the prince strode into the room and bowed.

Alexandra and Lucille greeted him with polite courtesies.

"Your Royal Highness, what a pleasure to see you again," Lucille said. "Please . . . sit down, and welcome. May I pour you some tea?"

With ragged nerves, Alexandra watched him take a seat. Today he wore a dark blue double-breasted tailcoat and fawn breeches with shiny black boots. The collar points of his clean white shirt stood high against his cheeks, and his cravat was tied immaculately at his throat. He looked undeniably handsome, and she had to force herself to look away to avoid staring, for her heart was suddenly racing like a mad monster in her chest, and she despised herself for reacting this way to him.

"Thank you, Your Grace," he replied as he chose a spot on the sofa directly across from Alexandra. Lucille offered him tea and a selection of sweetbreads.

The usual light drawing room conversation ensued while Nicholas spoke to them about his impressions of London since his arrival and described the crossing from Petersbourg, which he declared a smooth and pleasant journey.

He was the epitome of politeness and gentlemanly behavior, and Alexandra had to remind herself a number of times that he was here to protect Randolph from ambitious social climbers like herself. She realized she must therefore straddle a fine line between her obvious attraction to this infuriating younger brother and her plans to marry the future King of Petersbourg.

"Will you and Prince Randolph attend the theater while you are visiting London?" Lucille asked, and he revealed their plans to attend a play at Covent Garden the following Tuesday.

Alex sipped her tea and wondered how easy it would be for Mr. Carmichael to obtain tickets to that performance.

"I hope you will not deem it too forward of me," Nicholas said as he set his cup and saucer down on the table, "if I extend an invitation to you both to dine with us at St. James's Palace this evening. Randolph is aware it is brief notice, but he would welcome your attendance if you are not previously engaged. If you do have other plans, however, he has instructed me to extend the invitation to tomorrow evening, or the evening after that."

Lucille nodded enthusiastically. "We would be most honored to join you this evening."

He then turned his charming gaze toward Alexandra, and her body flushed with heat. While her heart beat traitorously in her breast, she realized that securing a proposal from the future king was going to be much more complicated than she had initially imagined, for each time she locked eyes with this man she seemed to forget all about her vengeance, which had been a strong driving force in her life in recent months.

"Randolph will be most pleased." He rose to his feet. "A coach will be sent to fetch you at eight o'clock. Following dinner, an informal musicale has been arranged. Do you enjoy Mozart, Lady Alexandra?"

She nearly stumbled at the direct question but quickly gathered her aplomb. "Very much so."

"Excellent. Then I will look forward to seeing you both later this evening." With that, he walked out of the drawing room.

"There, you see?" Lucille said. "Randolph *was* taken with you!"

Alexandra crossed to the window and watched Nicholas leave the house and return to his coach.

"That remains to be seen," she replied, "for I am curious to know how many *other* ladies were invited to dine at the palace this evening. I expect Prince Nicholas will make a few more calls before the hour is out."

She sat back down and fought hard to ignore the butterflies that continued to flutter in her belly for a full hour after he left.

*   *   *

There were exactly five young ladies, including Alexandra, invited to dine at St. James's Palace that evening, and they were all unique in some way.

The girl by the fireplace was petite but large breasted. The one seated on the sofa was tall, with a dark complexion—an odd quality in an Englishwoman.

The two girls at the window both appeared rather flighty, for they giggled constantly to each other.

As for herself . . . well, she was not like any of them.

Prince Randolph entered the drawing room shortly after Alex and her stepmother arrived. She and all the other ladies performed deep curtsies.

This evening, His Royal Highness wore conventional dinner attire—fawn breeches with ivory stockings and buckled shoes, a chocolate brown coat with tails, and a fine silk cravat.

He bowed exuberantly in return and flashed a charismatic smile that sent the two girls by the window into another fit of foolish giggling.

"Please," Lucille whispered under her breath, "will someone stuff a couple of pork pies down their throats and put the rest of us out of our misery?"

Alex nudged her. "Behave yourself, Mama. He is coming this way."

She curtsied again as Randolph reached them. "Your Royal Highness."

Lifting her eyes, she smiled flirtatiously while on the inside her stomach churned with dread at the notion of fawning over this man whose family was responsible for her own father's death. If only she could win back the crown with an army of rebels wielding swords and muskets, instead of being forced to lower herself in this way. It would be so much more satisfying to use military force as King Frederick had done twenty years ago. It would at least spare her the indignity of competing with half the female population of Britain to win the heart of a man for whom she felt nothing but disdain.

"What a pleasure to see you both here this evening," the prince said. "I am pleased you could attend."

She remembered how his brother had extended the invitation to the following two nights if she and Lucille had not been available and suspected there would be five more "unique" young ladies joining the prince for supper and entertainments tomorrow night as well.

And the night after that.

She had her work cut out for her.

"We were most pleased to accept," she replied, sweeping those thoughts aside and struggling to focus instead on how handsome he was. It was a fact she could not deny.

They chatted about light matters for a few minutes. The prince mentioned his intention to attend the play at Covent Garden the following week; then his sister, Princess Rose, was announced. Again, everyone in the room bowed or curtsied as she entered wearing an attractive dinner gown of blue and silver crepe.

Randolph immediately invited Rose to join them.

"My dear sister," he said, "allow me to present Her Grace, the Dowager Duchess of St. George, and her lovely stepdaughter, Lady Alexandra."

A spark of recognition lit in the princess's eyes, and she smiled warmly.

"What a pleasure to meet you both," she said. "Randolph has told me so much about you, Lady Alexandra. It appears you made quite an impression on him last night."

Alexandra took a deep breath and let it out. Perhaps it would not be so difficult after all. Perhaps she *could* seduce him quickly and efficiently. Then be done with it.

"You are most kind to say so, Your Royal Highness," she replied.

Randolph gestured with a hand. "It appears my sister cannot keep a secret. What is a prince to do, I ask you, when his heart is exposed to the world?"

Everyone laughed graciously; then Randolph turned his eyes away. "If you will permit me to leave you both in the capable hands of my sister," he said, seeming suddenly distracted, "I shall go and greet the others."

His departure poured a bucket of cold water on Alexandra's confidence, and she made the mistake of letting out a disappointed sigh.

"Oh, don't mind him," Rose said. "He is only doing his duty as a proper host."

"No need to explain," Alexandra replied. "I understand. He is an excellent ambassador for your country. You must be very proud."

"Yes, very proud indeed," Lucille repeated.

"I am," Rose said. "I count my blessings every day, for he is the most wonderful brother in the world. And what about your family, Lady Alexandra? I understand you have three sisters. Are they much younger than you?"

"They range in age from thirteen to seventeen," Alex replied, "and they are lovely girls, each one."

"So they are not yet out in society," Rose noted.

"Not yet."

Rose smiled and turned her pretty green eyes to Lucille. "Their time will come soon enough, and I am sure they will enjoy themselves immensely—with their eldest sister to lead the way."

"Indeed," Lucille said.

Alexandra nodded. "You are very kind. Now please tell us about your homeland. Is it very different from England?"

"Not different at all," she replied. "Society is much the same, as is the countryside, and our constitutional monarchy was modeled after your own. I daresay you would feel quite comfortable there. Almost as if it were your *own* homeland."

Alexandra could have spit right there on the floor. Instead, she took a moment to steady her nerves and smiled warmly at Rose. "I truly hope I will see it one day."

They chatted for a brief while longer about Petersbourg's architecture and some of its talented artists and writers, but were interrupted by the entrance of another guest who entered the drawing room rather discreetly, as if hoping not to be noticed. It was of course none other than Randolph's wayward brother Nicholas.

His and Alex's eyes locked instantly, and a spark of fire exploded in her belly as he set out on a direct and determined path toward her.

He did not stop to speak to anyone else.

It was as if no others existed in the room but the two of them.

Bracing herself hard and fast against the oncoming storm of his charisma, she smiled politely and flicked open her fan.

Chapter Five

"Good evening, ladies." Nicholas gave a small bow.

"Good evening," they all replied.

He turned to Lucille and wasted no time at all in requesting a private moment with Alexandra. "May I have your permission, madam, to escort your stepdaughter to the gallery?"

Alex recognized the look of shock in Lucille's eyes—for it was a bold request that pushed the limits of proper decorum.

For a few tense seconds she appeared to be at a loss for words, then recovered her composure and said, "I am sure Alexandra would be delighted to view the palace collection."

Chivalrously he offered his arm. Alex could do nothing but accept his invitation and curse her body's treacherous response to him.

This will pass, she told herself as they exited the room and moved farther and farther away from the company of others. *It is nothing but a physical attraction, and if you carry on as planned, he may prove useful. Stay focused. Do not become distracted.*

It was not so easy to stay true to her objectives, however, when her heart was fluttering like something with wings. Could he feel it? Did he know?

"Did the palace coach arrive at the correct time to fetch you?" he asked, not long after they left the drawing room.

"Yes, thank you," she replied. "The footman knocked upon our door at eight o'clock precisely."

She didn't know what else to say after that. She was afraid to engage him in conversation. She did not wish to intermingle.

Thankfully, he did not ask any more questions on the way to the gallery, but then he led her inside and took her straight to a spectacular framed canvas of a nude woman, sleeping innocently while Jupiter uncovered her from beneath a gossamer white sheet.

"Are you familiar with Jean-Antoine Watteau?" he asked.

Alex swallowed over her shock. In the flickering light from the candles in the overhead chandelier, the painting appeared erotic, like something out of a wicked dream. She stared at it for a sweltering moment.

"Yes. It is quite breathtaking."

That was an understatement. Watteau was known for painting a world of charming goddesses playing at love. She felt rather exposed all of a sudden and feared that Prince Nicholas knew all her deepest secrets and had brought her here in order to drag her into the open.

"There is something very intriguing about you," he softly said as he watched her profile in the candlelight. "In fact, I do not believe there is a single work of art in this room that can compare to your beauty."

Alex took an instinctive step back. "You flatter me, sir."

"It is not flattery. It is the truth, and I cannot keep it to myself. I confess I am taken with you, Alexandra, which may create a problem."

Oh, God, no. . . .

"Why?"

"Because I am duty bound to help my brother choose a wife and a future queen, and you are the most impressive prospect by far."

Her heart began to pummel her rib cage, for this was not what she wanted, yet it thrilled her at the same time.

He felt as she did. There was an undeniable spark of attraction between them, a potent connection that begged to be explored.

But she, too, had a duty to perform and could not possibly throw away her God-given destiny for something as reckless and superficial as her own physical passions, no matter now powerful they may be.

"You mustn't say such things, sir. You know my mind. I have been very clear about my intentions. You know why I am here."

"Because you want to marry a future king."

"Yes. Is this another test?"

He shook his head. "No. I asked you here to speak to you in private because you have been a constant presence in my thoughts since the first moment we met and I believe you are cheating yourself."

This was not what she had expected, and it was becoming more and more difficult to breathe. Her strong physical attraction to this man was like some sort of trap from which she could not escape.

"You surprised me at Carlton House," he continued. "Even tonight, I did not intend to steal you away from my brother, but as soon as I saw you, I found myself deeply involved, and I wanted to be the man you were pursuing."

She shook her head. "Please do not speak so."

Before she knew what was happening, he moved closer and cradled her chin in his hand.

His touch was warm. His eyes were dark and earnest. She couldn't seem to feel her toes.

"I understand that I am not the one you came for," he

said. "But I wish to court you, Lady Alexandra. With your permission, I will speak to your stepmother."

A fierce resistance rose up within her. "No, you mustn't do that."

"Why? Do not tell me you feel nothing for me. I know you do. Something wonderful occurred between us on that terrace. I saw it in your eyes then, as I see it now."

Heaven help her, she could not possibly deliver a truthful answer, so she took a moment to sharpen her wits, tramp down on her emotions, and redirect the conversation.

"It must be difficult in your position," she cautiously said, "to always walk in your brother's shadow."

He said nothing for a moment, then pinched the bridge of his nose. "Yes, it is always a challenge to play a role, no matter what that role is." His eyes lifted. "You are playing one this evening as well, are you not?"

She backed away from him, flicked open her fan, and waved it in front of her face while she struggled to fight off a powerful wave of apprehension.

She felt very transparent in front of him, and that was not safe.

"What are you suggesting, sir?"

Had he discovered something?

He moved closer again, and her thoughts grew frantic.

"I merely suggest that in order to do your duty you will *pretend* to be in love with my brother, and you will make yourself available to him if he should consider you worthy of his crown. You are striving to be what he wants, to captivate him and attract him so that he will propose."

She snapped her fan closed and lowered it to her side. "Do you treat all the ladies like this?"

He frowned. "What do you mean?"

"I know of your reputation—that you have a talent for seduction and you think nothing of stealing and breaking innocent female hearts. As I said before, I cannot help but wonder if this is another test. Are you attempting to seduce me in order to discover if I am prone to infidelity?"

He moved closer and crowded her up against the wall. "No," he said with a chuckle, as if he found her conjectures amusing. "That is not why I am seducing you."

"So you admit it, then?"

"Of course I admit it," he replied with another chuckle. "I thought I was quite clear on the matter."

She forced herself to remain steady on her feet. "Yes, I believe you were, but permit me to repeat myself, sir. I did not come to St. James's Palace this evening for *you*. I came for Randolph, so whatever you think exists between us does *not* exist. It is on your side only, not mine, which is why I am going to forget about this conversation entirely. It never happened. Do you understand?" She brushed past him. "I wish to return to the drawing room now."

She turned and walked away from him.

A shiver of nervous tension coursed up and down her spine as she felt him follow. Just the *idea* of his nearness was riveting to her in every way.

Oh, God, this was going to be torture.

Chapter Six

A few days later, Alexandra watched from her window as Prince Nicholas again stepped out of his coach, exactly as he had done before when he came to invite them to St. James's.

He was persistent. She would give him that.

Lucille joined her at the window. "Is someone here?"

"Yes, Prince Nicholas has come to call. Does he not have anything better to do?"

And why does Randolph not come himself? Why must he send his handsome younger brother?

Lucille cheerfully smoothed out her skirt and pinched her cheeks to summon some color. "I suspect he has come to deliver another invitation. This is most excellent. It proves you have passed all the tests so far."

"We shall see." Alexandra sat down by the unlit fireplace and picked up her embroidery. A few minutes later, the butler announced Nicholas's arrival.

"Welcome," Lucille said.

She offered him tea, but he remained standing.

"Good afternoon, ladies. Permit me to extend an invitation to you both to join me in the royal coach this afternoon for a leisurely drive to Hyde Park. My brother is there now, enjoying an afternoon stroll, and with high hopes he sent me to fetch you."

Lucille blushed the color of a ripe red apple. "Why, of course we would be delighted to join you!"

"But we couldn't possibly intrude upon your kindness," Alex quickly added. "We shall take our own coach, though it is very generous of you to offer."

His blue eyes narrowed with roguish determination. "I assure you, my lady, it is no intrusion. In fact, Randolph would be most disappointed if you refused."

Alexandra did not wish to argue in front of her stepmother, but returned his determined gaze with an equal hint of warning.

She had told him, in no uncertain terms, how she felt. How dare he disregard her wishes?

"Well, there you have it!" Lucille stepped forward and plunged herself into the fray of their stubborn, clashing stares. "We simply cannot disappoint the future King of Petersbourg."

"No, we cannot," Nicholas replied with a satisfied grin.

Alexandra forced herself to nod politely and went to gather her gloves and bonnet.

* * *

"Is it your intention to spoil my chances with your brother?" Alex asked irritably as they arrived at the park and she took hold of Nicholas's hand in order to descend from the coach. "I hope that is not the case, sir, for I would very much like us to be friends."

Despite the fact that she was wildly annoyed with him, she simply could not afford to lose his favor.

Lucille had already walked off to speak to a lady she had met at the Carlton House ball, which left Alex stranded alone with this infuriatingly handsome obstacle.

"I assure you," he replied, "I have only the most honorable intentions in regard to your happiness. There is nothing that matters to me more."

The coach behind them drove away, and Alexandra looked up at him in the blinding sunlight. His gaze feathered across her skin and down to her neckline, which unnerved her beyond words.

"You make me uncomfortable," she confessed.

"How so?"

He had to ask?

"You spoke candidly the other night," she explained, "but I hope I was also candid in return. I am not looking for a torrid affair with you or any other man. I am devoted to Randolph." She looked around. "Where is he? I would be grateful if you would take me to him."

Nicholas inclined his head curiously. "How can you be devoted to someone you only just met?"

She returned her attention to those captivating blue eyes that were such a torment to her in every way. "I could say the same to you, sir. You hardly know me, yet you declared yourself after three short minutes in a gallery. And from what I know of your reputation, you are notorious for leading unsuspecting ladies down a pretty but perilous garden path."

He studied her face carefully. "So it is my reputation that has ruined your opinion of me."

"Yes, but does it matter either way? The result is the same."

"It matters to *me*," he replied, "for I would also like us to be friends."

Lucille returned to join them. "It is quite crowded here today, is it not? I wonder if Prince Randolph is nearby." Rising up on her toes, Lucille raised a hand to shade her eyes from the sun. "I do not see him. Do you see him, Alexandra?"

"No, Mama," she replied. "Not yet."

"Shall we walk then?"

Nicholas clasped his hands behind his back and strolled casually beside Alexandra.

"It is quite a large park," she coolly mentioned. "We might not encounter him at all."

Knowing this man's motives, Alexandra realized he could easily have lied about his brother even being here. He might say anything to lead her astray and tempt her away from her goals.

"We will search every corner," he helpfully replied.

They chatted about the weather for a while. Then Lucille cried out, "Oh look, there he is!"

Alexandra turned. *Indeed.* It appeared that Nicholas had not been toying with her after all. His brother *had* graced the park with his presence—but was presently kissing the gloved hand of a blushing young lady in a bright blue dress.

Lucille quickened her pace and kicked up a bit of dust as she left Alexandra and Nicholas behind.

"I believe my stepmother is awestruck," Alexandra said.

"Then perhaps *she* should marry Randolph."

It was a rather tempting suggestion, Alex thought, but it wouldn't give her what she wanted.

They approached the squealing pack of young women, who all appeared ravenous for a single taste of handsome royal meat. They seemed perfectly prepared to fight to the death for it.

"My word," Alexandra said. "I'll never get within fifty paces without being torn to shreds."

Nicholas watched the spectacle with dark disdain. "That's always the way of it, and it pains me to say that I've become immune. It has been like this in Petersbourg for years. It doesn't shock me in the least. Not any longer."

"I cannot imagine ever becoming immune to something like *that*." They watched the appalling spectacle for a few minutes more. "No wonder he came to England," she said with a sigh. "Though I suspect he must be disappointed to encounter the same thing here, when he had only hoped to escape it."

"My thoughts exactly."

She turned to him. "I must assure you, sir, that I am nothing like those women, and if you will permit me, I wish to apologize for their behavior. They do not represent the majority."

He regarded her intently. "Apology accepted, but I beg to disagree. I believe they *do* represent most women—at least the ones who are seeking a proposal of marriage from Randolph. Except for you. As you say, you are not like them. Why is that?"

She sensed he wanted to know it for himself, not for his brother, but she would answer the question regardless, for it was information that could improve her chances with Randolph, and she genuinely hoped that Nicholas would eventually give up his pursuit when he realized it was futile.

Which it was. She would not let it progress any other way.

"I suppose I am different because I have been living outside of society most of my life," she explained. "After my uncle sent us away, we gave up our hopes for grand marriages. Or perhaps I am jaded."

He stared at her in a way that made her feel apprehensive.

"Aren't we all?" he replied.

A fast breeze blew through the treetops. She laid a gloved hand on her bonnet to keep it from flying off and looked up at the sky. "Where did that come from?"

Nicholas looked up as well. "Life is a mystery, is it not? Do you wish to be escorted to my brother now?"

She wanted to say, "No, not yet," but it was a thoughtless impulse. Mr. Carmichael had invested a great deal of money with the understanding that Alex would do whatever it took to secure the Petersbourg throne—even push and shove her way through a crowd of silly young females. There had even been some suggestion that she should entrap Randolph in the worst possible way, but she was determined not to let it come to that.

"Will you help me?" she said to Nicholas. "If you truly believe I am not like the others, can you not find it in your heart to talk to your brother on my behalf so that I might avoid this sort of thing?"

He glanced at his brother. "But *why* do you want to marry him? And please do not insult me by telling me you are in love with him, because I know that is not true."

She sighed. "I've already told you of my situation, and I will not lie. I am ambitious. I wish to do something meaningful with my life." At that, she looked up at him. "Have you ever been knocked down by someone, Nicholas? Have you been treated unfairly? If so, then you will understand how it has a way of rousing you to struggle to your feet and fight back harder than ever before."

He considered that for a moment. "So there is a hint of vengeance in your scheme," he bluntly suggested.

Vengeance? If he only knew how close he was to the truth.

"I would not call it that," she cautiously replied. "I simply have something to prove, that is all, and I am proud. I want the very best for my sisters and me. They deserve happiness, and so do I. I make no apologies for that."

"Nor should you."

"I believe people should have the freedom to improve their situation if they so desire," she continued, "and to embrace their destiny, and to follow their hearts, no matter how difficult a road it might be to achieve a certain thing."

His eyebrows lifted. "Those are inspiring words, Lady Alexandra."

They both looked at his brother, who was now stroll-

ing toward the river. Lucille was following the crowd, but
she turned and waved at them to follow.

Nicholas offered his arm and Alex accepted it, but
they did not hurry to catch up. In all honesty, she was not
ready to end this conversation, which came as a surprise
considering how she felt about this man.

"I must warn you," he said. "It is not easy to be a royal."

I know. Otherwise my family would still be alive.

But of course, she did not speak those morbid words.
Instead she grinned lightheartedly at Nicholas and gestured toward the crowd of women. "Oh, yes. Clearly your
brother looks miserable at the moment."

Randolph had just taken the hand of a young girl, no
more than twelve years old, and he was waltzing across
the grass with her while everyone laughed and applauded.

"I'm afraid he is a bit of a flirt," Nicholas said.

"I've noticed."

They reached the crowd of onlookers and joined in the
applause.

Randolph spotted them at last and bowed chivalrously
to his dancing partner, who blushed and giggled. He excused himself from his admirers and came striding with
good cheer toward them.

Alex leaned close to Nicholas. "Will you help me, then?
I would be forever grateful."

He looked her fondly in the eye. "I cannot say no to
you, my lady. Your happiness is mine, so I suppose I have
no choice in the matter."

Her heart turned over in response to those words. No
one had ever said anything like that to her before. It caught
her off guard and she felt suddenly flustered.

"Good afternoon, Lady Alexandra!" Randolph said as
he reached them. Lucille came trotting along behind him.
"I am delighted that Nick could convince you to visit the
park today." He held out his arm. "Would you care to take

a stroll with me down to the water?" He turned to Lucille.
"With your permission of course, madam."

"Permission granted," she cheerfully replied.

Alex let go of one prince's arm and did not look back
as she walked off with the other. But in the privacy of her
own mind she wished overwhelmingly that Nicholas was
the one who would wear the crown, because *he* was the
one she desired.

*   *   *

Nearly a half hour later, Prince Randolph escorted Alex
back to Lucille, who was waiting under the shade of an oak
tree with Nicholas.

"What a lovely afternoon for a stroll," Lucille said. "Did
you enjoy yourselves? What do you think of our park, sir?"

"It is almost as delightful as the pleasure of Lady Alexandra's company," Randolph replied. "I have sent for the
coach, which should be along at any moment. I do hope
you will both attend the play at Covent Garden on Tuesday.
Do you have tickets?"

"We do indeed," Lucille replied.

"Very good then. Ah, look. Here is your driver. Nicholas, will you see the ladies safely home?"

"It would be my pleasure to do so."

The coach pulled to a halt on the lane, and the ladies
bid the prince farewell before allowing the footman to
escort them into the vehicle. Alexandra seated herself on
the elegant blue leather upholstery and took a deep breath.

She was relieved that was over. There were far too many
moments when she'd found it difficult to manage a sincere
smile because she felt no spark of attraction whatsoever
for Prince Randolph. Not that she'd expected to fall in love
with him. In fact, she'd expected to fight a long-standing
battle with her contempt for him.

When it came to his roguish younger brother, however, her blood rushed with excitement and no amount of self-restraint seemed to make any difference.

She could not bear it. It was going to drive her mad.

"How was it?" Lucille asked. "He seemed quite enraptured. He must have been if he was willing to leave all those other young ladies behind. You were the only one he singled out to escort along the path."

"He was very charming," she flatly said.

"Charming? That is all you have to say about it?"

Alex was not in the mood for Lucille's blunt interrogation. There was a sickening knot in her stomach the size of a turnip, and she just wanted to sit quietly for a moment. "He was charming and gentlemanly and everything else, but please don't speak now. Nicholas will be here shortly."

Just then, his large form loomed in the open doorway of the coach. He gripped the handrail and swung inside.

"You are so kind to see us home," Lucille said to him.

He smiled at her. "I trust it was a pleasant afternoon for you?"

"Oh, it was much more than pleasant! We are both so grateful that you decided to pay a call today. Perhaps tomorrow you will knock on our door again and there will be some other grand adventure awaiting us!"

Lucille looked out the window while Alex cautiously locked eyes with Nicholas.

As the coach rolled along, they watched each other but did not say a word. The tension, however, was palpable, for she knew his feelings. He had made them excruciatingly clear.

She, on the other hand, must keep her traitorous feelings secret from everyone. She could not reveal even the smallest measure of her heart.

As the coach pulled to a halt in front of the house, he stepped out first and assisted Lucille out of the vehicle.

"Thank you again," she said. "We enjoyed ourselves immensely. And please tell Randolph that we will look forward to seeing him at Covent Garden."

"I will deliver the message," he replied.

Without looking back, Lucille sauntered to the front door and waited while Alex took hold of Nicholas's gloved hand. As she stepped down, however, he did not let go. He clung to her fingers and she had to pull them firmly from his grasp.

"When I watched you go off with my brother," he said in a low, gruff voice, "I didn't like it. I was jealous. I am *still* jealous."

Startled by his unexpected confession, Alexandra wet her trembling lips. "I beg your pardon?"

He glanced up at the front of the house to ensure that Lucille could not hear what he was about to say. "I know I said I would help you, and I will because I want you to have what you desire. But I believe you are mistaken about what you think you want, Alexandra, because I believe you desire *me*."

Her heart began to beat very fast. "I don't know what you are talking about."

"Yes, you do." There was a dangerous, almost angry level of persistence in his voice.

Meanwhile, she couldn't seem to make her feet work in order to walk away from him.

"We've only just met," she argued, as if she did not feel the same way . . . as if she could convince him that whatever attraction he felt was no deeper than paper when, in reality, a wild fever had stirred her blood as well. Even now, here on the street, the intensity of it struck her like a firestorm. "Surely whatever you are feeling will pass soon enough," she added. "You will find some other woman to dally with."

"Dally?" He frowned. "Again, you judge me by my reputation. You think I am not capable of commitment."

His indignation both surprised and intrigued her. "Well? Are you?"

"Of course I am. I have loved before, and contrary to what the world thinks of me, I wish to love again."

She darted a glance at the house and expected her stepmother to call her in at any moment, but Lucille continued to wait.

"What happened to this woman you loved?" Alex asked before she could stop herself. "I am hesitant to ask where she is now. Not ruined, I hope."

A muscle clenched at his jaw. "Did you ever stop to consider the possibility that I was the one who was jilted and left for another?" He looked down at her lips, then shook his head, as if he did not wish to reveal any more ugly details. "Let us simply say that I am not cavalier about matters of the heart. I know how it feels to want something and to be ultimately disappointed."

Oh, what was it about this man that aroused her so? Each time he spoke, she was captivated. Whenever she looked at him, she shivered with desire. She had felt nothing close to this while walking in the park with his brother. That had been proper and polite. Artificial. Deceitful, even. Most definitely a chore.

She had not known that an attraction like *this* could even exist.

"Perhaps one day," she said, still determined not to become reckless of mind, "you will find another special woman to love, but I am afraid it cannot be me. I believe you are mistaken in your impression of my feelings. You do not know me at all. You are laying your affections in the wrong place."

But heaven help her, she was plagued by her feelings as

well, and he was not wrong about that. He saw her exactly as she was, and she had lied to him just now.

One giant, heartbreaking lie on top of so many others.

"I must go," she said.

He reached out to stop her. "Wait."

The raw command in his voice caused her to halt in her footsteps, but she did not dare turn around.

"I will bring the coach around to escort you and your stepmother to the theater on Tuesday," he said. "Be ready for me at seven o'clock."

She was furious with him for ordering her about in such a manner and for igniting her passions when she did not wish for them to be ignited, yet she could not bring herself to refuse.

"Very well. Do not be late," she replied with an equal force of command, though she hated herself for her surrender as she hurried to the door.

Chapter Seven

The following day, the St. James's Palace coach pulled up in front of the house on Grosvenor Square, but this time Nicholas did not step out.

Instead, Alex found herself watching with stark disappointment—which vexed her terribly—as a servant knocked on the door, delivered what appeared to be a letter, returned to the coach, and drove off.

Was it a note from Nicholas, or was it an official communication from the palace?

It was not easy to maintain an appearance of calm, but Alex managed to gain a stranglehold on her emotions, for she could not possibly let anyone learn of her foolish infatuation with the future king's younger brother. She must work harder to smother it.

"A letter from the palace, Your Grace," the footman said as he entered the room.

Despite all her best intentions to remain indifferent, Alexandra's heart sank with disappointment as she watched the footman deliver the letter to Lucille, who picked it up off the silver salver.

"Oh look, there is something here for you, too, Alexandra. Not one but two letters from the palace." She held out the second letter, which Alex accepted with the pretense of disinterest.

"Come, come, what does yours say?" Lucille broke the seal on her own. "Mine is an invitation for us both to join Prince Randolph on Thursday for a tour of the Egyptian Hall."

Alexandra turned her back, broke the seal, and stared at the letter briefly while her heart began to pound out of control. "That is what mine says, too."

Then she politely excused herself and hurried to her room—in order to read Prince Nicholas's personal letter in private.

My dear Lady Alexandra,

Please accept my most sincere apologies for my behavior when we walked in the park together and later parted ways at your door. It is not my custom to allow my passions to overtake my good sense, and I am still struggling to come to terms with how I behaved and what I must accept—that your ambitions are engaged elsewhere.

For that reason, I must honor your wishes by bowing out of the race.

I also believe that I would be doing a disservice to my country if I deprived the people of Petersbourg of such a strong and beautiful queen.

I will therefore offer my assistance to you, for I am nothing if not your devoted servant in all ways. I will advise my brother to recognize your superior qualities, and I will dedicate myself completely to the task of helping you achieve all that you desire.

I will not stand in your way, nor will I speak of my affections again.

Please accept my apologies, but I must send another servant to deliver you to Covent Garden on Tuesday. Ran-

dolph will look for you in the lobby at intermission. I will arrange it on your behalf.

Yours sincerely,
N.

Alex sank into a chair and lowered the letter to her side. Every inch of her being was sizzling with shock.

She read the letter again. *I will dedicate myself completely to the task of helping you achieve all that you desire. . . . I will arrange it on your behalf.*

She should be happy. She was now very close to the ultimate fulfillment of her destiny, but her heart was turning in another direction, for she knew Randolph did not touch her heart the way his brother did. The sparks had turned to flame that first night on the terrace, even before she knew his name. The very instant he spoke, she had felt the power of their attraction. It was not something she could explain in rational terms, even while her intellect was scolding her and demanding that she forget him.

Suddenly all that seemed to matter was the strange fever that was overtaking her body in the most intoxicating way.

Sitting forward, she chastised herself for feeling disappointed that he had decided to withdraw his pursuit, and would not escort her to the theater on Tuesday. Her benefactor would be appalled if he knew her thoughts—but heaven help her, she wanted Nicholas to keep fighting. She wanted to write back to him now and tell him not to accept defeat so quickly. She might yet change her mind, but what kind of idiocy was that?

She was the true hereditary heir to the Petersbourg throne, and her family had been forcibly removed and banished to a place where they all perished tragically.

It was her duty to return to her homeland and restore the true monarchy. She wanted to serve the people and be a kind and benevolent monarch. They were currently ruled by a power-hungry revolutionary, but they deserved so much more than that—and it was no secret that they wanted it, for the country was divided. The Royalists and the New Regime could not agree on anything.

Cupping her forehead in a hand, she wondered what to do with this letter.

She should not keep it. She should destroy it, for what if she became queen and it fell into the wrong hands?

Without giving it another thought—for if she read it again she might very well succumb to weakness—she rose from her chair, lit a candle, and held the letter over the flame.

As she watched it disintegrate, her heart squeezed with misery at the price she must pay in the name of duty, and it took no small measure of discipline to keep from rescuing the letter and patting out the flames.

As soon as it was gone—reduced to nothing but a small pile of ash on the desktop—she turned and made a solemn vow not to spend another moment dreaming about Prince Nicholas, for he was the most dangerous of men. He had the power to divert her from her goal, and she could not allow him to do that. No matter that he fired her blood and made her body yearn to be touched.

His brother made her feel no such things, and yet it was he whose children she must bear.

Suddenly the thought of bearing Nicholas's children possessed her, and she felt a deep pang of longing.

She pushed the thought away. It was no use dwelling on what could not be.

For those reasons, and a dozen more, she vowed to forget about Nicholas once and for all. She would focus on her duty, no matter what the cost.

Chapter Eight

On the night of the play at Covent Garden, Alexandra and Lucille took their seats in the center of the fifth row.

"I wish Randolph could have escorted us himself," Lucille whispered, "instead of sending a servant to do it for him. Is there any possibility that he has escorted another woman here this evening? Are we second choice, do you think?"

"I don't know, Mama. We shall have to wait and see." Alex looked up at the only empty box, which was reserved for Randolph, his sister, Rose, and the regent, and wondered if her stepmother was correct. Perhaps another more purposeful young lady—not distracted by the wrong man—had put her hooks into Randolph already and was well on her way to becoming the future Queen of Petersbourg.

Just then, Lucille turned in her seat, then quickly faced forward again. "Good Lord. Sit up straight, Alexandra. Your benefactor has just walked in."

Alex turned to see Mr. Carmichael taking a seat at the rear of the theater. She faced the stage again and kept her eyes fixed on the velvet curtains while she comprehended the situation.

This was the first time she had encountered her benefactor since her debut into society. He had always remained on the fringes, never interrupting her social engagements or her interactions with Randolph.

Was Mr. Carmichael here to observe her progress? Did he somehow know she had become diverted from her goal—a very expensive goal, which he had financed himself with the hiring of the house in Grosvenor Square, not to mention the servants, the carriage, and all the gowns?

"Is he not worried the prince will recognize him?" Alex quietly whispered. "He was once secretary to my father. Surely his face is known in Petersbourg."

Lucille shook her head. "King Frederick would recognize him, most definitely, but not Randolph, for he was only seven when they removed Carmichael from the palace. Since then he has remained invisible to the revolutionaries who now hold power. He has not dared return to court."

For a few tense seconds Lucille and Alex sat in silence while members of the orchestra tuned their instruments in the pit. It was a frenzied discordance of notes that did not help Alex to relax.

She could feel Mr. Carmichael's gaze burning into the back of her head, watching her every move, no doubt wondering why she hadn't accomplished more by now. Shouldn't it be the heir to the throne sending her secret love letters and not his younger brother?

But Mr. Carmichael would not know of that. There was no possible way. At least she hoped there was not.

"I don't want him here," she whispered to Lucille. "He makes me uneasy. I will not be able to focus my attentions on the prince if Mr. Carmichael is breathing down my neck."

Lucille glared at her. "You hardly have a choice in the matter. He bought the tickets for the seats we are now occupying, not to mention our gowns and jewels. Without him, we would be nowhere. We would be stuck back in our little house in Wales, counting farthings to pay our debt to the landlord."

Alexandra's chin shot up. "Do not tell me I do not have choices, Mama, for I suspect the gowns and jewels we are wearing are a product of my family's lost wealth. Where else would Mr. Carmichael obtain such resources? Unless he comes from money himself . . . Is this his private investment?"

Lucille stiffened. "I do not know where his money comes from. All I know is that he was your father's loyal servant until the day he died, and he saved your life. He smuggled you to safety after both your parents had been erased from existence. So do not forget that when you speak to him."

The audience rose to their feet just then and began to cheer and applaud. As Alex stood to join them, she looked up at the box where the prince and princess were stepping elegantly into view.

Randolph was dressed in his impressive scarlet regalia, while Rose wore a sparkling tiara and a gown of ivory and gold silk. They were a striking couple, impossibly good-looking. It was no wonder the people of Petersbourg accepted them as monarchs. They certainly carried off the role with grace and aplomb.

As the applause died down and the audience took their seats, Alexandra struggled with her pride—a dark and bitter monster inside of her.

Or perhaps it was not pride but jealousy. She could not pretend to be immune to the anger she felt from the loss of her family and position and the obvious rise of these people who had seized their crowns through the use of military force and murder. The idea of marrying this flagrant usurper was not an easy one to swallow, yet it was a price she had deemed worth paying. It was a sacrifice that would rightfully reestablish her father's descendants as sovereigns.

As she sat down and the lights in the theater were extinguished, she tried not to think about her wedding night with a man she did not love. Then something drew her eyes to the box overhead.

Nicholas. He entered—looking incredibly handsome in his formal evening attire. He sat down behind his brother but did not look at the stage as the curtains finally drew apart. Instead, he looked down at Alexandra, as if he had already ascertained where she was seated and did not need to search.

Something inside her melted like butter on a hot stove, and all that existed in that heated moment of connection was the beautiful man in the theater box, who had written her a most intimate and passionate love letter.

Then the play began, and she turned her attention to the stage.

*　*　*

When the curtains closed for intermission, Alex and Lucille followed the crowd out to the reception area. They barely had a moment to breathe before Mr. Carmichael approached.

"Good evening, Your Grace," he said. "I trust you are enjoying the performance?"

"Very much so, Mr. Carmichael," Lucille replied. "And you?"

Alex cleared her throat as she glanced down at the ruby ring on his forefinger and the fine silk coat he wore. He was a handsome older man—tall, slim, and very distinguished. He carried himself with the arrogance of a royal, though he did not possess a title, other than that of former secretary to the late King of Petersbourg.

"And what is your impression of the production, Lady Alexandra?" He took the opportunity to look her over from head to foot, while she struggled to remember her stepmother's advice about being grateful for what he had done for her all those years ago—smuggling her away from danger and arranging for her secret adoption by an English duke.

"The costumes and set decorations are extraordinary," she replied, "and the characters are intriguing, though not entirely realistic."

He regarded her with some amusement. "You are a critic, I see."

"Not always."

Other theater patrons mingled about, conversed, and laughed.

"And how is the situation progressing with the prince?" Carmichael quietly asked.

"Very well," she replied. "We have enjoyed many pleasant encounters this week."

"He singled her out at the park the other day," Lucille helpfully added. "She was the only young lady he chose to escort along the path. They walked alone for quite some time."

Carmichael raised a brow. "That is excellent news, but I see you have not yet spoken to him this evening."

"Not yet," Alexandra replied, "but it is not easy to engage a man in conversation when he is over our heads in a private theater box and we are seated below."

She felt her stepmother's irate gaze shoot toward her like a slap across the cheek.

"Prince Nicholas has indicated, however," Lucille quickly added, "that his brother will seek us out this evening. I expect he will enter the lobby at any moment."

Carmichael glanced over his shoulder. "Be careful around the brother. He is a known libertine and an irresponsible rake. He takes advantage of his status as a royal, and has a reputation for misusing the ladies. You should not associate yourself with him too closely."

This unexpected warning from Alexandra's benefactor was like a knife in her heart, for though she was committed to her duty, she *had* developed feelings for Nicholas, however foolish they may be, and felt a passionate need to defend him.

"To the contrary, he has been very kind to us," she argued. "He escorted us personally to the park that day, and has assured me of his support in my quest to be considered as a worthy candidate for Randolph, who relies on his brother's judgment and advice."

"You don't say." Mr. Carmichael regarded her with surprise. "Did he tell you this himself?"

"He has been very helpful," Lucille added.

"He most certainly has," Alexandra said.

Carmichael said nothing for a moment, but she saw a muscle flick at his jaw.

"You seem displeased," she said.

"That is because you will not heed my advice."

She swallowed over the sudden impulse to say something she might later regret. Instead, she responded in a calm voice, "Rest assured that I know exactly what I am doing, sir, and I must demand your cooperation. Please keep your distance while I perform the necessary tasks."

The crowd fell silent all around them, and Alex leaned to peer around Mr. Carmichael's tall frame, which was blocking her view of the stairs.

"The royal family has just descended from the theater box," Alex said. "You must leave us now."

Carmichael had no choice but to back away, where he soon melted into the crowd.

"You were very rude to him," Lucille scolded. "What did I tell you about treating him with the respect and gratitude he deserves?"

Alexandra faced her stepmother. "I was not rude, but I will not be treated like his pawn."

Her stepmother raised her chin defensively.

Alexandra continued, "Please tell Mr. Carmichael not to distract me like this in public again, or he will soon find himself on the outside of this arrangement."

Lucille grabbed hold of her arm. "It is you and I who will find ourselves on the outside, if he withdraws his financial support."

Alex wrenched her arm away and immediately turned toward Randolph. "Your Royal Highness." She greeted him with a curtsy.

He offered his gloved hand to help her rise. "Lady Alexandra. What a pleasure to see you. Are you enjoying the performance?"

"Yes, it is breathtaking," she replied.

Princess Rose approached as well. "Good evening."

Alex studied her briefly. "Good evening, Your Royal Highness. How lovely you look. That color is most becoming on you."

Rose smiled. "And may I return the compliment? What a pretty shade of blue."

Nicholas joined them at that moment and Alex swallowed over a cumbersome knot of confusion, for she had come into this believing herself capable of ruthlessness. The news about her family had given rise to an inner ambition she had never known before.

But now she was battling a potent wave of self-doubt and uncertainty. One moment she felt as formidable as a steel sword, and the next, when she locked eyes with Prince Nicholas, she burned with desire and was tempted to throw everything aside for passion and desire.

They shared a brief look, and she wondered if he knew her defenses were weakening. There had been no communication between them since the letter. She had not replied, nor had he come to call for any reason.

His brother turned to her. "I have it on good authority that you will be attending the ball at Almack's tomorrow evening, Lady Alexandra. Would it be too forward of me to take this opportunity to request the honor of a dance?"

"It would not be forward at all," she replied. "I would be most pleased to accept."

An awkward silence ensued. Nicholas quickly filled it by turning to the princess. "And Rose, would it be too forward of me to request the honor of a dance with you tomorrow evening?"

She laughed. "Of course not, dear brother. I will look forward to it."

Everyone smiled and nodded politely; then the bell rang to indicate the end of intermission.

Nicholas turned to Lucille. "Your Grace, I will have the coach brought around to the front of the theater following the last curtain call. If you would be so kind as to meet me here, I will escort you and Lady Alexandra home."

He intended to see them home? But she thought . . . she thought . . .

Oh God, she couldn't think.

"How generous of you, sir." Lucille and Alex curtsied to the royals, and they all made their way back into the theater.

*　*　*

"My word," Lucille said irritably as a young man in a shabby jacket pushed by. "What is the world coming to when one must attend the theater with merchants and solicitors?"

Alexandra turned as she felt a warm hand cup her gloved elbow.

"The coach is waiting for us," Nicholas said in her ear. Then he offered his arm to her stepmother. "Your Grace, may I assist you to the vehicle?"

Alexandra had never seen the dowager blush before, which only confirmed the inconceivable level of his charm.

"Will Prince Randolph be joining us?" Lucille asked as they reached the vehicle.

"I am afraid not, Your Grace. He is invited to Carlton House to discuss matters of state with the regent. I will be joining them there as well after I deliver you safely to your destination." He handed her up into the coach.

He then held out a hand to Alexandra. She slid her fingers across his open palm and relished the brief moment of contact.

Settling herself comfortably inside the cozy interior, she waited for him to join them, but he merely stuck his head inside the door to ensure they were both seated.

"Are you not coming with us?" she blurted out, then regretted it immediately, for she had revealed too much.

"I beg your pardon," he said. "I have forgotten something inside. If you will wait but a moment, I promise I will return."

With that, he closed the door behind him, and Alexandra sat back with relief. She worked hard to slow her breathing and smiled to herself—for he was coming right back—then felt the watchful eye of her stepmother examining her movements and expressions.

"Mr. Carmichael was right about one thing," Lucille said, adjusting her cape around her shoulders. "That man *is* dangerous."

"Whatever do you mean?" Alexandra asked.

"Did you see the way he looked at me when he helped me into the coach? He is too charming for his own good.

It's no wonder he has a reputation with the ladies. He knows how to flaunt his looks."

Somewhat relieved that her stepmother was not referring to her own response to him, Alex chuckled softly. "Let us be honest, Mama. I saw you blush. You quite enjoyed it."

"Well, that is neither here nor there," she haughtily replied. "What matters is your reputation. You mustn't let that man charm you. Remember your objectives." She was quiet for a long moment while they waited. "I don't like him," she said.

"Why?"

"I just told you why. He is a danger to you. I can feel it. He may pretend to be aiding you, but I would not be surprised to learn it is nothing but a cunning ploy bent on seduction. Heaven knows how many women he is encouraging. Promising them a good word delivered to his brother if they will toss a few favors in *his* direction . . ."

"Oh, Mama, now you're being ridiculous."

"Am I?" She wiggled self-importantly on the seat. "He is far too handsome. Try not to look at him during the ride home. Think only of Randolph."

Alexandra squeezed at her reticule. "I could say the same to you."

Just then, the coach bounced under Nicholas's weight as he climbed onto the iron step, pounded on the side of the vehicle to signal the driver, and swung inside.

"My apologies, ladies." He took a seat across from Alex.

The coach lurched forward and they rolled on in silence toward Grosvenor Square.

Alexandra kept her eyes downcast for the first few minutes, for her stepmother was right about one thing. It was not easy to look at him without falling under his spell. Even Lucille had fallen victim to it, by her own admission.

Eventually, Alexandra could resist temptation no longer and found herself taking a slow perusal of his legs, which were gorgeously muscular beneath his dark trousers.

"Are you looking forward to the ball at Almack's tomorrow evening?" she asked before she had a chance to consider the ramifications of such a question or how it would appear to her stepmother.

His gaze traveled from the dark window glass to Alexandra's face, and he tilted his head to the side as if studying her with some curiosity. "Yes, I am."

It was a perfect opportunity for him to request a dance with her, as his brother had done at the theater, but he simply added, "And I am sure it will be a most enjoyable evening."

He looked out the window again and said nothing more.

Disappointment pooled in her belly, but she had no right to moan about anything, for she had rejected him quite blatantly a number of times and he had given his word in the letter that he would say nothing more about their previous intimacies.

She should be relieved that he was treating her with indifference, but to her utter dismay, she was dissatisfied.

Then his eyes turned to hers. "Perhaps you would honor me with a dance as well, Lady Alexandra."

And just like that, the world came alive again and her heart swelled with relief.

God in heaven, what did this mean?

"I would be delighted," she replied.

They gazed at each other across the dimly lit interior, and suddenly her future was not so clear after all. What she thought was most important to her—the crown that belonged to her family—suddenly seemed less vital. Her heart was pointed in quite another direction this evening, and it felt astonishingly liberating to finally admit to it.

They continued to gaze at each other in the flickering lamplight, and she knew without a doubt that he still wanted her, though he was trying very hard not to. As was she.

"I expect it will be a full house tomorrow evening," Lucille announced, intentionally interrupting their staring fest with a brusque reminder that they were not the only two people in the coach.

"I expect Your Grace is correct," Nicholas replied, without the slightest hint of discomfiture.

He glanced only briefly at Alexandra again before engaging her stepmother in a conversation about the weather—always a safe and acceptable topic.

When they pulled to a halt in front of the house, he helped Lucille out first, then offered his hand to Alexandra.

This time, however, as she exited the coach, Lucille did not walk on ahead. She waited beside Nicholas, as if she knew she must stand guard against any clandestine whispers of an improper kind.

"It has been a pleasure escorting you both home this evening," he said as he walked them to the steps. "Until tomorrow," he said with a bow; then he departed.

Alex and Lucille slipped inside and handed over their capes and gloves to the butler, but before Alex could make haste to her bedchamber Lucille stopped her. "Not so fast, young lady. I wish to speak with you in the library."

With sinking dread, she followed her stepmother across the hall. Lucille closed the double doors behind them.

"What did I say to you about keeping your eyes off Nicholas, but there you sat, practically throwing yourself at him."

"I did no such thing."

Lucille scoffed. "Do I look like a blind fool? Clearly you are smitten with the man, and I daresay he looked to be enjoying every minute of it. Have you forgotten why we are here in London? It is not for you to go traipsing about, flirting indiscriminately with the first handsome buck who pays you a compliment."

"I have not forgotten," she retorted, "and I have not been flirting indiscriminately with anyone, much less a *buck*—handsome or otherwise."

Lucille squinted. "Don't lie to me, gel. I know an infatuation when I see one, and he is the worst possible man to take up with in such a way, for he will spoil any chance you may have with Randolph. If it was another man, we could perhaps keep such a scandal secret, but he is Randolph's brother! I forbid you to dance with him tomorrow night. You must make some excuse and direct all your attentions to the man who will occupy the throne."

"I beg your pardon," Alexandra argued, "but you cannot forbid me from dancing with Nicholas. If I lose his favor, I may lose everything. Let us speak of this no further."

With her heart about to beat out of her chest, Alex strode quickly to the door.

"Impudent gel!" Lucille scolded. "Come back here at once, or I shall tell Mr. Carmichael what you have just said to me, and he will not be pleased!"

Alexandra swung around and spoke with heated restraint. "Tell him if you wish, but it would be a grave mistake. Do you *want* him to withdraw his support?"

"Of course not," Lucille replied.

"Then do not stand in my way. Trust that I know what I am doing and, no matter what path I choose, I am still the rightful heir to that throne. When it comes to my future, there is much I have yet to decide."

Lucille stared at her with wide eyes. "What do you mean? You overstep yourself."

Alexandra felt a muscle clench at her jaw. "Do I indeed?"

Then she gave her stepmother a fierce look of warning before she turned and exited the library.

*   *   *

Stinging raindrops had just begun to fall like pebbles from the sky when Nigel Carmichael galloped through the misty darkness onto Westminster Bridge.

He still wore his formal evening attire from the theater, and cursed the inclement weather as he reined in his mount halfway across the bridge.

The wind gusted violently, and he was forced to hold on to his elegant top hat, while his opera cloak blew open.

At long last, he heard the sound of approaching hoofbeats through the noise of the rain and spotted a horse and rider coming from the opposite side of the Thames. The rider trotted closer and came to a halt beside him.

"You could have chosen a more sheltered location," the Duke of Kaulbach said. "I am already drenched to the bone. What news have you about the princess's progress?"

"I spoke to Alexandra this evening. She assured me that all is proceeding according to plan, and that Randolph has singled her out on more than one occasion. I am hearing some talk in the clubs that she is the current favorite, though I have watched Randolph mingle with the public. He is charming toward most women. There are many who are nursing high hopes, I can well imagine."

The duke's horse tossed his head as a fierce blast of wind roared across the bridge and the rain struck their faces.

"Then Alexandra must work harder to seduce him. Have they been alone together yet?"

"Only briefly. She is always chaperoned. We must take great care not to let her out of our sight."

"I am quite sure she is not in any danger. We are the

only two people in England who know of her lineage, except for the dowager. Can she be trusted?"

"I believe so."

His Grace paused as he considered everything. "You must encourage the girl to be more brazen. If he chooses another, we will be forced to rely on other means to restore her to the throne—and I doubt we could raise enough capital for that. Seduction is the most efficient way."

"Not enough capital to fund an army, you mean—"

"Yes, for if such a thing were possible, I would have already done it."

Carmichael tipped his head forward to shield his face from the stinging rain, and a stream of water poured from the brim of his hat. "I don't believe an army will be necessary. She seems well motivated. She is strong willed. Beautiful as well. I have no doubt she will capture the hearts of the people the moment she sets foot in the country and blinds them with that dazzling smile."

The duke nodded gamely. "That is exactly what I wish to hear. God is on our side this time."

Carmichael nodded. "Let us hope so." He paused. "And your son, the marquess—is he prepared to do his part?"

The duke paused. "I regret to say he has been misbehaving lately. We had a rather heated argument last night and he has left England for Petersbourg. But I have no doubt he will come around and help Alexandra to settle in once she arrives."

"That is excellent news. In that regard, what have you heard about the health of the king?"

"He grows weaker every day."

"I see." Carmichael paused. "Well, then. Now is the time to act. We are doing the proper thing, Your Grace. It is long past time we restored the true monarchy to the throne."

The duke steered his horse in the other direction toward Lambeth. "I daresay you rouse my blood, sir. Let us hope Princess Alexandra is up to the task." He began to shout over his shoulder as he trotted away, "We shall meet again, Carmichael! But for now, continue to keep me informed, and keep that priceless jewel on track!"

Chapter Nine

A dull hum of conversation ensued in the main hall of Almack's Assembly Rooms on King Street the following evening while a few immaculately dressed couples took part in a decorous country dance.

Alexandra glanced up at the large crystal chandelier overhead and watched the orchestra in the balcony above, then perused all the guests, looking for a very particular face.

"I see Prince Randolph has not yet arrived," Lucille mentioned. "But oh, my word, look at that. . . . What a dreadful gown. Did no one say anything to her? Will no one help her to have good taste? It's rather sad, is it not?"

Alexandra ignored Lucille's observations as they were greeted by the wife of the Austrian Ambassador.

A short while later, Alex was invited to dance with a young viscount, and following that little triumph, a handsome eldest son of an earl escorted her onto the floor.

At last, Prince Randolph and Princess Rose were announced, and the crowd fell silent and parted with elegant bows and curtsies. The royal guests conversed with the patronesses for quite some time while Alex watched the door, wondering impatiently when Nicholas would arrive.

A full hour must have passed without any sign of him. Later, when his brother approached her to claim his dance, she smiled warmly, laid her gloved hand upon his, and joined him on the floor for their set. All eyes were upon them as he led her through the figures of a traditional Scottish reel.

"My brother speaks highly of you," he said when the proper moment presented itself.

"I am flattered," she replied.

But had Nicholas been singing her praises as a potential future queen, or was Randolph now aware of his brother's true feelings, and had she been disqualified from the race?

Glancing quickly to the left, she noticed her stepmother observing intently and thought how much easier this would be if she felt for Randolph only *half* of what she felt for Nicholas. Then there would be no need for a charade. There would be no urgent decisions to make.

She smiled at Randolph and tried to imagine herself married to him but was no longer certain she could be such a gifted actress for the rest of her life. It was one thing to wear a mask for the duration of an evening but quite another to deceive someone into a wedding and beyond until an heir was born. Especially when she was in love with his younger brother.

She made an effort to flirt with Randolph with her eyes, but he hardly seemed to notice as they joined hands and moved across the floor. Eventually, she could resist temptation no longer. She asked the only question that mattered.

"And where is your brother this evening?"

Randolph gestured toward the door. "As it happens, he has just arrived and is speaking to your stepmother this very moment."

Alex turned to look.

Sure enough, there he was—the one man she could not banish from her heart and mind. Dressed in a royal blue frock coat and a waistcoat of white-embroidered satin, he looked more handsome than ever.

The dance came to swift finish, and before she knew it she was being escorted back to Lucille.

"Good evening, Lady Alexandra." Nicholas bowed to her. "I wonder if I am too late. May I still claim my dance?"

Lucille piped in like an army trumpet, "But surely you must give the poor girl a chance to rest her feet. She has just come off the floor."

"Quite right," Nicholas replied, surrendering to Lucille's greater wisdom. "How ungracious of me. Perhaps I could escort you to a quiet chair instead, my lady, where we will sit for the duration of the set."

It was most certainly an unwise decision, but without hesitation she offered her hand to him. Together they crossed the ballroom and put some much-needed distance between themselves and her rigorous chaperone.

"I apologize for my tardiness this evening," he said.

"You are indeed quite late, sir," Alex replied.

"If you must know, I almost did not come at all."

He picked up two glasses of punch from a passing footman carrying a tray, and handed her one.

"Why?" she asked. "Did you not wish to see me?"

She let go of his arm and they faced each other.

"Quite to the contrary," he replied. "Though I am personally agonized by this situation, I will always wish to see you whenever possible."

He took hold of her elbow and led her to a few unoccupied chairs in a dimly lit corner where they both sat down.

"That is very kind of you to say. I, too, wish to say something—something I have not been able to express until now." She paused while his eyes searched all the corners of her face, which only served to intensify the fever that was heating her blood, simply from the nearness of him. "The letter you wrote . . . I . . . I was touched by it. Touched very deeply."

His scintillating blue eyes fixed upon hers. "I wasn't sure," he said. "I thought perhaps I had offended you, but when you spoke to me in the coach last night, I knew there was still hope. You had not cast me aside completely." He looked down at her hands upon her lap. "I fear I cannot hide what I truly feel, though I am compelled by duty to do the right thing."

She swallowed over her restlessness. "Does your brother know how you feel?"

"No," he replied. "I have told him nothing."

"And you believe the right thing is for you to step aside," she said, needing to reconfirm the particulars. Was there still a chance for them?

"I confess I am torn," he replied. "I believed it was the right thing to do when I wrote to you, but every moment since has been more torturous to me than I can possibly convey. The mere idea of never sharing another private moment alone with you has been enough to drive me almost mad with regret for ever writing that blasted letter in the first place."

A wild thrill of renewed hope flooded through her body.

He still wanted her. The desire was not gone. Heaven help her, she was losing sight of everything that mattered, but for the first time she didn't care.

She took a sip of her punch and turned her eyes to the dancers.

"If you were to confess your feelings to your brother," she carefully said, "my opportunities would be greatly altered. It seems my fate is in your hands, sir. I am at your mercy."

He took a moment to consider that. "But would that fate not be altered for the better, my lady, if you chose love over duty?"

Still so afraid, so unsure, she fought to keep her true feelings concealed and slid him a surprised look. "Are you presuming that I am in love with you?"

"I presume nothing," he replied. "I have always known my place. I am second in line for everything."

Alexandra downed her punch in a single gulp. He was far too honest, which made this all the more excruciating.

"My apologies," he said, taking the empty glass from her hands and setting it on the floor under his chair. "It was not my intention to make you uncomfortable."

"I am not uncomfortable," she replied, without looking at him. She feared that if she did, he would see straight into her soul and there would be no turning back. "But I wish you wouldn't say such things. You don't understand. My life is very complicated."

"As is mine," he told her. "There are things you don't know about me, Alexandra. Things I wish to tell you, but I cannot. Not yet."

Her mouth went dry, and she swept her tongue across her lips, feeling very confused while her mind went to battle with her emotions and desires. Oh, how desperately she wanted him. How she ached to move closer and touch him. "Why are you doing this to me, Nicholas? You have tempted me constantly toward something I made clear I did not want. And yet . . ."

It was the first time she had used his given name—an intimacy to which she should not have surrendered—but everything was spinning out of control so quickly.

A footman came by and collected their empty punch glasses, which reminded her that they were not alone here and they were no doubt being watched.

"I must return you to your chaperone," he said, "but I cannot bear the thought of letting you go. All I do is dream of touching and holding you. . . . I beg of you, Alexandra. Do not reject me, for surely you are meant to be mine."

Her breaths came fast and short. Her body was on fire with longing.

The music stopped.

What would happen next?

"You promised you would not do this to me," she whispered. "You said you would let it go."

He shook his head. "I would if I could, but I see now that it was an impossible promise I should have never made. I want you for myself, and I must warn you that I intend to fight for you. By God's grace I will have you in my bed. You will not marry my brother. You will choose *me*."

In one last attempt to cling to her sense of duty and ambitions, she scoffed. "Such bold declarations. This is exactly what I was warned against. It is why you have earned such a reputation."

He rose to his feet. "My reputation has nothing to do with this and you know it, because you feel the same passion as I. You wanted me the first moment we met, and even then, you had no real interest in my brother, outside of the fact that he is the best catch of the Season—a golden prize—and you are ambitious."

She stared up at him for a heart-stopping moment, then, half in a daze, placed her gloved hand in his.

"Follow your heart, Alexandra, and consider my suit as well."

A moment later they reached Lucille, who watched them with suspicious eyes. Alexandra had to force herself to let go of his arm.

"Thank you for the honor of your company, Lady Alexandra," he said with a bow. "Enjoy the rest of your evening."

With that, he walked out and left her trembling.

* * *

When they returned home from the ball, Alex and Lucille were surprised to discover Mr. Carmichael waiting for them in the library with urgent business to discuss. He sat before a roaring fire with a glass of brandy in his hand, as if he were lord and master there.

Lucille began to apologize profusely. "We are so sorry to have kept you waiting, Mr. Carmichael. We had no idea you intended to pay a visit this evening; otherwise we would have returned earlier. Shall I ring for biscuits and tea? Or a late supper, perhaps?"

He turned his impatient eyes to Alexandra and swirled his brandy around in the sparkling crystal glass, then gestured for them both to join him.

Lucille moved quickly to the sofa and sat down while Alexandra remained standing.

He tapped a finger repeatedly on the armrest as if he was very displeased about something, then finished his brandy and rose to pour himself another.

"What happened at Almack's this evening?" he asked, returning to his seat by the fire.

"Why do you ask?" Alexandra challenged.

Lucille let out an apologetic little laugh while Mr. Carmichael sank back into his chair.

"I ask because I heard something of what occurred and I wonder what you have to say about it. Have you lost your nerve, Alexandra? Have you completely given up the dream of reclaiming your throne?"

Alex lifted her chin. "What exactly did you hear?"

Did he have spies in every corner of this city?

A log shifted in the grate, and a few bright sparks flew up into the chimney.

"I heard that Prince Randolph was seen with the beautiful widowed Countess of Haverston. He danced with her twice, and they disappeared for nearly an hour. Did you not notice?"

No, in truth, she had not. She'd had eyes for only one man all evening.

Relieved, however, that Mr. Carmichael was not here to scold her for the time she had spent with Nicholas, she relaxed her shoulders and sat down next to her stepmother.

"Was there some gossip about it?" she asked.

"Indeed there was. Lady Jersey had to put out a few fires, and Lady Castlereigh suggested that the countess's subscription to Almack's be permanently revoked. I daresay the countess has done irreparable damage to her reputation, and I hope the prince does not attempt to rescue her by offering marriage."

Alexandra felt her eyebrows pull together in a frown, for the notion of another woman sitting upon *her* throne and giving birth to the future King of Petersbourg was enough to curl her toes, and in light of her feelings lately, she was surprised by the intensity of that reaction. "Do you think that is a possibility?"

Mr. Carmichael shrugged. "It is difficult to say. Quite frankly, I am shocked by this news. I cannot believe that the prince would engage in such unseemly behavior. It is the sort of thing one would expect of his brother, Nicholas, but not of *him*."

Alexandra shifted uncomfortably on the sofa cushion.

Carmichael pointed a finger at her. "Mark my words, young lady, if you don't soon win a proposal, he'll wind up trapped by some other ruthless, ambitious female and you will be stuffed back into your little house in Wales, wondering why you hadn't been more efficient when you had the chance."

Alexandra drew back slightly. "By 'efficient,' do you mean fast and loose? Would you have me compromise my morals and risk my reputation and honor in the process? What if he decided such behavior was not becoming of a queen, and he cast me aside, as I suspect he will do with Lady Haverston?"

Feeling a little sick to her stomach, Alexandra stood. "If you will excuse me, sir. I am fatigued and must retire for the night."

Praying he wouldn't call her back, she left him in the library to finish his brandy while Lucille sat speechless on the sofa.

* * *

"I am not pleased," Nigel said to Lucille. "She is becoming impudent. She does not seem to understand what is at stake. Certain risks must be taken."

"She was always a high-spirited girl," Lucille explained. "Even the duke could not control her when he was alive. Sometimes I thought he doted on her too much, but other times I felt he knew he could not win an argument with her—or any sort of battle of wills—so he simply gave in to what she wanted. She was never intimidated by authority."

Nigel tapped his finger on the armrest again. "What would you have me do then? I have invested a great deal of money to put her back on the throne so that we may have a true monarch after the next succession. But I cannot orchestrate such an outcome if she will not do as I tell her to do."

"As I said before, she is strong willed." Lucille paused and chose her words carefully. "Perhaps you might be more successful if you won her trust and behaved as a loving father would. I believe that is what she truly desires. Perhaps, to use an old adage, you might get further with honey than with vinegar."

Nigel set his glass down on the table, stood, and moved to the window, where he clasped his hands behind his back and looked out at the darkness.

"Thank you, Your Grace," he said. "I do see the wisdom in your counsel." He turned and smiled warmly. "You have been most helpful to me. I suppose I have been without a home for too many years and this loneliness has hardened my heart. I have forgotten how to be trusting, but you make me see that there are other ways to live."

Lucille blushed. "Oh, Mr. Carmichael, you exaggerate. I merely hope to offer some helpful information about Alexandra's character, which might aid you in getting what you want from her."

He regarded her with a cunning look of approval. "But you did so much more than that, Your Grace. You have given me hope. I believe I may have my own happy ending to pursue. There is more to life than politics, isn't that so?"

She laughed and agreed.

"I must strive," he said, "to remember that. Now, won't you please join me by the fire? Tell me about your late husband, the duke. Were you very young when you married him?"

* * *

Alexandra closed the door of her bedchamber, tipped her forehead against it, and closed her eyes.

She did not like all this strategic maneuvering, yet she had come to London determined to pursue that path. Now that she was here, however, and had met the prince and his handsome younger brother, nothing seemed quite the same. It was no longer a chessboard with black and white squares. This was her life, and she had her heart to consider.

And what of the wedding night? If she chose duty over love, how would she ever survive it when Randolph came to her bed and she longed for the touch of another man?

Opening her eyes, she found herself looking down at a letter on the floor, which must have been slipped under her door earlier that evening. It bore the red seal of the Royal Palace of Petersbourg.

Bending quickly to pick it up, she broke the seal and unfolded it, then hurried across the room to the dressing table, where she held it up to the candlelight.

My dear Alexandra,

Tomorrow, I will accompany my brother on a tour of the Egyptian Hall in Piccadilly, to which you are also invited. It is a public event, and we expect a great crowd.

I must see you. Please find a way to break free from the group and meet me outside the door. I will wait for you on the street and will think of nothing else until that moment.

Yours, with all my heart,
N.

Alexandra sank into a chair and read the letter a second time. What would her stepmother say if she knew what scandal was brewing in Alex's mind? What kind of madness was this? Did she truly wish to throw away her only chance at reclaiming her family's crown? Could she give it all up for love?

If that's what this was. She had no idea. What if it was just a passing fling on his part? A temporary fit of passion on hers?

Rising from her chair, she read the letter one more time, then did a difficult thing.

She tossed it into the fire and watched it burn while she consoled herself by planning how she would succeed in sneaking away from the group in the museum tomorrow.

For she fully intended to do it. Her heart insisted upon it. Not even one of Mr. Carmichael's incessant lectures about duty was going to stop her.

Chapter Ten

It was a miserable day for a trip to the Egyptian Hall. Rain was coming down in cold buckets from the sky and had filled the streets with puddles.

Alex, however, was undaunted. Not long after the museum tour began, she managed to slip away unnoticed through the constantly shifting crowd.

Shivering in the dampness as she walked out the front door, she paused next to a column in the shelter of the overhang and peered up and down the street.

At last, a quiet, husky voice spoke to her from the shadows. "You came."

Alexandra turned to discover her love—yes, that's what he was—standing behind the opposite column, dressed in a fur-trimmed double-breasted greatcoat, black boots polished to a fine sheen, and a stylish top hat. He held his leather gloves in his hands, and when he began to move toward her in that slow, sensual gait it was all she could do to keep from falling into his arms. She wanted him desperately, with unquenchable passion, despite what her sensible mind had to say about it.

"Yes," she replied. "I shouldn't be here, but I couldn't bear another moment away from you."

And there it was . . . surrender at last. Her true heart revealed.

Something flashed in his eyes. A look of relief. Or triumph, perhaps. He was pleased she had confessed such a thing.

Striding forward, he said, "Do not let yourself entertain any regrets about this, Alexandra. You are thrusting duty aside and choosing happiness instead. It pleases me to know you are here for no other reason but love."

"Do not call it that," she pleaded. "It is too much. I don't know what this is. It may be a temporary infatuation. Rebellion perhaps. I admit, I am mystified."

He stared at her for a long moment, then glanced away. "Come with me now. My coach is just over there."

"My stepmother will notice my absence."

"Five minutes is all I ask. Lift the hood of your cloak."

Surrendering yet again to her natural impulses, she raised her hood and followed him up the street to that illustrious black vehicle parked at the corner. It gleamed brightly, washed clean by the driving rain, and was illuminated by a single beam of sunlight that had pierced through the clouds.

He handed her up into the dry, private confines of the coach while the rain roared like a beast on the roof.

"I apologize for the weather," he said as he climbed in, shut the door, and joined her on the seat.

Oh, she was done for. While he removed his hat, whisked the water from the brim, and unbuttoned the top of his coat she was fascinated by his every move and couldn't take her eyes off him. He smelled clean, like shaving soap. His hair was thick and wavy. She wanted to run her fingers through it. He was the most beautiful man she had ever seen.

After setting his hat and gloves on the seat beside him, he reached out to lower the hood of her cloak and looked carefully into her eyes. He seemed to be admiring every detail of her face.

His hand rested on her knee. Her heart ignited with uncontrollable passion.

Next, without uttering a word, he slowly peeled off each of her gloves and set them on the seat behind him. He then touched the pad of his finger to the sensitive inside of her wrist and drew a little heart there.

Alex trembled.

"May I kiss you now?" he asked, leaning closer and touching his cheek lightly to hers.

"Yes . . ."

And just like that, all her dreams of the Petersbourg crown flew out the window and nothing mattered but the soft, warm touch of his lips.

Tilting his head to the side, he deepened the kiss and slid his hand around the nape of her neck. Her body grew warm with rapture. All her nerve endings sparked with fire as his tongue swept into her mouth.

Knowing it was not possible to block this desire, she tipped her head back to allow him greater access to her throat and ran her hands across the tops of his shoulders.

He let out a low groan of arousal that helped her to understand what it meant to be a woman, not a girl. She, too, sighed with pleasure and relaxed into his embrace.

He pressed his open mouth to hers again, and this time she was better equipped for the explosion of sensation and met the kiss with equal insistence. Light flashed suddenly in the window and a thunderous rumble shook the coach. Alex pulled back, startled and unsettled.

"I must go," she said breathlessly. "My stepmother is probably searching for me at this very moment, and if she learns where I've been—"

"It doesn't matter." He took her face in his hands. "I will marry you. If we are engaged, she will have no more hold on you, at least not for long."

Alexandra pressed her hands to his chest, for if she gave in to the smallest temptation to go on kissing him like this, there would be no turning back.

"You don't understand," she said. "My life is not what you think. There are things you don't know about me."

"Then tell me now. I want to know everything."

Her stomach dropped. She couldn't tell him. Not now.

But when? Could she *ever* reveal such a thing to him? What would it mean for the succession if she married the younger son? The throne would not be hers, and there might be another civil war if the people of Petersbourg discovered the truth. She did not want to be the cause of that.

Lightning flashed in the windows again, followed by another thunderclap.

"I really must go." She reached over him for her gloves, pulled them on, and made for the door.

"Wait." He caught her by the hand. "I must have you."

"Please, Nicholas."

She flicked the door latch and stepped out into the rain. He followed her, and together they hurried back to the museum.

"Meet me again tomorrow," he said. "*Please.* In the garden at Grosvenor Square."

Not wanting to linger too long on the street, she nodded. "Fine. I will be there at the gate at two o'clock when my stepmother takes her afternoon nap. Now let me go, and do not follow!"

With that, she rejoined the museum tour.

* * *

Throughout the evening and all the next day, the memory of that kiss filled Alexandra with yearning as she anticipated another secret rendezvous with Nicholas that very day.

It wasn't easy to hide her feelings from Lucille, however, who asked more than once what she was daydreaming about when she was caught staring off into space.

When the clock finally struck two and Lucille announced she would retire to her bedchamber for her nap, Alex mentioned casually that she might take a walk in the garden, for it was such a lovely day.

A short while later, wearing her blue-and-white-striped walking dress and a pale blue bonnet with a wide brim that shaded her eyes, she left the house and crossed the street to the gate, where she took note of a coach parked at the curb with two black horses and a dark-coated driver.

At first she thought it might be the palace coach, but upon closer scrutiny, she noticed it bore no crest.

A flicker of apprehension coursed through her, for she had lived too long with the knowledge of her father's execution and had never felt truly safe in her surroundings. She was always glancing over her shoulder, locking doors behind her.

With growing unease, she wondered if she should return to the house, but there was no time to mull it over before the door of the coach swung open and a gentleman stepped out.

Nicholas.

Oh, thank God.

"Come this way." He waved her over. "The driver will take us around the square."

Still somewhat shaken, Alexandra hurried to the coach and climbed inside. He followed her in, shut the door, and drew the blinds.

"I thought I would go mad waiting for this moment," he told her as he removed his hat.

The coach lurched forward, but Alexandra was oblivious to the movement, for she was lost in the husky rumble of his voice and the captivating blue of his eyes as he slid closer and immediately pressed his lips to hers.

A wild passion flared through her, and she took his face in her hands, fearing that he might slip through her fingers if she didn't hold tightly enough.

The kiss was rougher this time, more aggressive, but she drank it in without restraint. She wanted this man badly enough to deny what she had accepted as her destiny. She would do anything for him. She would walk through fire or climb the highest mountain.

Perhaps others were wrong about her future and her true destiny lay elsewhere, for life was not all about politics and duty, was it? What about love? This affair may be sudden and impulsive, but here was a man she could not give up, not for any amount of power, wealth, or status in the world. She had no wish for a throne if it meant she could not have him.

"Say you'll marry me," he whispered in a quiet voice of husky allure as he eased her down onto her back and settled his hips snugly between her thighs.

"I cannot resist you," she said. "I cannnot resist *this*."

"Then don't." He thrust his hips and pushed against that yearning place that begged to be touched.

She threw her head back. "Oh, Nicholas, how I want you."

"Then have me. I am yours."

She kissed him again and pulled him close. "I've never done anything like this before. You're the only man I've ever wanted."

"You have no idea how happy that makes me."

"Truly?"

"Yes, and one day soon you'll understand why." He laid openmouthed kisses down the side of her neck. "How long can you stay?"

"Not long," she replied. "A few more minutes, then I must return. My stepmother does not sleep long in the afternoons. As soon as she wakes, she will look out the window. We must be careful not to stop in front of the house. She must not know we were together."

His hand slowly slid up her thigh, and she squirmed with longing.

"What if she knew I offered marriage?" he asked. "Would she not agree?"

Alexandra blinked up at him. "She would not be pleased."

He frowned. "Why not? I am second in line to the throne. Is that not good enough?"

"She wants me to marry your brother."

His body went still. "Well, I don't care what *she* wants. It only matters to me what *you* want."

"I want *you*," she breathlessly replied as she pulled him close. "But there are others, my benefactor for one, who would oppose it."

She wasn't sure what Mr. Carmichael would do. It could be dangerous.

Nicholas let out a deep, guttural groan of need.

"Oh . . . ," she sighed as he kissed her neck. "We could run away together. Then it would be too late for anyone to stop us. We could live abroad if you wanted. I would give up everything for you, even my chance at the throne." Oh, God, what was she saying?

He drew back slightly.

"What's wrong?" she asked.

"Nothing."

"Yes, something is wrong. What is it?" She leaned up on her elbows.

"I'm just . . ." He raked a hand through his hair as if he could not conceive of what she had just confessed and could not even form words. He sat back on the seat. "I am pleased you feel that way."

"I do. I do."

Quite unexpectedly, he took her face in his hands and

looked into her eyes with fierce conviction. "But if you agree to marry me, I will have something important to tell you."

"Tell me now."

He hesitated, then shook his head. "Not until we are both sure this is what we want."

"I *am* sure," she told him. "Aren't *you?*"

He hesitated, and her heart sank.

"I need to know that you are sincere. That you will truly give up everything for me," he said. "I need to be sure you will not change your mind."

The wheels of the coach rattled ominously beneath them.

"Do you not believe me?" she asked.

"I was burned once before. Remember?"

Alexandra nodded. "Yes, I remember every word you've ever spoken to me, but what are we going to do?"

At last he faced her. "Let us do it then. Run away with me. We can leave in the morning, travel north to Scotland, and be man and wife in a few days—with or without your stepmother's permission. Once it is done, there will be no reversing it, and it won't matter about the scandal here in London. We will begin anew in Petersbourg. I will introduce you as my wife, and we will send for your sisters, who will be presented at court. We will be the happiest couple who ever lived. You'll see. I promise."

She gazed into his eyes and couldn't seem to say yes. Not without telling him the truth.

"You seem unsure." He looked hurt. Almost frightened.

"No," she quickly replied. "I am not unsure. I want this. Truly, I do."

Clasping her hand in his, he raised it to his lips. "You are everything I've ever hoped for, Alexandra, but never really imagined I could have."

She smiled. "I am yours. Nothing will ever come between us." She wouldn't let it. She would do whatever it took. "But I must go."

He did not yet release her. "Can you sneak out before dawn?"

Her heart beat riotously at the prospect. Was this really happening? "Yes." Turning to look out the window, she said, "This is a good place to let me out. I can walk home across the garden."

Nicholas pounded a fist on the wall, and the driver pulled to the curb.

"I won't sleep a wink tonight," she said with a laugh, barely able to contain her excitement as she kissed Nicholas one last time. "I've never been so happy. I never imagined my life could turn out like this!"

"Nor I," he replied as she stepped out of the vehicle. "In the morning I will be parked here on the street outside your house in the same spot I was this afternoon. Do not disappoint me or you will break my heart."

"I promise I won't."

He shut the door and drove away, and Alex walked briskly along the wrought-iron garden fence, skipping occasionally while making plans for her future. She would tell Nicholas the truth about her heritage in the morning. Best to do it before they crossed the border into Scotland.

Oddly enough, the notion of confessing to him did not frighten her, for she was quite certain he would understand, because he loved her.

And he would protect her. He would protect her against all enemies.

PART II
Where Truths Are Revealed

Chapter Eleven

St. James's Palace

His Royal Highness Prince Randolph of Petersburg strode into the drawing room, instructed the butler to bring up a bottle of champagne, and immediately sent for Rose and Nicholas.

The champagne arrived first; then Rose entered the room, stopped just inside the door, and regarded him with surprise. "Good Lord, what has happened? You have that look about you."

He picked up a glass of champagne and held it out to her. "You know me too well. I have good news. Come and celebrate with me."

Nick came striding in just then, looking as if he'd just risen from bed. His hair was disheveled, and he was shrugging into a jacket. "What's going on?" he asked. "The way Spencer was banging on my door just now, I thought there was a fire."

"Rand says there is something to celebrate," Rose explained with a curious lift of her eyebrow as she accepted the glass he offered.

"I'll have one of those," Nick mentioned. He followed Rand to the table. "Now tell me what is going on, and it better be good."

Rand poured him a glass of bubbly and held it out. "It's the best damn thing I've had to say all year. Perhaps you should both sit down."

His siblings moved to the sofa while he remained standing.

"Your plan worked," he said to Rose. "I have just proposed to Lady Alexandra Monroe, eldest daughter of the late Duke of St. George, and she has accepted me."

Nick frowned. "But we've been in England only a fortnight. You're sure about this? Wouldn't you like to sow some oats first? Meet a few other ladies perhaps? Act like *me*?"

Rand chuckled and shook his head. "I'm not you, Nick, and I doubt I could have kept up the charade much longer. Besides, she's the one. I knew it the first moment I saw her. She is meant to be Queen of Petersbourg. I can feel it."

Nick stared at him for a moment, then raised his glass. "Obviously there's no point in arguing. You will charge ahead as usual, straight into the thick of it."

Rand turned to his sister, who was staring up at him with wide eyes.

"I cannot believe it," she said. "I had no idea it would happen so quickly. But does she know who you are? Have you told her yet?"

Rand downed his champagne and set the glass on a table. "No. She has been working hard to resist what exists between us, and I needed to be sure she would be willing to give up the dream of marrying a future king. Today she agreed to throw duty aside for love. She even agreed to elope with me to Scotland and live abroad if we had to. It is exactly what you imagined, Rose, when you concocted this plan," he added. "She has chosen me over the future crown."

"So you are absolutely *certain* she genuinely loves you," Rose said, not yet convinced. "There is no chance she already knows the truth?"

"No chance at all," he replied. "Nick and I have been very careful. Ah, Rose, if you only knew what it has been like. When I am with her, I feel as if she understands my plight, for it is her own. She once wanted to marry for love, but bears the burden of duty to her family. She is conflicted, and I wish to rescue her. I cannot wait for the moment when I reveal the truth. I am certain, without a doubt, she will be overjoyed."

He poured another glass of champagne.

"When will you tell her?" Nick asked.

"Tomorrow morning. As we are leaving London."

"Leaving London?" Nick stood up. "But we've only just arrived."

Rand raised a hand to calm his brother. "Have no fear. I don't mean us. As I said, she agreed to run away with me to Scotland and forsake all her responsibilities. We plan to meet at dawn."

Nick shook his head. "Are you mad? You are the future King of Petersbourg. You cannot elope without a word to anyone. The people will be furious and disappointed, not to mention how Father will react. It may start another rebellion, for we are hanging by a thread as it is. The people will not stand for this. The Royalists will use it to damage Father's popularity. They will say that a real king would never do such a common thing."

Rand sat down and regarded his sister and brother with steady eyes.

"I appreciate your concerns," he said, "but I am not that foolish. I only wish to ensure that she is as devoted as she claims. When she walks out her door at dawn tomorrow, I will know that it is an act of love. I will then tell her the truth and suggest a proper royal wedding in Petersbourg. She will probably weep tears of joy, knowing that she will have love, as well as the thing she wanted most to begin with—a grand future for herself and her sisters.

She will be greatly relieved that her stepmother will not disown her but will be prouder of her than ever for winning the race against all the other ambitious young ladies in this country." He walked to the window and looked out. "Though I despise that turn of phrase. Calling it a race . . ."

Rose stood up and raised her glass as well. "Well then. I am very happy for you, Rand, and pleased also to anticipate the joy of having a sister. Let us drink to true love." She paused and cleared her throat, as if she were fighting tears. "And whatever it takes to achieve it."

He turned to her and bowed. "I owe you my happiness, Rose. I never imagined it was possible, but your brilliant plan has worked—for somehow I've managed to find the one woman in England who has no interest in my crown."

With that, they raised their glasses and sat down to plan their journey home to Petersbourg—with his future queen at his side.

Chapter Twelve

That night after the household was asleep, Alexandra sat at her desk by candlelight with a quill in her hand.

She could not leave without a word to anyone in the morning. She could not simply disappear without explaining herself to her stepmother, who would notice her absence and worry that she had been abducted by revolutionary spies.

She knew her sisters would understand, for they were young and romantic, and she was not concerned for their welfare. The scandal over this elopement would be quite great, no doubt, but she was confident that Nicholas would take care of everything. Once they were married and living in Petersbourg, he would send for her sisters. They would be presented at court and make their own spectacular debuts in their new country.

She may not become queen, but she would be happy in love, and it would be enough.

For that reason, a letter was the only way. With luck, by the time her stepmother read it she and Nicholas would be well on their way to Scotland and no one would be able to stop them, not even Mr. Carmichael.

A wave of euphoria pulsed within her as she imagined stepping into the coach in the early hours of the morning.

Just to see him again—to touch him and know that he

loved her and was willing to take this risk in order to
spirit her away . . . It fueled her determination to an immeasurable degree. He had rescued her from her bitterness,
her jealousy, and her empty vengeance. She owed him
everything.

But heaven help her, she could barely think clearly
enough to dip her quill into the ink, for her feet were tapping on the floor, and she couldn't seem to keep the butterflies from fluttering wildly in her belly. She was the
luckiest woman on earth!

Nevertheless, she persevered. . . .

Dear Mama,

*Please prepare yourself for what I am about to confess. I
have decided I cannot live a lie. I must marry for love, not
duty or vengeance or ambition, and I must therefore give
up the Petersbourg crown. I take solace in the fact that I
do not believe my true family would have wished for me to
sacrifice my happiness for the sake of tradition. I cling to
the hope that any person's life is worth more than that,
no matter who they are—common or royal—and that in
heaven, my father and mother believe the same.*

*Surely, heaven is a place of the heart where love and
honesty without greed is the right way. I believe it must
be true. My heart is telling me so. Something very powerful is driving me toward the love I feel for Prince Nicholas. Everything is telling me to let go of my ambition and
give up my goal to marry the future king.*

*I do not love Randolph; therefore I cannot be his queen.
I will fail miserably if I am forced to sacrifice my heart
for a man I do not love.*

*Please forgive me for acting in accordance with my
conscience and breaking the agreement we had with Mr.*

Carmichael. Please tell him I will repay all our debts to him. His generosity will not be forgotten.

Also, please tell June, Alice, and Frannie that I will send for them once we are settled in Petersbourg. Their futures are now secured.

Sincerely,
Alexandra

She laid the quill down on the desk and sat back to watch the ink dry.

A tear spilled across her cheek, and for the first time in her life she realized what true happiness was.

She wished the same for her stepmother and sisters. She prayed they would, one day, know it for themselves.

* * *

Please, God, don't let her change her mind, Rand thought as the coach rolled onto Grosvenor Square at dawn.

It was still dark. The streets were quiet and empty, but the birds were chirping in the treetops. There was a fresh dewy coolness in the air.

Before stepping into the coach, he had paused a moment outside St. James's Palace to breathe in the exquisite aroma of hope—for at last, he had succeeded in achieving the impossible. He had found a woman willing to marry him for love and not the throne.

Why, then, did he feel such intense trepidation?

He'd had his heart shattered once before, he supposed, and did not wish to repeat the experience. The cynic inside him almost wished he had not thrown caution aside so completely over the past week and given free rein to his emotions, but there was no turning back now. He had offered his whole heart to Alexandra, and now he must be courageous enough to follow through. He must believe, in the very depths of his soul, that she would not disappoint him.

For if she did not come, he was not quite sure what he would do. He doubted he would ever trust another woman again for as long as he lived. He might possibly declare war on the entire female race.

Finally, the coach pulled to a halt a few doors down from her home. He tried to sit back patiently and wait, but it was no easy task. He had been very confident in the drawing room the day before while explaining his plans to Rose and Nick.

Nick had expressed some concern about his impulsiveness, but Rand had defended himself and his actions.

Because he *loved* Alexandra. She was the only woman he wanted at his side when he became king.

He laid a hand on his stomach. It was swirling around and around.

Dammit. All he wanted was for her to dash out her front door at this very moment to be with him forever, no matter what their futures held.

He was half-tempted to proceed with this mad plan to elope to Gretna Green—like any common man—and forgo the pomp and ceremony of a royal wedding.

All in exchange for a simple wedding night mere days from now.

His blood quickened at the thought.

Sitting forward, he watched the front of her house.

* * *

Nearly two hours later, Rand pounded his fist against the back of the seat and cursed his bloody impatience. The sun had risen in the sky quite some time ago, but Alexandra had not come to him.

Had she changed her mind? If so, what was he to do about it? Go knock on the door and demand to hear from the butler why she had not left her house unchaperoned at this ungodly hour to run away with him and elope to Scotland?

Rand burst out of the coach, stepped onto the walk, and paced up and down along the garden fence, never taking his eyes off the front of the house.

Where the bloody hell was she? She had seemed so sure of her decision yesterday, and he had believed her to be genuine.

Had he been wrong? Did she decide in the end that he wasn't good enough? In which case he would forever wonder how things would have turned out if he had told her the truth yesterday.

Why hadn't he? Why hadn't her acceptance been enough? Was he completely unable to trust a woman? She had told him yes in no uncertain terms, yet he continued with the charade, requiring her to prove herself one more time by leaping over another hurdle and sneaking out of her house at dawn.

He stopped pacing, tore his hat off his head, and raked his fingers through his hair. Perhaps he had taken it too far and this was his punishment.

He paused in front of the team of horses and looked up at the front of her house again.

A milk cart passed before him, obstructing his view.

A fish merchant went down the front steps to the servants' entrance to make a delivery.

Clearly the household was awake and functioning; therefore, Alexandra could not possibly slip out now. It was too late. There would be no eloping today.

He wondered—he hoped—that she might have simply overslept. He, on the other hand, had not even gone to bed last night. He had not wanted to be late. He had not wished to disappoint his future bride or leave her waiting in the street, uncertain of his love for her.

As she seemed to have done to him.

The sound of raucous laughter from a group of grooms-men farther down the square startled him, and his anger ignited into a roaring fire of resentment.

He tried to tell himself that he must not assume the worst. Perhaps her stepmother had discovered her inten-tions and locked her in her room.

Perhaps she had been taken ill.

Or perhaps she had changed her mind.

Rand circled around to the door of the coach and climbed back inside. He had humiliated himself quite enough.

"Move on!" he shouted, pounding hard against the roof-top. "Take me back to St. James's!"

He wasn't quite sure what he would do when he got there. It would take some time to settle his anger—directed mostly at himself, of course.

He should have known better. How many times would he put himself through something like this? Would he never learn? He was a prince. A future king. He should know by now that true love was not for him. Not even a brilliantly executed charade could make it so.

He cupped his forehead in a hand and squeezed his eyes shut.

Chapter Thirteen

Two hours earlier

Shortly before dawn, Alexandra piled the pillows on her bed in the shape of her body and tossed the coverlet over them, feeling certain that it was an effective ruse to indicate that she was merely sleeping late.

She then fastened the buckle on her valise and tiptoed across her bedchamber to the door, which she opened very slowly. It creaked on its hinges, and she winced, for she did not wish to wake anyone at this hour. She wanted to leave the house and be rolling out of London long before her absence was even noticed.

A floorboard creaked under her feet as she made her way gingerly to the stairs. She stopped abruptly and listened for any sounds of movement in the house.

All seemed quiet, so she proceeded to the top of the stairs and carried her bag down to the first level, stepping lightly onto each stair.

Crossing the front hall on her tiptoes, she was about to reach for the front doorknob when a voice spoke to her from the library.

"Alexandra! Stop where you are."

Heart leaping to her throat, she froze.

"Mama," she said. "What are you doing up at this hour?"

She decided in that moment that she would not let anyone stand in her way. Nothing her stepmother could say or do was going to change her mind, for she wanted this. She wanted Nicholas more than she'd ever wanted anything.

Lucille, still wearing her dinner gown from the night before, strode forward into the hall. In her hands, she held a newspaper.

Alexandra glanced down at it and was not at all prepared for the unexpected flash of dread that sparked in her belly.

"What do you want?" she asked, thrusting all fear aside.

Lucille glanced down at her valise. "You cannot go," she said. "I understand what you are feeling, truly I do, but you must listen to me."

Alexandra took a deep, slow breath while her stomach turned over in knots and her heart pounded wildly with anxiety. "No, I do not think you understand at all. And how did you know what I meant to do? Why are you awake at this hour?"

Lucille regarded her with what appeared to be pity, which grated upon her steely pride.

"Your maid found your letter after you were asleep," Lucille explained, "which she brought to me. Do not look at me like that, and do not blame her, the poor girl. She didn't like doing it, but when Mr. Carmichael took her into his employ she was told that her first loyalty was to me, as your guardian."

Alexandra reached for the doorknob again, determined to flee from this discouraging world—a world of manipulation and mistrust. All she wanted to do was escape into the hazy summer dawn with the man who loved her for herself and had encouraged her to choose her freedom.

"No, wait!" Lucille darted forward with her hand outstretched. "Hear me out. I am quite certain you will thank me afterward."

Alexandra knew her stepmother well enough to recognize that her plea was sincere. She was not here to satisfy Mr. Carmichael's ambitions. This was something else, and Alex felt strangely compelled to listen.

"Speak quickly," she said. "If you've already read my letter, you know that Nicholas is outside and I am sure you understand I do not wish to keep him waiting."

Lucille held out the newspaper. "Read this. Front page."

Slowly, Alexandra set down her valise and took hold of the paper.

It was too dark to read anything in the front hall, so she entered the library, where the fire and candles were lit. The warmth touched her cheeks as she crossed the threshold, but her heart was freezing over with dread.

Sitting down in the wing chair that Mr. Carmichael had occupied recently, she glanced over the page in search of whatever it was that Lucille wished her to see before she dashed out the door to elope.

Suddenly there it was, like a death bell ringing in her ears.

PRINCE NICHOLAS A DISGRACE TO THE THRONE!

Prince Nicholas has yet again proven himself unworthy of any connection to the crown, and some are calling for his resignation as private secretary to our future king.

Lady M—, daughter of the esteemed Duke of Tantallon was recently seen leaving the Hanover Hotel at dawn on the morning of May 10 following a political assembly which her father had attended the night before.

She is said to have been intending an elopement with the prince, but was caught in the lobby by her mother, the duchess.

The minority Royalists—growing increasingly vocal in recent months—have begun a new campaign at the

Hanover Hotel and call for a return to the direct line of descent in the royal succession.

Alexandra slumped back in the chair and let the newspaper fall to her feet. Staring into the flames of the fire, she fought against the sudden nausea rising up within her.

He had seduced another daughter of a duke into eloping with him only six weeks ago? How did he accomplish it? Did he lead the young lady to believe she needed his approval to win Randolph's heart? Did he kiss her passionately and convince her that he was her one true love?

"Oh, God," Alexandra whispered, vaguely aware of her stepmother sitting down across from her.

"I'm sorry," Lucille said. "I could see how you felt about him. He is a charming, handsome man, without a doubt, but I have heard other stories like this. I knew what kind of man he was. I tried to warn you, but you wouldn't listen. I am only glad I stopped you in time."

"I am glad, too," Alex replied, steeling herself against the terrible agony of heartache rising up within her. Why, God? Why? How many more times must she suffer a hurtful truth about someone she allowed herself to love and trust?

She had no intention of shedding a single tear, however. Not over him. She would not crumble into a fit of weeping. She would remember who she was.

Lucille laid a comforting hand on her knee. "I hope you will not be too heartbroken. I hope you will recognize that he was not worthy of you. We came to London to win a proposal from Randolph, and he is still available if you will let go of this foolish infatuation. Will you consider that?"

Alexandra pulled her eyes away from the flames in the hearth and regarded Lucille steadily. "You mean to say, even after this, there is still a chance?"

"Mr. Carmichael is now suggesting that we adopt another strategy. He had hoped you might marry Randolph and produce an heir without anyone knowing of your true identity—because while that tyrant of a king is alive your safety cannot be assured. But now, with Randolph quite possibly consorting with that scandalous countess, there is a dangerous possibility that he might marry her, which would complicate matters terribly. The king would no doubt prevent news of the scandal from entering Petersbourg, and a royal wedding, even to that disreputable widow, might win back the country's support for the New Regime. But there is something else you must know. The king is unwell. In all likelihood, he will not be with us much longer, and Mr. Carmichael believes we might be better off stepping out into the open straightaway. He believes you may be able to speak to Randolph directly and discuss matters of state. You could convince him that taking you as his wife would appease the Royalists and put an end to the divide."

Alexandra pulled herself out of the humiliation of her botched elopement and regarded her stepmother with astonishment.

"Mr. Carmichael wishes me to reveal my identity? I thought that was forbidden. He said my life could be in danger if the New Regime knew of my existence, not to mention my ambitions."

"That is true," Lucille said. "But with the king's death the announcement of your existence will breathe new life into the Royalist cause. Surely we can convince Randolph that you are the answer to his prayers. Once his father is gone, he will need all the help he can get, and you may be just what he needs to save his monarchy."

"It is not *his* monarchy," she heard herself say with more than a little umbrage.

Alex stood up and walked to the window, where she looked out onto the square and saw that shadowy black coach waiting at the curb.

Nicholas was inside. *Her Nicholas.* The man who had captured her heart and convinced her his love was genuine.

Had she truly been tricked by a scoundrel, just like that poor ruined girl at the Hanover Hotel? If so, was she even capable of leading a country that was already in turmoil, with no sense of itself?

A quarter of an hour earlier, she thought she had all the answers. Now she felt like a fool.

Turning to face her stepmother, she said, "How likely is it that Randolph might propose to this woman who has seduced him into her bed?"

Perhaps she and Randolph were kindred spirits after all. Perhaps he, too, had lost himself to his passions and forgotten the great duty that rested upon his shoulders—which was the safekeeping of his dynasty.

It was something Alexandra understood very well.

"No one is sure," Lucille replied. "But Mr. Carmichael has it upon good authority that they have already become intimate, perhaps even at the palace. It is the perfect trap. Passion is dangerous, as you well know. It has trapped and weakened many a king."

Alexandra turned again to look out the window at the coach in the rising light of dawn. "Indeed, I know very well," she replied. "Perhaps I *can* talk some sense into Randolph. Perhaps we can discover a common Achilles' heel in each other. And a common strength." She faced her stepmother. "Does Mr. Carmichael truly believe I will not be in danger if I reveal my identity? Do *you* believe it?"

Lucille stood up. "I believe you are brave enough to face that possibility and meet it head-on. And I have never been more sure that this is your true destiny."

Alexandra looked out the window one more time.

She had loved him. Truly, she had, and she'd believed, with all her heart, that it was real. A part of her still wanted to believe it and her soul was reeling in a deathlike agony, but she would listen to her head this time.

You saw the story in the paper. He seduced another woman and convinced her to elope with him only six weeks ago. He is a rake and a libertine. You knew it from the beginning.

Turning to face her stepmother, Alex spoke in a firm voice. "Thank you for your intervention. I will be forever in your debt. I would like to arrange a formal meeting with Prince Randolph to discuss his marriage. I shall present him with a solution to the problems in his country."

Lucille approached and pulled her into her arms. "I have never been more proud of you. And I am sorry about Nicholas. I want you to know I understand, for I was young once myself. I remember what it feels like to fall in love. There are moments you would do anything to be with the one who is the perfect light in your world."

Alexandra shuddered at the words. Quickly she stepped back.

"Please do not mention it again, Mama. I do not want to think of him. I want to put it behind me."

Fighting against a raw, unwelcome pang of regret, she picked up her valise and returned to her room to dress for the day.

Chapter Fourteen

Rand did not imagine it would be quite so humiliating as this, but he had brought it all on himself, opening a bottle of champagne before Alexandra had actually crossed the threshold to run away with him.

"Where is she?" Rose asked, stopping in her tracks as she greeted him at the door.

His sister was dressed in a peach gown of silk and lace— much too formal for this hour of the day—but clearly she had expected an engagement announcement.

Her eyebrows pulled together with concern, and her excitement deflated notably as she glanced over his shoulder, expecting to see Alexandra behind him.

"She changed her mind," he explained as he removed his hat and gloves and shouldered his way past Rose toward the stairs.

"I'm so sorry, Rand. Truly . . . I know how you must feel."

"Never mind," he replied, taking the stairs two at a time to the top. "I don't wish to discuss it now."

"But did you see her, or speak to her?" Rose called out.

"Not yet."

With steely purpose, he strode into his bedchamber, slammed the door behind him, and paced back and forth for a few minutes.

He wondered if he should have stayed longer or gone to knock on the door. Perhaps there was a perfectly reasonable explanation and he had given up too quickly—jaded as he was by past experience.

Acting far too impulsively for his own good, he sat down at his desk and pulled out a box of stationery. Hunting around for a quill, he found one at last and dipped it into the ink jar.

Perhaps this could all still be resolved. Perhaps there was some reasonable explanation. . . .

* * *

Alex was lying on her bed staring absently at the ceiling when another letter slid under her door. It swished across the floor and landed squarely at her bedside.

Slowly sitting up and regarding it with bitter antagonism, she wondered from where it had come. Was it another love letter from Nicholas? If so, should she even break the seal?

Damn him all to hell. He had humiliated her in the worst possible way and nearly caused her to lose sight of her true destiny.

Staring at the letter with something close to murderous rage, she stood up, crouched down, swiped it off the floor, broke the red seal, and quickly unfolded it.

My dearest love,

I do not know what happened to you this morning. All I know is what happened to me.

I waited more than two hours past dawn for you to arrive, but in the end, I was disappointed. Please write and tell me you are safe. If it was wrong of me to return to St. James's Palace without you, I will turn around and collect you immediately. But if you have changed your mind about us, I beg to understand why.

What happened? Please know I am your devoted servant and all that matters to me is your happiness. Whatever the problem is, I will fix it. I assure you I have the means, if only you will trust me.

Yours devotedly,
N.

Alexandra crumpled the letter into a ball and uttered an unladylike oath before she pitched it fast across the room.

How could he do this to her? Clearly he was a compulsive philanderer, and she had let him fool her. He was fooling her still, because heaven help her, she continued to want him with every spark of heat in her body.

Bloody hell!

But no. No! She would not allow herself to pine for him, nor would she be tempted by the look of him when she saw him tonight, for surely he would be present when she spoke to Randolph.

Hurrying angrily to pick up the offensive correspondence, she stuffed it into the top drawer of her desk and slammed it shut. Three times in rapid succession.

She realized suddenly that this was the first time she had not destroyed a letter from him by fire. Perhaps that was what weakened her position when she arrived at St. James's Palace a few hours later to speak to Randolph, but was greeted at the door by the man she loved, who looked at her as if she were the devil himself.

Chapter Fifteen

"Your Royal Highness," Alexandra said decorously as she curtsied very low. The butler reached to take her cloak, which she removed and handed over. "I did not know if you would be here this evening. Allow me to introduce Mr. Nigel Carmichael, my benefactor."

She gestured toward him.

"Your Royal Highness," he said, "I am pleased to make your acquaintance."

Nicholas glared at him with icy contempt. "It was *you* who contacted me about an urgent meeting with Randolph tonight."

"That is correct," Mr. Carmichael replied. "There is much to discuss. Lady Alexandra will explain everything when she is granted a private audience with him."

Nicholas turned his cold eyes upon her, and she shivered at the threat she saw there.

"My brother is not at home," he informed them. "Consequently you will have to speak to *me*."

Alex frowned. "But we already made arrangements, and we were assured we would speak to Randolph directly."

Those blue eyes narrowed with a dark fury that unsettled her. How bold he was in front of her benefactor.

"Be that as it may, I wish to speak to you in private, Lady Alexandra," he said. "If you will excuse us, sir."

It was an arrogant request from a disgraced son of a tyrant king, and Alexandra felt Mr. Carmichael stiffen beside her.

"That would be highly inappropriate, sir," he said. "I am here as Lady Alexandra's guardian. Any discussions you wish to have with her will occur in front of *me*."

A muscle flicked at Nicholas's jaw, which suggested he was highly agitated, as if *she* were the one who had betrayed their love that morning.

Oh, how she longed to set him straight.

"I beg your pardon, Mr. Carmichael," she said, "but I believe I will speak to Prince Nicholas in private, as he has requested."

"You can wait in the library," Nicholas added. "Spencer, show him in, and bring him a brandy. We may be a while."

Not entirely comfortable with her decision to speak to Nicholas in private—for she might throw a rather large and expensive piece of crystal at him—Alexandra nevertheless did not look back as she followed him to the drawing room.

He waited for her to enter, then shut the doors behind him.

With crazed, fuming emotions, Alex regarded him from across the room. *"How dare you?"* Honestly, she was fit to be tied!

He strode forward. "How dare I do *what*? Wait two hours in front of your house like a lovesick fool? Or perhaps it was the fact that I have not produced my brother this evening, when that is clearly what you came for." He stood less than an arm's length away and stared into her eyes with angry disbelief. "Was I not good enough for you?" he asked. "Did you wake up this morning and change your mind? Did you decide you would prefer to be queen after all?"

Alexandra struggled not to stumble backwards into the

deep abyss of her passion for this man. He was too handsome, too forthright, and the way he looked at her now almost made her lose her head.

"You seduced me," she said. "And you neglected to mention how you seduced and ruined another young lady at the Hanover Hotel barely six weeks ago. What have you to say about *that*?"

His head drew back in surprise. "That is why you did not come? Where did you hear this? And when?"

"Just this morning," she explained, "when I had my hand on the door and was about to leave everything behind and destroy my reputation for the blind love I felt for you. But my stepmother stopped me just in time, thank God for that."

The anger in his eyes drained away like water through a sieve and was replaced by something else. Relief. Or perhaps it was joy.

Joy?

"Oh, my darling," he said, taking a step closer. "Why did you not tell me? Why did you not come outdoors and confront me?"

She took an abrupt step back and held up a hand. "Stay where you are, sir, and do not call me darling. That is not what I am. Not to you. And *how* could I tell you? Why *should* I have? It was all there in black and white. I did not wish to hear your side of the story. I am quite sure you would have come up with some convenient explanation to turn me blind and infatuated again."

"You're not blind," he insisted. "You see the truth. You have always seen the truth, which is why I fell in love with you."

He closed the distance between them, slid his hand around the back of her neck, pulled her into his arms and, despite everything, the nearness of him sent a crashing wave of love into her body.

The sensation broke her will, and she gasped.

"You hurt me," she told him, revealing far more than she ever intended while she tried to push him away. "I hated you, and I hate you now. I came here to speak to Randolph. Why are you doing this? I have important things to say to him."

"Then say them," he whispered in her ear.

He held her even tighter—so tight she could not move—and all the fight drained out of her. "Please let me go, Nicholas."

Drawing back slightly and cupping her face in both his hands, he gazed into her eyes with what appeared to be some amusement and shook his head.

"You don't understand, do you?"

"Understand what?"

He chuckled softly. "I have no intention of letting you go, Alexandra, because I know you are in love with me, as I am in love with you. You are the most exquisite creature I have ever beheld in my life, and I want you as my wife. My queen. I did not do those things that caused you pain. That was my brother. I would never hurt you. Do you understand *now*?"

She frowned up at him. "No, because you are making no sense, Nicholas. Is this some sort of trick? What are you saying?"

He stepped back, spread his arms wide, and regarded her with complete seriousness. "Please do not be angry with me. I never meant to hurt you, but I must tell you the truth now. I am not Nicholas. I am Randolph."

A jolt of shock shook her from within as she stood motionless, staring at him, not sure what to think or feel.

Thank God, after a few heart-stopping seconds of shock and denial, good breeding intervened and she dropped into a curtsy, as if meeting him for the first time. "Your Royal Highness."

Before he could utter a single word in return, she rose quickly to her full height and slapped him hard across the face.

"How *could* you?" she shouted while another, more rational part of her brain knew she was the quintessential pot calling the kettle black and had no right to be angry with him, for she had lied, too. In fact, she was still lying to him now.

Yet she was a woman who had suffered a broken heart that very morning, and unfortunately, rationality had little to do with anything. She simply needed to boil over and boil very hard.

"How could you lie to me like that and pretend to be someone you are not? You tricked me from the beginning. You tricked everyone."

He did not appear surprised by her outburst.

Recovering from the slap, Rand reached out to pull her into his arms again and buried his face in the crook of her neck.

"I am so sorry," he whispered. "I knew it was wrong, but I had to make sure I could find a woman who would love me for myself, not because I am a future king. You are that woman. You were prepared to throw everything aside for me when you believed I would not sit on the throne. And you were jealous and hurt this morning when you thought I had seduced another. You have no idea how that touches me."

With her heart pounding wildly in her chest, Alex let him hold her for a moment while she struggled to make sense of the situation.

He was the future king, and he wanted her to be his queen. She had passed his test, and with complete authenticity, because she truly *would* have thrown everything away for him.

For those reasons, and so many more, she could not help

but celebrate the fact that he was not that rakish libertine who had seduced and ruined another duke's daughter six weeks ago. That was not him. He was not that man, and she had no reason to doubt his intentions. He truly was the man she had come to adore, future king or not. And he loved her. He loved her!

"I don't know what to say," she replied, with no notion of how to proceed from here. It was exactly what she'd wanted, to marry the Crown Prince of Petersbourg, and it appeared she had somehow unwittingly succeeded in that quest.

Though all of that was not at the forefront of her mind at the moment. All that mattered was that her dearest love was holding her in his arms and declaring himself and there was no more cause to resist. He was no longer forbidden. He was the golden prize.

He pressed his lips to hers and kissed her passionately. Her body grew instantly aroused, and she met his kiss with equal ardor and abandon.

She had wanted this man from the first moment on the terrace at Carlton House, and all the tender touches and sweet kisses and intimate encounters since then had fueled her passions into a roaring hot blaze she could no longer control.

She sighed with delight, and his kiss turned into a smile upon her lips.

"To be alone with you," he said, "is a luxury even I, as a royal prince, could not afford before now. But here you are, and you know the truth. I believe I will go mad if I have to stop touching you."

"As will I," she replied with mounting desires. "Is the door locked?" she asked, imagining that Mr. Carmichael might come stomping through the palace, determined to preserve her reputation.

It was the last thing she wanted: to hear his fist pounding on the door when all she wanted was more of this magical kissing—and a chance to explain herself.

To tell Randolph everything.

"Yes," he replied. "It is locked."

No longer Nicholas. He was Randolph now.

Sweeping her off her feet, he carried her to the sofa and laid her down upon the soft cushions, then covered her body with his own.

"I apologize," he said, "for taking such liberties with you, but I don't know how much time we have left before your benefactor will decide this is unacceptable, and I must have you, Alex."

"I want you, too," she breathlessly replied as his mouth covered hers in a passionate kiss that crushed all sense of propriety.

His lips blazed a trail down the side of her neck while his hand slid across her rib cage and down her hip, over the top of her thigh to her knee until she could hardly bear the pleasure of it.

As he settled himself between her legs, she was astonished by the instinctive carnal knowledge she possessed as she wrapped her legs around his hips and hugged his body close.

The fire in the hearth snapped and crackled, and she became more aware of the sound of her own labored breathing and his uninhibited groans of pleasure as he thrust his body closer.

Randolph rose up, braced his upper body on both arms to look down at her. She regarded him in the magic of the firelight.

Should she tell him to stop? Yes, of course she should. This was beyond proper. But when his mouth found hers again, so hot and luscious, she couldn't bring herself to do so.

His lips traveled lower to her cleavage, and he laid soft

kisses along her neckline, causing her skin to tingle hotly with longing. Then he dipped his tongue into the tight confines of her corset.

"Randolph, please," she whispered, wiggling against the inconceivable pleasure of it.

"I must taste you." His voice grew low and husky with desire. "Did you say yes, yet?" he asked. "I can't remember. I've been very presumptuous, assuming you want to be my wife."

"Of course I want to be your wife," she replied, "but there are things I must tell you first." But she couldn't think. She could barely breathe from the excitement of his kisses and the spellbinding touch of his hands.

"You can tell me anything."

He cupped her bottom and pulled her tight up against his pelvis, pulsing smoothly and firmly. Their bodies moved together, and soon he was sliding his hand up under her skirts.

Alex gasped with pleasure and spread her legs wide, wanting to do nothing but coast down this tantalizing river of desire.

"That's it, darling," he whispered. "Relax for me. I only want to touch you."

"It feels so good," she replied.

"That's because we are meant to be together."

He used the palm of his hand to stroke the tingling core of her desire, and a tidal wave of pleasure washed over her.

Nothing had ever felt so good, and her virgin body convulsed in tiny spasms of delight.

"Do you like that?" he asked.

"Yes." She squeezed her eyes shut and floated away into an enchanted oblivion.

"Then let me try something else."

Gently he slid a finger into her depths while she clutched

at his shoulders, digging her nails into the fabric of his jacket and squeezing it in her fists.

"I feel your virginity," he said. "How innocent you are. Am I hurting you?" He breathed the question into her ear and made her clench tight with yearning.

"No."

Her voice sounded different. It was gruff and low in her throat.

"I want to touch you, too," she told him, thrusting her hips forward and running her hands down the length of his back to his strong, muscular buttocks.

His mouth covered hers in a devouring kiss of ravenous hunger, while his fingers still worked below. In the heat of her passions, she was vaguely aware of his other hand working the fastenings of his trousers and lifting her skirts.

It was all so intoxicating—this need she felt deep between her legs. It was like some kind of trance, and she couldn't resist the urge to push her hips forward.

Then, all at once, he was there.

Their bodies went still.

Her eyes fluttered open, for she was intensely aware of his manhood pushing against her, with no more barrier of clothing between them.

He was firm and hot. She could feel the silky tip of his erection poised at the entrance to her body.

"Let me inside you," he whispered. "I give you my word I will marry you as soon as it can be arranged. Will you have me, Alex? Please say yes. I will take precautions to prevent a child, but I must have your pledge. I will not let you change your mind again."

"I won't change it," she promised. "For I, too, must have this."

A tear spilled from her eye, which she quickly wiped away.

She remembered very clearly the last time she cried, when her adoptive father passed away. Since that day, she had endured the cold cruelty of the real world and had learned many things that caused her heart to freeze over with ice. But she was dripping wet at the moment, melting like a sentimental fool in this man's arms. He made her remember how it felt to be hopeful and grateful.

And loved.

"I need to tell you things," she said.

"You can tell me anything."

Then suddenly he pushed into her, deeply and thickly, and the pain was more than she could bear.

Her body tensed. She sucked in a breath. She thought she had been prepared, but she was not. She had no notion it would hurt so much, yet she was not sorry. She did not want him to stop, nor did she regret any of it.

"Are you all right?" he asked, holding very still while he touched her tearstained cheek with the tender comfort of his lips.

She managed to nod, though she was finding it difficult to breathe, for he filled her so completely.

"Am I hurting you?" he asked.

"A little."

"It will go away soon." He distracted her with a deep kiss of unfathomable sensation.

She touched her tongue to his and soon he was moving over her with smooth and masterful grace while her body melted into the warmth of his arms and, just as he promised, all the pain disappeared.

"Oh, Randolph," she sighed. "I never imagined . . ."

She had come here tonight prepared to negotiate for political power, but instead she was lying with the man her heart truly wanted and her body and soul were somehow dissolving into a heated pile of rapture that cared nothing for politics or crowns.

Randolph's pace began to quicken, and she opened her eyes to watch him in the firelight.

He was looking down at her, clearly overcome by his own desires. A film of perspiration shone on his forehead and he breathed heavily, pushing into her faster and more vigorously. Then he shuddered and convulsed and pulled out of her quickly, rising up onto his hands and knees.

"God," he groaned, taking hold of himself and convulsing again.

"What's wrong?" she asked, for she had no knowledge of these things.

He glanced down. "I'm not sure I was quick enough to withdraw. I didn't want to." His eyes met hers. "But it doesn't matter. We'll be married soon."

A glow of happiness smoldered within her, and she grabbed hold of his neckcloth to pull him close for another kiss. Their tongues collided and meshed, and her heart raced with excitement.

"Oh, Randolph, I didn't know it would be like this."

"You must call me Rand," he replied. "It's what my friends and family call me."

"And which am I?"

He returned her smile with a mischievous grin that touched her all over again. "You will soon be both, but you are also something more."

"And what is that? Or am I fishing for compliments?" She coquettishly arched her back and hung on to his lapels.

He chuckled as he fastened his trousers. "You shall never be in need of compliments from me, darling, for I will worship you until the day I die."

After he helped her lower her skirts, she snuggled close to him on the sofa. They lay together for a long while in the quiet drawing room, listening to the fire crackling in the hearth, stroking each other gently, kissing dreamily.

Alex cleared her throat. "Rand," she said. "There is

something I must tell you." Dread vibrated down her spine at the thought of it and she wished she had told him sooner, but she had become so distracted by the pleasures he offered.

"What is it?" he asked.

She leaned up on an elbow to meet his gaze, and he regarded her with affection. It gave her the strength she needed to continue.

"There is something you don't know about me, but before I confess it, I must assure you that everything that has happened between us has been real, and what I feel for you is genuine. I adored you even before I knew you were the future king. Will you remember that above all else?"

He shifted uncomfortably beside her, then leaned up on an elbow to hear the rest.

Chapter Sixteen

"I was not born in England," Alexandra told him.

Randolph inclined his head curiously.

"And I am not the true daughter of the Duke of St. George," she continued. "I was born in Switzerland, but was smuggled out of that country when I was only three days old and adopted by the duke." She paused while a gust of wind howled down the chimney and attacked the flames in the hearth. "I knew nothing of this until the duke died six years ago. That is when Mr. Carmichael came to my door."

"Switzerland . . ." The color drained from Randolph's face. He sat up on the sofa.

She, too, sat up beside him and adjusted her skirts while he retied his neckcloth.

"I suspect that has some significance to you," she said.

He nodded but did not explain what he knew of it. "Continue."

Her stomach churned sickeningly, but she maintained her composure. "My real father was Oswald Tremaine, King of Petersbourg, who was deposed by the military during the Revolution, which occurred under your father's command."

She kept her eyes fixed upon his while he stared at her with shock. "Is this a joke?" he asked.

"No, it is the truth, and I am quite sure it was not the least bit amusing to my mother when her husband died in a foreign country and she was left alone to give birth to me. And it was certainly no laughing matter when she died holding me in her arms."

His eyes darkened with fury and he stood quickly, as if she had just poured a bucket of ice water on him.

"Perhaps I didn't express that very well," she added.

"Is there any better way to express it?" He began to pace back and forth in front of her. "Good God, Alex! What does this mean? Are you telling me you are a Tremaine princess? A legitimate heir to the Petersbourg throne? To my *father's* throne?"

She held out her hands to calm him. "Yes, that is correct, but it is not my intention to take it away from you."

"Then what *is* your intention?" he asked, looking utterly appalled. "What were you plotting when you came to Carlton House that first night? You kept your identity secret, even from the regent." His eyes narrowed suspiciously. "Unless he knows. Does he?"

"No, of course not. No one knew, except for my stepmother and Mr. Carmichael. We were afraid for my safety."

"Your safety? What in God's name are you hinting at?"

Alexandra stood up. "Surely you must know the answer to that. My parents were forcibly removed from the palace, and they are now lying cold in their graves. I could not be sure of anything."

"I was there the night they were 'forcibly removed,'" he told her. "I witnessed everything. No harm came to them. They were put into the protection of my father's military commanders."

"But what happened after that?" she asked. "How could you possibly know? You were only a boy."

He cupped his forehead in a hand and continued to pace.

"Are you suggesting they were assassinated? Or that *you* might be in danger of such an end? That is ridiculous."

"Is it?" she replied. "There are those who maintain that my father was murdered."

He swung around to face her. "Who says this? I demand that you name them!"

"I cannot. To do so would be to sign their death warrants for high treason. Besides . . . I don't know their names."

For a long moment he stared at her. "Good God, Alexandra. What are you playing at?"

"Nothing!" she shouted in protest. "But I have read the reports. I know that my father was taken to a remote location in Switzerland with very few witnesses. The military denied any wrongdoing of course, but there are those who have heard rumors. You may not believe it, but you are a Sebastian. You are your father's son."

"What is that supposed to mean?"

"I know where your loyalty lies."

He crossed to the side table and poured himself a glass of brandy, which he quickly swallowed. He poured another, which he handed to her.

"Make your point," he said. "What do you want?"

She accepted the glass and held on to it without bringing it to her lips. "I just want *you*," she replied. "That is all. Nothing more."

His voice was ice-cold. "How am I to believe that? You have been lying to me from the outset."

"Might I remind you that you have been lying to me as well?"

"But I told you the truth *before* . . ." He stopped himself and gestured toward the sofa. "How can I not think this was a trap? Because I assure you, I am not in the habit of making love to virgins."

She set the glass of brandy down on a table. "Nor am I in the habit of offering my virtue to every man who sends me love letters. Not that very many have. You are the only one. In fact, what happened between us tonight had nothing to do with politics or crowns. I told you my feelings were real, and I would have married you even if you were nothing but a clerk or a merchant. The only reason I did not run away with you this morning was because of what I read in the paper."

He sank down into a chair and slouched back, stretching his long legs out in front of him and cupping his forehead in a hand. "How will I ever know if that is true? How can I be sure you didn't know who I was all along, and have orchestrated all of this?"

Alex laughed bitterly. "Do you really think I am a powerful puppet master who can manipulate events to my liking? I was heartbroken this morning when I learned about the lady at the Hanover Hotel, and I have never felt more powerless. All I wanted was you, yet I was told you were a shameless seducer of women." Now it was her turn to pace. "And tonight I arrived here, determined to ignore my broken heart and negotiate openly with your brother, but then you revealed a shocking truth—that you are a complete impostor. You proceeded to make love to me, which was no small distraction, and I am still reeling from it. So please, Randolph, do not assume I am manipulating things to my liking, for my whole world has just turned upside down. I have no idea what will happen next, and all I want to do is go back in time to the moment you took me in your arms and promised that I could tell you anything and it would be all right."

His dark brows drew together with uncertainty; then he practically sprang out of the chair.

Alex backed up in fear.

"If you are lying to me," he growled as he took hold of her arm.

"I'm not. I swear on my life! I told you everything."

She pulled away from him. "I have confessed my feelings, and I have given myself to you, body and soul. I was a fool for you tonight, and I did not mean for it to go as far as it did. It all happened so quickly."

He turned away from her and walked to the window, where he looked out at the blackness of the night.

"I am still uncertain of my destiny," she continued, "and my desires. I don't know what I am meant for. The only thing that was clear to me tonight was the pleasure I felt in your arms, and the fact that you said you loved me. That was all that mattered, and all that matters to me now is that you forgive me for keeping the truth from you, as I have forgiven you for the same. What matters is our future together."

He turned to face her. "You have put me in a difficult position, Alexandra. Because, you see, I was fooled once before by a woman who told me she loved me. She played the part very well, but she was merely ambitious, not to mention in love with another man. Love can be blinding that way."

Alexandra's heart pounded heavily. She could barely get air into her lungs.

"Earlier tonight, you told me I was not blind," she said. "You believed I saw the truth because I loved you even when I didn't know your real name. I am asking you now to see the same sort of truth. I am not that woman who betrayed you, and it shouldn't matter where I was born or who my father was. Nor should it matter that I kept something from you, because you did the same to me. Does that mean you do not love me? You have already stated and shown me otherwise, and I still believe you. All I ask is the same in return."

The firelight reflected in his eyes while he stood before her, contemplating all that she had said. "Are you really Oswald's daughter?"

"Yes."

"And your family is all gone."

"Yes."

He paused. "What about your benefactor downstairs? Who is he? What are his ambitions?"

Taking a deep breath, Alexandra spoke truthfully. "He was my father's secretary and a loyal servant for many years. He is a Royalist, of course, and wants to see the House of Tremaine restored to the throne."

Randolph regarded her with a mixture of mistrust and pity. "You are very naïve, Alexandra, if you believe that is all he wants." He turned and moved closer to the fire. "In any case, my father will know everything there is to know about him if he was your father's secretary during the Revolution. They would have known each other all those years ago." He turned to face her. "Has he spoken of my father to you? Has he uttered any words of treason?"

She moved closer. "You wish to know if he means to inspire a civil war and depose your family?"

"Yes." When she did not reply straightaway, he prodded further. "Well? What are his intentions? And I warn you, Alex, if you lie to me, you will be committing treason as well."

She swallowed uneasily and bit back the resentment she felt at such a threat. "He has never revealed such a plan to me, though he has spoken many times of the turmoil in your country—how the people are divided between the Royalists and the supporters of the New Regime. I believe it is his intention to bring peace by uniting our two bloodlines, and that is my intention as well. So do not accuse me of treason. It offends me greatly."

He picked up a log from the iron canister and tossed it onto the grate. A flurry of bright sparks flew up the chimney.

For a long moment, he watched the log begin to burn; then he turned to face her.

"I have proposed to you," he said, "and I have made love to you. As a gentleman, that leaves me little choice about the future. You could be carrying my child, and I am therefore trapped." He strode closer. "But make no mistake about it, Alexandra. Remember that I am no ordinary gentleman. I am a future king, and I will not bring enemies into my father's court."

"I am not your enemy," she insisted. "I want what is best for Petersbourg, but more importantly, I want you. Do not forget that I said I would marry you before I knew who you were. There is love between us, Randolph, and you know it."

His eyes narrowed. "There are many who say a king has no business marrying for love, and I am beginning to think they are right. Perhaps it is time I accepted that." He looked away for a moment. "You must leave me now. Go home. I will need to consult with Nicholas."

The ice in his tone chilled her heart, but she had said all she could. He knew the facts, and the last thing she wanted was to make him feel as if she were tightening the trap.

"I understand," she said. "There is much to consider. What shall I say to Mr. Carmichael?"

Rand pulled the bell rope, then walked to the door and held it open for her. "Tell him that I am Prince Randolph, and that I am considering your proposition. You will have your answer in the morning. Spencer will see you out."

Slowly, Alex made her way to the door, but hesitated before leaving. "I will not tell Mr. Carmichael what happened between us tonight," she said. "That is private between you and me, and I give you my word that I will not hold you responsible for it. The intimacies that occurred

between us were never meant to be a trap. I did not plan it
that way."

He regarded her with cool, callous eyes, then simply
nodded to acknowledge her pledge.

Alexandra curtsied and turned to the butler, who was
just coming up the stairs.

"Our guests will be leaving now," Randolph said.

"Very good, sir," the man replied.

Alexandra followed the butler down the stairs but felt a
pang of anxiety when the front door opened and the true
Prince Nicholas walked in.

He was dressed in formal evening attire with an elegant opera cape and top hat. He was just removing his hat
and gloves when their eyes met.

Charmingly, he smiled and bowed to her. "Lady Alexandra, what a pleasure to see you."

She reached the ground floor and paused at the newel
post to offer the obligatory curtsy. "And what a pleasure
to see you, *Nicholas*."

His eyebrows lifted at the sound of his true name upon
her lips.

"Ah," was all he said.

"Indeed," she replied. Turning to Spencer, she added,
"Please tell Mr. Carmichael that I will wait for him in the
coach."

"Very good, my lady."

Nicholas bowed again, then dashed up the stairs to
speak to his brother.

Alexandra waited politely for the butler to open the
door for her while deep down she wished she could find a
way back into the drawing room—to bear witness to the
heated conversation that was surely about to occur.

Chapter Seventeen

Rand looked up when the door of the drawing room swung open and his brother walked in.

"What happened?" Nick asked. "I just met Lady Alexandra in the main hall and she addressed me as Nicholas. You told her, then? How did she take it? Will there be a wedding?"

"Pour us both a drink," Rand replied, not rising from his chair.

Nick moved to the side table and poured two brandies, then joined Rand in front of the fire.

"Did she explain why she didn't meet you this morning?" Nick asked.

"Yes, and the reason is your fault for she heard about Lady Margaret at the Hanover Hotel. The dowager showed her the newspaper before she left the house at dawn, and naturally she took me for a rake. That is why she rejected me, and I cannot blame her. Not for that, at least."

Nick frowned. "How the devil did she get ahold of that paper? It's six weeks old, and it was printed in Petersbourg."

"Her benefactor obviously has connections, but that is not the half of it. Lady Alexandra is not who we thought she was, and we have some decisions to make. It may be a late night. Cancel your plans, if you have any."

Nick leaned forward and rested his elbows on his knees. "Consider it done. Tell me everything, and start at the beginning."

* * *

The following morning, Alexandra woke from an uneasy slumber and could not eat breakfast, nor could she explain to her stepmother why she was not hungry. She certainly did not wish to describe what had occurred on the sofa at St. James's Palace the night before. It was enough that she had revealed Randolph's masquerade to Mr. Carmichael and the fact that she, too, had confessed her true identity.

Which explained why she could not eat this morning. She entered the breakfast room, breathed in the scent of eggs, ham, and toast on the sideboard, and felt unbearably nauseous. All she could do was pour herself a cup of coffee and hold it to warm her hands.

"Are you not hungry?" Lucille asked, tapping the shell of her boiled egg with a small silver spoon.

"No." Alexandra sat across from her at the table. "I couldn't sleep. I have no idea how this will be resolved, and I am tormented by the thought that Randolph believes I have behaved dishonorably. I did care for him—as you well know—for you were the one who stopped me from eloping with him." She raised the steaming cup of coffee to her lips and regarded Lucille over the rim. "But perhaps you regret that now."

Lucille set down her spoon. "There is no need to punish me. I had no idea he was the true heir to the throne. If I had known, I most certainly would have let you go."

Alexandra leaned back in her chair. "So now we all know the truth."

At that moment, the clatter of a coach and horses outside caused them both to turn their eyes to the window.

"Could it be him?" Lucille asked, perching forward in her chair.

Alex rose to look outside.

"Yes, it is the palace coach." Her stomach careened with nervous butterflies and a terrible fear that this would all end very badly and collapse around her like a giant house of cards.

"It is not the proper time of day for a social call," Lucille said. "It must be a matter of utmost importance." She stood quickly and dropped her napkin to the floor. "I should have chosen a prettier gown. This shade of blue does nothing for me. You look lovely, however. Shall we move to the drawing room?"

Alexandra watched from the window as the coach pulled to a halt and the footman opened the door.

Out stepped His Royal Highness Prince Randolph, wearing a dark greatcoat and black top hat.

Alex's heart skittered like a stone skipping over water at the mere sight of him. How handsome he was. All she wanted was to hear the sound of his voice, to feel his breath in her ear and the soft touch of his hand upon her skin. To return to the erotic pleasures of the night before, when she had not known her world was about to shatter.

Alexandra turned bravely to face her stepmother. "The time has come. Let us go and hear his decision."

* * *

"Welcome, Your Royal Highness," Lucille said, dropping into a deep curtsy as he entered the drawing room. "Won't you please come in?"

He was impeccably dressed, but his eyes were weary, as if he had not slept.

"Good morning to you both." He turned to Lucille. "I

am here to request a moment alone with Lady Alexandra to discuss a matter of personal importance."

The implication was obvious to Lucille. She nodded and moved efficiently to the door. "Of course. If you will excuse me. I will wait in the breakfast room."

With that, she swept out and closed the doors behind her.

Alex regarded Randolph curiously in the morning light.

"Would you care to sit down?" she asked, gesturing toward the sofa.

"No," he coolly replied, wedging an instant emotional distance between them, deep as a canyon.

Steadying her nerves, she watched him clasp his hands behind his back and glance around the room at the furnishings and the portraits on the walls. The vase of flowers on the mantel. *Tick, tick, tick,* went the clock.

At last, he spoke.

"I was up all night discussing the matter with Nicholas," he explained, "and he is of the opinion that a marriage between us may be good for the country, and might put an end to the political turmoil that exists between the disputing factions. He believes enough time has passed, and that the birth of an heir descended from the House of Tremaine, if presented a certain way, could be a most celebrated event."

Alexandra moved closer. "And what do *you* believe?"

He turned and walked to the window. "I have always trusted my brother's opinions. He has a good sense of the people."

Her stomach flipped over with nervous, cautious hope, for she would do anything for a second chance with Randolph. Anything.

How odd that she had never intended to love the Prince of Petersbourg. In fact, she had hated him—or at least the idea of him—since the day she learned the truth about her real family. When she discovered he would travel to England to seek a bride and future queen, her pursuit of his hand had been an act of duty and vengeance.

Yet now here she stood, the morning after she'd given her innocence to the man she vowed never to love, and her heart was breaking in two, because he was not the same. Gone were the heated flirtations she had come to live for. Gone was the thrill of their passion, which she had seen in his eyes on so many wonderful occasions. Instead, this morning he looked completely disenchanted with her.

"For that reason," he continued, "I wish to make you an offer of marriage. Whatever concerns you may have had in the past for your safety, or the safety of your family, may be put to rest. As my wife, you will be under my protection, and no harm will come to you. Though I warn you now, there will be those who will disapprove of this marriage. The country is divided, remember. You may have your supporters, but we also have ours."

This was certainly no fairy-tale ending. In fact, Alex felt slightly ill from the loss of his affection, but she reminded herself that it was not so different from what she had originally envisioned. And perhaps there was still hope. Perhaps in time she could prove to him that her love was true.

"What about your father?" she asked. "I do not suspect he will be pleased. Will he not wish to have some say in the matter?"

Randolph looked away. "My father has not been well in recent months, and I doubt he will have the strength of will to oppose it."

Not been well? She had not known of this.

Randolph looked at her intently. Was he waiting for an answer?

If so, what was *she* waiting for? This was a marriage proposal from the future King of Petersbourg, a union that would secure the restoration of her family's proper place in history.

And she loved him. More than anything.

"I accept," she said at last, though for some reason when the words passed her lips she dropped her gaze, for she could not look him in the eye.

This was not what she had been dreaming of these past few days. It was not even close.

The clock ticked away in the stony silence of the room until slowly he strode closer. "Tell me one thing," he said. "Why did you not come to me sooner with this petition? Your benefactor obviously knew that you would have many supporters among the Royalists. Why did you begin with a charade?"

Alexandra took a seat on the chair opposite the sofa. "It was common knowledge that you had no interest in a political marriage," she explained. "You wanted to marry for love, so that is what we sought to achieve."

His eyes darkened. "*Love.* You sought to achieve *love.* Through lies and deceit. Do you feel you succeeded?"

"I'm not sure yet," she replied. "But before you judge me too harshly, remember that you sought to achieve it through dishonesty as well. You lied to the woman you claimed to love."

A muscle clenched at his jaw, but his eyes never veered from hers. "We could go on and on like this," he said, "around and around, knocking the ball back and forth. Clearly we are both guilty of some form of deception."

"Indeed we are, and I have forgiven you for yours. Have you forgiven me?"

His Adam's apple bobbed, and his shoulders heaved with a deep, resigned sigh. "I won't lie to you, Alexandra. I don't know what I feel for you."

His words were like a knife in her heart, for she and Randolph had come so far to reach this moment. He had taught her to love and had inspired her to give up her vengeance, which had been a driving force in her world for six years. She had never felt so happy as she did on the day she decided to run away with him. But it was all gone now. That happiness was no more. This felt more like a funeral.

"Is there any hope for us?" she asked.

He blinked slowly and bowed his head. "I have been hunted all my life by ambitious women and their overbearing mothers, and just when I thought I found the one woman in the world who wanted me for myself, I discover she was a fortune hunter all along."

"Please do not call me a fortune hunter," Alex said. "That is not what I am."

They both looked away from each other and said nothing for a grim and somber moment.

"Where does this leave us?" she asked. "You have proposed, and I have accepted. Now what?"

His eyes, at last, met hers. "You will accompany me back to Petersbourg, and we will give the public what they want—a spectacular royal wedding."

"How lovely it will be for them," she said.

"Lovely indeed," he replied.

Her heart throbbed painfully, and she was half-tempted to leap out of her chair and shake Randolph senseless for being so unforgiving, because she loved him. She *loved* him! Could he not see that?

Yet at the same time she understood his skepticism. She was the true heir to the throne he would one day occupy, and she was a member of the enemy Royalist cause that opposed his father's rule and deemed him a usurper. And she had practically accused him of murder. How in the world would she ever convince Randolph that she was faithful and true?

"When will we depart for Petersbourg?" she asked.

"In three days. Arrangements are already under way. The regent has been informed that I have found the bride I was seeking, and he will reveal my true identity and announce our engagement at a political assembly tomorrow evening."

"The regent knew all along?"

"Yes. We couldn't have done it without his support and assistance. I daresay he was rather amused and inspired by the whole affair."

"It will cause quite a stir," Alex replied, "when members of the *ton* discover they have been tricked."

"Perhaps," he replied, "but the dust will settle soon enough with the announcement of our military alliance." He paused. "You see, I did not come here for the sole purpose of seeking a bride. My father has commissioned four new navy ships to be built here in England. Compared to that, our little royal wedding is merely incidental."

Making a sincere and noble effort to maintain her dignity before such a clear reminder that she was no longer the center of his world, Alex stood up and held her head high. "Ah. Then it will be a most auspicious event tomorrow evening. I must consider what to wear."

He stood up as well. "In that regard, I hope you will accept this symbol of our engagement."

He reached into his jacket pocket and withdrew a ring, which he held up in front of her.

"Is that a ruby?" She felt almost dizzy at the sight of it. It was a magnificent stone surrounded by diamonds.

He reached for her hand and slid the ring onto her finger. "Yes. It belonged to your mother."

Alex's heart flipped over in shock as she admired it.

Her mother's ring. It fit perfectly. How could this not be some divine act of providence? How could her and Randolph's accidental meeting on the terrace that first night have been anything other than fate?

She laid her hand over her heart. "This means so much to me, Randolph."

He stood before her, tall and handsome in the morning light, his strong physical presence a vivid reminder of the intimate pleasures they had shared the night before, and despite everything, she clung to the hope that one day he would love her again.

"I will speak to your stepmother now," he said, "and make the necessary arrangements. Then I will send the coach to fetch you tomorrow evening at seven o'clock."

"Very well."

As he walked out the door and she imagined the first formal night of their engagement taking form at last, she had no notion that those carefully laid plans would not come to pass.

She did not know that the coach would not come for her.

Nor would there be a political assembly at the palace to announce their engagement, or any celebrations in Petersbourg.

All because of a letter that was delivered to St. James's Palace that afternoon.

A letter that would change everything . . .

Chapter Eighteen

After Rand spoke to the dowager duchess about his intentions and received her blessing for his and Alexandra's marriage, he stepped into the coach and told the driver to circle once around Hyde Park before returning to St. James's Palace.

As soon as the door swung shut behind Rand and the vehicle rolled forward, he tipped his head back against the seat and shut his eyes while struggling to focus on what he had achieved. Not only had he committed to a marriage that would produce his future heirs, but he had also found the fabled Princess of Petersbourg and ensured that her presence on the throne beside him—as his wife—would keep her from raising another rebellion as his enemy.

Had she trapped him with this charade?

Yes, she most certainly had, but he had done the only thing he could. Not only did he maintain his honor as a gentleman, but he also would cast a strong and sturdy net over her in return.

Why, then, was his chest aching with regret?

He sat forward and bowed his head very low as he rested his elbows on his knees and lamented over the manner in which this had unfolded.

He had wanted so badly to love her. He had wanted it more than anything. His insides were pitching and rolling with frustration over the fact that when he woke up this morning he had resented her so bloody much.

But he had been burned once before. How could he be anything but bitter?

Was there really no hope for him?

Lifting his head and leaning back in the seat, he chided himself for such thoughts. He was a future king, dammit, and he had made his choice. He had done what would be best for his country and the monarchy.

It was time, therefore, to lay indecision aside. No matter what he felt, no matter how disappointed he was about this turn of events, he would do his duty. He would not dwell on the past or long for what could not be. He would do everything in his power to make this a workable marriage, and he would make love to Alexandra again as soon as they were wed, in order to produce at least one male heir.

That part, at least, would not be unpleasant, for despite all the lies and this incomprehensible agony, he still desired her with a lust that was so powerful, it made him wonder how he would ever keep his mind on the callings of his reign.

A short while later the coach arrived at the palace and Rand barely had a chance to step out before Rose and Nick hurried out the door to greet him.

"Thank heavens you're back," Rose said. "We received a letter this morning."

He noted his sister's pale complexion and red puffy eyes. "What is it?"

Nick gestured for him to join them inside. "The letter has come from John Edwards."

Edwards was their father's Chief of Staff at Petersbourg Palace.

Rand's heart skittered sideways as he entered the main hall. "What does it say?"

They paused briefly while Spencer took Rand's hat and gloves.

"Edwards wrote that Father has taken a turn for the worse," Nick explained. "The palace physician does not believe he will last more than a fortnight. The letter was dated a week ago. We are not even sure if he still lives."

Rand faced them both. "Then we must leave England straightaway."

"That would be best," Rose replied. "Whatever plans you have made must be canceled. We must try to get home before . . ." She couldn't finish.

Rand pulled her into his arms. "Do not worry, Rose. All will be well. Think only of our reunion with him. Perhaps the physician is wrong. Maybe by the time we arrive, Father will be up and about, eating strawberry sugar cakes and calling us all fools for doubting his fortitude."

Rose withdrew from Rand's embrace and spoke bravely. "I hope so."

He turned to Nick. "Has the regent been notified?"

"Yes. I sent a messenger this morning, and I have already arranged for a ship to take us across the North Sea. We will travel with the same captain who brought us here. He assured me that he will have his crew ready to depart the moment we reach the docks."

Rand paused to consider these developments.

"I will need to inform Lady Alexandra. She has just agreed to become my wife and must therefore accompany us."

Rose's eyebrows lifted, and she frowned with concern. "So it is settled, then? She has accepted you?"

"Yes."

Nick laid a hand on his shoulder. "Congratulations. Is there anything else you need me to do?"

Rand looked his brother in the eye and knew they were

thinking the same thing—that Rand might return to Petersbourg to find himself king.

"Send word to the regent. Tell him I will not be able to attend the assembly tomorrow evening. Explain why, and also tell him that in my absence he may announce my engagement to Lady Alexandra and the official amalgamation of our naval fleets. You may also tell him that I shall marry Lady Alexandra on board the ship."

"During the crossing?" Rose asked. "Good Lord, Rand! Are you sure you should rush into this so quickly? Nicholas has told me everything about her charade. She is a Tremaine! What if she is not to be trusted?"

"Leave that to me," Rand replied. "I know what I'm doing."

Besides, it was too late to reverse it. He had already taken her virginity, and she could be carrying his child. He couldn't very well cut her loose and presume she would not eventually use that child to lay claim to his throne.

He and Nick had decided it would be best to keep her close . . . *especially* if she was not to be trusted.

"This makes no sense to me," Rose said.

"I will explain everything to you later." Rand turned to Nicholas. "Go and meet with the Petersbourg Ambassador today and make the necessary arrangements. And Nick . . ." He paused. "Do whatever it takes, for we must keep Lady Alexandra in our sights and, most importantly, within our power."

* * *

"I beg your pardon?" Mr. Carmichael stood from his chair in the library. "He means to leave the country tomorrow?"

Lucille strode all the way in. "Yes! Alexandra is packing

her things at this very moment. Upon my word, I've never heard of such a rushed marriage that was not attached to some horrendous scandal. You don't think he has deflowered her already, do you? Good heavens." Her eyes went wide as saucers. "In which case, we must do all we can to hasten the marriage. On land or at sea. Whatever the prince wants. Which is why I wasted not a single moment in coming to you, sir, to inform you about what has transpired."

Carmichael said nothing for a moment while he considered the situation. Then he invited Lucille to sit down.

"At least he has proposed," he said, tapping his finger on the armrest. "And I agree. The sooner they are legally wed, the better. Let us not worry about the extravagance of a large wedding. Even a small shipboard ceremony will suit just fine. At least this way, she will enter the country as their future queen and there will be no reversing it."

Lucille settled herself into the soft chair opposite the desk. "She may do better than that if the king is as ill as they say. He may be gone by the time they arrive, and Randolph will wear the crown." She wiggled her bottom on the seat and fought to suppress a hopeful grin. "Wouldn't that be just the thing? Imagine it."

Mr. Carmichael poured her a cup of tea. "Your Grace, though I understand your aspirations, you must make an effort not to say such things in the presence of others. Some might consider it treason, to wish for the king's demise."

She covered her mouth with a hand. "Good Lord, I do beg your pardon." She accepted the dainty teacup he offered. "But please be assured I would never express myself in such a way among others. I only confess my thoughts to you because I believe we understand each other. We both want the same thing."

He set the teapot down on the silver serving tray. "We do indeed. You have been a loyal friend through all of this, Your Grace. I couldn't have managed any of it without you. If it weren't for your generous support, the House of Tremaine might have disappeared completely into oblivion, but now I feel quite assured that the true monarchy will be restored."

He raised his teacup as if to toast to her contribution, and took a small sip.

"And what will become of you, Mr. Carmichael?" she asked. "Petersbourg is your home country. Will you return to bask in the glory of your accomplishment, or will you remain here in England?"

He set down his cup and saucer and considered the matter carefully.

"I will travel home to Petersbourg," he replied. "And I will make it my own personal goal to keep an eye on our girl. She may find the new city to be a challenge in many ways. If she seeks advice, I shall be only too happy to oblige."

"You are very kind." Lucille set her own cup down as well. "I hesitate to confess it, sir, but I shall miss our frequent meetings to discuss my stepdaughter's future. It has become such a wonderful source of stimulation in my life. I daresay I have not felt so happy or useful in a great many years."

He leaned forward, reached for her gloved hand, and kissed the back of it. "You, in turn, have been my shining light, Lucille. Without you, none of this would have been possible. How will I ever repay you?"

She regarded him shrewdly. "Mr. Carmichael, what a shameless flatterer you are."

"Please call me Nigel." He leaned back in his chair with a smile and crossed one leg over the other.

"When exactly will you arrive in Petersbourg?" she asked, casually raising an eyebrow.

He tapped a finger on the armrest. "I shall board the first ship to leave London, directly behind yours."

She glanced up at the ceiling. "Would it not be more efficient to gain passage on the same ship? I can provide details if you like. The captain is a close neighbor of ours."

He leaned forward and touched her knee. "As I said before, Lucille, you are my shining light. What did I ever do to deserve such a woman as you in my corner?"

She gave a coy grin. "Oh, Mr. Carmichael . . . or rather, *Nigel*. How could we ever leave England without you?"

PART III

Where a Tempestuous Journey Begins

Chapter Nineteen

Alexandra stepped over the threshold of her private cabin aboard the *Abigail* and glanced about at the modest furnishings—the narrow bunk against the wall, her trunks that carried all of her possessions from London, stacked and secured. The rest of her things from her home in Wales would arrive at a later date when her sisters made the crossing to join her.

A small, high window provided only a measure of light, for the glass panes were coated in a film of powdery salt and the Thames was cloaked in a bank of fog.

When she had boarded the ship, the captain informed her that they would set sail within the hour, and she had done her best to reply cheerfully, while deep down she was uneasy about setting sail into the vast unknown with a man who still believed she had trapped him into matrimony.

A prince she had once vowed never to love.

The wedding was scheduled to take place that evening at seven o'clock in the captain's quarters—a conspicuously private event for the future king of a small but powerful European nation.

Though it was her nation, too, she reminded herself as she tossed her reticule onto the bunk and sat down. She would therefore make no apologies for the web of lies she had spun in order to secure her place on the throne. Nor would she ever again doubt her true destiny, for occasionally fate had a way of stepping in to intervene when a person hesitated or began to take a wrong turn. Hadn't that just been proven to her in more ways than one?

Footsteps tapped down the companionway just then. She stood up and in the next moment found herself curtsying to her future husband.

Wearing a dark brown square-cut tailcoat and fawn breeches with black boots and a high shirt collar and cravat, he filled the open cabin doorway with an almost debilitating force of charisma.

"I am pleased to see you arrived safely," he said. "I hope your quarters are adequate." He glanced around to examine the situation.

"Perfectly so," she replied.

Their gazes locked and held for an intense moment while Alex considered rushing forward and pressing her lips to his—for no other reason but to remind him of what they had done together a few nights before.

The compulsion passed, however, as he ducked his head under the bulkhead to enter the cabin.

She waited for him to say something that might breach the emotional distance that had swelled between them, but he maintained a casual indifference.

"It's not quite the prestigious royal wedding you expected, is it?" he said.

"It doesn't matter where we are wed," she replied. "Remember I was quite willing to join you in your coach two days ago and dash off to Scotland to be married over an anvil by a blacksmith."

It was the whole truth—the honest reality of her heart—and she wished he would believe it.

Then slowly he moved across the plank floor toward her.

She had no idea what he was thinking or feeling. All she could do was try to comprehend the desire she felt when his hand cupped the side of her neck and his thumb graced her earlobe.

"I have not forgotten it," he said. "I also remember why you changed your mind."

"Because I was under the impression you were a scoundrel," she reminded him. "Which was not incorrect. Your brother, Nicholas, is such a man, and I thought you were him."

His eyes held no humor, but the touch of his hand was wildly seductive. His hot breath in her ear made her knees go weak. "But I am not him. I am simply a man who was seeking a wife, and I have found one. So I would like to put the rest of this behind us, Alexandra, and begin anew. Can we do that?"

She took a deep breath and swallowed over the flood of emotions that were too complicated to understand, because she longed for the pleasure of his touch and wanted this marriage to succeed, but she did not believe he truly loved or trusted her. A new beginning would not necessarily be a happy one.

"Of course," she replied nevertheless. "There is nothing I want more than to be your wife, and I will do everything in my power to earn back your trust." *And the fiery heat of your passions.*

He let his hand drop to his side and stepped back.

The ship lifted, shifted to the side, and sank down on an unexpected swell next to the dock, and Alexandra reached out to grab onto something.

Before she could secure her balance, Randolph was at her side, steadying her against the unpredictable movement of the ship.

"You'll grow accustomed to it," he said.

"I certainly hope so. We haven't even left shore yet."

She thought she saw a flash of something in his eyes—was it desire?—but again, he backed away from her.

The ship creaked and groaned.

"Seven o'clock in the captain's quarters," he confirmed.

"I will be there. Not a moment late."

With that, he bowed, and she responded with a quick curtsy as he left.

The cabin seemed very quiet after he was gone, but her blood was pumping hotly in her veins.

She picked up the pillow and threw it at the door.

* * *

The captain's quarters were located at the ship's stern, with a row of paned windows that let in the pink glow of the sunset.

Unfortunately, the pretty horizon rose and fell with each volatile swell of the sea, which was why Lucille had been green as a bullfrog since the moment they left the dock. She was a good soldier, however, and had remained at her post to help Alexandra dress for her wedding and escort her through the narrow passageways of the ship for the ceremony.

As they entered the captain's cabin, Alexandra gave a nod to Mr. Carmichael, who stood before a glass-fronted bookcase containing a collection of rolled maps. He raised his stemmed sherry glass to greet them.

Her eyes then fell upon her future husband.

He was silhouetted against the glow of the sunset in the window, but she could nevertheless make out that he was dressed in his scarlet royal regalia, with a saber sheathed at his waist.

It was the first time she had seen him dressed as the true Prince of Petersbourg, and her heart beat violently with sexual exhilaration. Despite everything, he was still the most handsome man she had ever encountered. Even that first night on the terrace, when he smelled of brandy and horses and wore muddy boots, she had found him excruciatingly attractive. All she wanted to do was marry him and make love to him.

His brother, Nicholas, stood beside him. Princess Rose startled her by approaching from behind the door.

"Welcome," Rose said, addressing them both. "Please come in."

Randolph crossed to meet them. Effectively hiding all manner of conflict that existed between them, he took Alexandra's hand and kissed it. "You have come at last," he said with an appropriate measure of charm. "Shall we begin?"

"Of course." She, too, willed herself to bury her scandalous desires and all their political differences for the time being, and allowed him to escort her to the far side of the cabin, where the priest stood next to the captain in front of the upholstered window bench. The setting sun shone brightly upon their faces, and the sacred ceremony began. . . .

Chapter Twenty

It hardly seemed possible that Alexandra had just wed a future king. The ceremony had been a quiet affair with few witnesses other than family.

Presently, she was sitting up against the pillows in bed in her cabin, wearing a white nightdress and a matching silk robe, waiting for her husband to come and consummate the marriage—though one could argue that that particular deed had already been accomplished.

It would be different this time, however. They were now man and wife. He would likely make every effort to produce an heir, whereas last time he had exercised great restraint.

There would be other differences as well. Last time he had wanted her with unbridled passion. This time he would be guarded, perhaps even antagonistic toward her.

She had no idea what to expect, but of this she was certain: It would be an act of duty, not passion. At least on his side. For her part, she was already shamelessly aroused and brimming with desire. Her heart was beating at a feverish pace at the mere thought of being touched by him again.

The latch on the door lifted just then, and her husband walked in carrying a lantern. He was still wearing his scarlet regalia.

"My apologies," he said, hooking the lamp on a peg on an overhead beam. "It was not my intention to keep you waiting so long, but the captain was feeling gregarious. It isn't often he hosts a royal wedding."

Working hard to calm her nerves, Alexandra tossed the covers aside and rose from the bed. Her bare feet padded softly across the plank floor.

"No apologies are necessary," she replied. "You are here now. That is all that matters. Let me help you remove your sword."

Staggering slightly from the movement of the ship, she braced her feet on the floor, then unbuckled his sword belt and set it on top of a chair. She then returned to unbutton his jacket.

He said nothing while she freed each shiny brass button from the hold. All the while, his eyes held hers with an intense scrutiny that caused a rush of uncertainty in her mind.

Was he truly dreading this sexual act with her now that he knew her true identity? Or did he long for it, as she did? Was his body aching for it? If not, could she make it so? For she herself had every intention of enjoying it.

The lantern swung back and forth on the peg, throwing shadows across the walls.

"You are nervous," Rand said, watching her expression. The last button came free, and she slid the jacket off his shoulders, folded it, and set it on the trunk next to his scabbard. "Your hands are trembling," he added, "and you haven't looked me in the eye since the moment I walked in."

"Well . . ."

The ship took a sudden dip into the trough of a wave and she was tossed forward. "I am a bride on her wedding night," she explained, grabbing onto his shoulders to steady herself. "Is it not my duty to be nervous?"

Letting go of him, she stepped back.

He began to untie his cravat. "Is that all that exists between us now? Duty?"

Alexandra wet her lips and spoke without reserve. "I could ask the same of you, Randolph. In fact, I am quite curious to know your answer."

He carelessly tossed the neckcloth onto the trunk, pulled his shirt off over his head, and dropped it onto the floor.

At the sight of his smooth, muscled chest she couldn't seem to catch her breath. He stood before her like a gorgeous Greek god, naked from the waist up, regarding her with clear purpose and resolve.

"You are my wife now," he said, "and when I make love to you—which, I warn you, I will do often—I assure you that duty will be the last thing on my mind. And yours as well."

It was exactly what she wanted to hear.

"Very well then," she replied as he moved closer and set his hands on the curve of her hips, then slid them around to the small of her back and pulled her tight up against him.

Her body exploded with licking flames of fire, and she was not sorry that he seemed disinterested in any further discussion, for she did not wish to talk either. What was there to say after all? They were at an impasse in terms of their trust in each other, and their future as a married couple was still very uncertain and would remain so until they reached Petersbourg and determined the lay of the land. Perhaps there would be a public outcry. Or his father, the king, might demand an annulment on the grounds of fraud and deception. Why not just let go of all that and enjoy this?

Smoothly Randolph shifted his hips to settle more firmly against hers and covered her mouth in a fierce kiss that shocked and delighted her with its carnality.

This was nothing like the kisses they shared before. It was less tender, less tentative, but she relished it, for it stirred her blood like nothing else.

Sliding her hands up the length of his bare arms from wrist to shoulder, she hooked them around the nape of his neck and tilted her head to the side to gain better access to the lush, damp heat of his mouth.

Groaning passionately, he bent forward, scooped her up into his arms, and carried her to the bed. He set her down gently and removed his boots, unfastened his trousers, slipped them off, and came down upon her while the waves outside roared against the wooden hull of the ship.

She gasped at the sensation of his nude body, heavy upon hers. It was all happening so quickly. . . .

The ship rose and fell on the swells beneath them, and her body hummed with yearning. He was her husband now, and he did not ask for permission to take her, nor did he attempt to fight or suppress his sexual urges. He was driving forward like a galloping stallion, devouring her with his stroking hands and hungry mouth, proving to her that he did indeed want this. At least physically.

He caressed her breasts and slid his hand down over her hip and up under her nightdress, then tugged the white linen fabric up around her waist.

She, too, was eager for consummation. She had thought of little else since their coupling in the drawing room at St. James's. Her blood pounded through her veins in a feverish rush of desire that baffled her with its power.

When at last his hand found the damp, tingling center between her thighs she wanted nothing but the final joining of their bodies.

But even while she basked in the pleasure of his fingers probing the sensitive regions of her womanhood, she wanted something more. Something beyond the pleasure of this moment, for something was missing. . . .

Oh, how she wanted to regain the connection they once shared. She had no idea if that was possible.

"Take me now," she breathlessly pleaded in a desperate effort to salvage what was lost, her words caught in the intimate heat of their joined lips.

His tongue delved into her open mouth while his hips shifted and searched. He found success quickly, and slid into her without preliminaries, for she was slick with dampness and wide open with trembling desire.

Randolph shut his eyes and touched his forehead to hers as he worked in and out of her.

It was so much easier than last time. There were no barriers. No pain—only the sweet meeting of desire with fulfillment.

He pushed hard and fast, and she met each powerful thrust with one of her own.

Then the world spun circles before her eyes as he cupped her bottom and flipped everything over topside. All at once, she was sitting upright, searching for her bearings, as he guided her up and down over his glorious manhood.

"You are mine now," he said, pulsing his hips, "and God help you if you ever betray me."

"Do not speak of such things," she said with a frown. "Not now."

Leaning forward, she kissed him with ravenous hunger to keep him from repeating such a thing. He pushed hard and deep, and she choked back a cry of shuddering rapture. Wild sensation flooded through her from core to limb, and she collapsed weakly upon him.

He continued to slowly pulse, however, and turned her over onto her back, making sweet, slow love to her while he braced himself on both arms above.

Alexandra watched his expression in the flickering lamplight. He squeezed his eyes shut and let out a low groan of need as his body tensed and drove into her. She let her hands slide to the firm bands of muscle on his back and pulled him deeper inside until he growled and convulsed and finally shot his seed into her womb.

For a long moment afterward they lay together on the bed while the ship rose up and slid down into the waves. Alex could feel his heart beating against hers and reveled in the sensation while she ran the tip of her finger lightly up and down the damp, warm flesh of his back.

It was odd how her body felt satisfied while, deeper inside, she was not yet fulfilled . . .

In that moment, he lifted his head and rolled off her onto his back. He stared up at the ceiling, then sat up and gripped the edge of the bunk.

A knot of dread formed in Alex's stomach. She sat up as well. "What's wrong?"

He shook his head and didn't reply for the longest time. Then at last he spoke. "I don't know how this is going to work."

Oh, God. . . .

She sat up on the bed. "I don't know either, but somehow it will. We managed to get through today, didn't we?"

He stood up—naked and gorgeous in the swinging lamplight—and pulled on his trousers. The ship creaked and groaned beneath them. "I can't be here now," he said. "I should go."

"Why? There's no hurry. It's our wedding night, and I thought we both found pleasure just now."

"That is precisely the problem," he explained as he bent to pick up his shirt. "I burn for you, Alex. I want you in my bed every second of the day, and there are moments I want to throw my whole heart and soul into yours."

She drew back in shock. It was not what she had expected to hear.

"But I also know that would be a foolish and unwise thing to do," he continued, "because I don't trust you. Not one little bit."

Her heart sank while she marveled over the fact that she did not feel the same way at all—for she trusted *him*. Since the first moment they met, she had trusted him enough to fall completely, foolishly, hopelessly in love. She would even have gone so far as to elope with him if her stepmother had not stopped her at the door.

Nevertheless, she could not lose sight of the problem here. "I am afraid you are going to have to find a way to overcome that obstacle," she said, "because I am your wife now, and we are bound to each other until death."

She was reminded suddenly of what he had said to her when they were making love.

God help you if you ever betray me.

"What is it that you think I will do?" she asked. "Try to take your throne away? Seek vengeance upon your family? Or leave you for another man?"

He was now buttoning up his scarlet jacket with great haste. "All of the above, not necessarily in that order."

He picked up his sword belt and buckled it around his waist.

Alexandra knew not what to say. Did he truly believe she was capable of all those things? Did he not know how passionately she desired him?

"I am your wife now," she insisted, "and one day I will be your queen. I give you my word that I will be faithful and dutiful. I will not betray you, try to steal your throne, nor will I ever stray from our bed. But let me also be clear with *you*, Randolph, so that there will be no more secrets between us. I want the throne of Petersbourg, and I want my son to sit upon it one day. *Our* son. But for now, and for as long as I live, I will be your faithful queen. Do not doubt it. To do so is to insult my honor."

He had stopped what he was doing and was now staring at her with dark, brooding astonishment.

"I want to believe you," he said, "and I wish things were different."

"They *can* be. Just take off your clothes and come back to bed. Sometimes I feel this is the only place where you will let go of your doubts and simply follow your heart."

"It is not my heart that gains a foothold when I am in bed with you," he said, striding closer. "It is something else entirely. Something that borders on obsession."

She pulled her nightdress off over her head, dropped it to the floor, and stood naked before him. "I feel it, too, and when I become consumed by it I think no more of politics or justice or power. All I want is to feel you inside me."

He halted where he stood and let his gaze travel down the length of her body. She shivered with desire and closed her eyes, willing him to come to her. To touch her. Anywhere he pleased.

The ship creaked ominously as it rolled in a heavy swell, and she staggered slightly but never opened her eyes. For a moment she imagined he might simply walk out and leave her standing there, rejected, but then she felt the pad of his thumb rub across her erect nipple.

Sucking in a quick breath of arousal, she continued to brace both feet on the floor and ride the waves.

His warm hand cupped her whole breast while his tongue darted out to taste the other nipple. She quivered at the sensation, then threw her head back and took his head in both hands, running her fingers through his thick hair as he sucked and kissed her breast.

The next thing she knew, he was carrying her back to the bed and setting her down upon it. Only then did she open her eyes and look up to see him climbing over her.

Overcome by erotic sensation, she spread her legs wide. He kissed down the center of her quivering belly and at last settled his mouth at the throbbing juncture between her thighs.

He licked and sucked and drove her mad with ecstasy until she could no longer keep the pleasure at bay. She climaxed instantly, without warning, and her body convulsed upon the bed while she gripped his head in both hands to ensure he didn't stop until it was over.

When at last her legs fell open and she was completely sated, she heard the pleasing sound of his sword belt unbuckling again.

"You see this is what I am talking about," he said as he unfastened his trousers and lowered his body to hers. "I burn for you, Wife, and I want you in my bed every second of the day, no matter what the cost."

"Then do not deprive yourself," she told him on a breathless sigh of rapture. "You may have me whenever you please."

And with that clear message of encouragement, he slid into her with infinite grace.

"I fear you will be the death of me," he whispered as he kissed the side of her neck and drove slowly in and out of her.

"But won't it be a very pleasurable death?" she replied. "One that we can enjoy together?"

"You are speaking of something different, I believe," he said as he pushed deep.

He spoke no more words after that, but it was not an occasion for conversation. They each had desires to fulfill, fires to quench, hungers to feed.

For the rest of the night they satisfied their relentless lust for each other, and Alexandra felt quite certain that she had finally achieved greatness. She had found the man of her dreams, who made her feel like a true queen, and she had fulfilled her destiny—for she was on her way to the court of Petersbourg and would soon wear the crown that had been taken from her family.

And she was now confident that she could, in time, win back her husband's love.

Chapter
Twenty-one

At dawn the following morning, Randolph rose quietly from bed, got dressed, and left Alexandra sleeping in her cabin. They had made love countless times during the night and had slept very little. He was physically and mentally exhausted, yet he could not seem to drift off.

He went to his own cabin and changed out of his wedding attire, washed and shaved, then dressed for the day and pulled on his caped greatcoat.

Alone, he moved through the ship's passageways and climbed the companionway to the foredeck, where he spoke briefly to the officer at the helm. The man informed Rand that the winds had calmed during the night and for that reason their speed had been greatly diminished. They were nearly at a dead stop at the moment.

Indeed, as Rand looked out over the silvery waters of the North Sea under a pale blue sky, the surface was like glass and the sails could do nothing but hang flat. It was eerily quiet.

He thanked the officer and strode to the bow to watch the sun rise from the watery horizon. Closing his eyes, he breathed in the salty fragrance of the sea and listened to the sound of a nearby member of the crew who began to hum softly to himself while he coiled a rope.

For a long time Rand stood at the rail and wondered

about his father's condition and if he would still be alive to meet Alexandra when she and Rand arrived.

What would his father make of Rand's decision to marry her? His father had led the Revolution against the Tremaines, who had ruled the country for more than three hundred years. Perhaps he would view this as a step in the wrong direction—a move that would reverse all his efforts to shift the balance of power. Rand's father had never been a fan of King Oswald. That was no secret.

Rand turned when a hand came to rest on his shoulder.

"Couldn't sleep?" Nicholas said, leaning forward on the rail and squinting into the sunrise.

"Not a wink," Rand replied. "Too much to think about."

"It was your wedding night, Brother. I hope you didn't spend the whole of it *thinking*."

Rand gave no reply. He simply stood at his brother's side, looking out over the water.

"Strangely quiet out there, isn't it?" Nick said.

"Yes. Here we are, in a mad rush to get home to our father's deathbed, and the wind will not cooperate. It feels as if we are being held hostage. I don't suppose Carmichael had anything to do with it."

They shared a knowing look.

"How the devil did he get on this ship?" Nicholas asked. "I certainly didn't extend an invitation. Did you?"

"No," Rand replied. "It was the dowager. There might be something going on there besides their shared ambition to put Alexandra on the throne."

"You suspect they are engaged in an affair?"

"Yes. They seemed like a pair last night. The duchess is unquestionably enamored, and he will no doubt use that to gain acceptance at court. If he marries her, he will be Alexandra's new stepfather, and stepgrandfather to our children."

"The future heirs to the throne." Nick regarded him

shrewdly. "Where does he intend to stay while he's in Petersbourg? Surely not at the palace."

"He'll be residing at the Hamilton Inn."

"I'll send someone there to keep a close eye on him."

Rand nodded. "Good. But I'm afraid I'll need your help to keep an eye on Alexandra as well. I don't trust myself."

"What do you mean?"

With a heavy sigh, Rand leaned forward over the rail. "It would be easier if I felt I could be objective, but I seem to lose my head when I am with her. You know how I am, Nick. When I fall for a woman, I fall hard, even if I don't want to."

Nick faced him. "Do you regret marrying her?"

"I'm not sure yet. All I know is that I have grave doubts. She is like the serpent in the garden. She is very seductive and I cannot resist her."

"It's not such a terrible thing, you know, to enjoy making love to your wife."

Rand considered his brother's wisdom. "Perhaps for any other man that would be so," he replied, "but I am a future king and she has elevated ambitions. I cannot let down my guard."

A strong westerly wind blew across the deck just then. It lifted the hems of their greatcoats and fluttered their cravats. The mainsail billowed and flapped heavily.

The first officer called out an order to the crew: "All hands to the windlass!"

"Looks like we'll be on our way again soon," Nick said. "I just hope we get there in time."

Rand raised the collar of his coat to keep warm against the chilly sea breezes and regarded his brother curiously. "Do you ever think of that night twenty years ago, when they removed the Tremaines from the palace?"

Nick said nothing for a moment, then turned and looked

up at the top of the mainmast. "We've never talked about it, have we? Not in all these years."

"Why is that, do you think?"

He shrugged. "It wasn't something I cared to remember."

Rand nodded. "Nor I. I'll never forget the sound of the mob outside the palace, demanding that the king answer for whatever it was that had driven them to revolt. I didn't understand it at the time. Father locked him and the queen in the wine cellar. He said it was for their own protection. I believed him of course. The next morning they were gone, and when I asked where they were, he told me he had removed them from the palace and taken them to a secret location where they would be safe. It was a month later that the king was reported dead." He paused. "Do you think there is any truth to the rumors?"

"That he was executed?" Nick replied. "Good God, no. Father would never order such a thing."

Rand met his brother's gaze squarely. "Are you quite sure about that?"

Nick frowned. "Yes. Aren't *you*?"

After a moment's consideration, Rand leaned forward again and rested his forearms on the rail. "I don't know. But if there is any truth to it, it would explain Carmichael's desire to overthrow us, for he was deeply loyal to Alex's father. At least that is what I understand of it. Alex believes that is what happened, and for that reason I cannot be sure she is not motivated by a very dark vengeance. I cannot be sure of anything."

Nick laid a hand on his shoulder. "Whatever you need, Brother, I am here. You need only say the word and I will investigate any wrongdoing, set any plan in motion."

Rand inhaled a deep cleansing breath. "Thank you. It is good to know I have you at my side, watching my back, for I feel as if, by marrying Alexandra Tremaine, I have just kicked a hornets' nest and the insects are swarming."

"I am sure it's not as bad as all that," Nick reassured him.

"We'll know soon enough, when we step off the ship in Petersbourg with the future queen on my arm. Let us hope it doesn't incite another revolution."

"Indeed. It wouldn't do to witness a repeat performance of that night twenty years ago, when the mob chanted for the death of the king. This time it could be you."

Rand regarded his brother uneasily. "What is that old adage? You get what you give?"

"We weren't the ones who overthrew the monarchy," Nick reminded him. "We were just children."

Rand nodded. "Let us hope the people remember what Father did for them."

"And let us hope he did not do the wrong thing."

They both clasped their hands behind their backs and faced the horizon as the sails caught the wind and the ship sliced through the cold, frothy waters of the North Sea toward their home country.

* * *

That night, Alexandra, Randolph, Nicholas, and Rose were invited to dine privately with the captain in his quarters at eight. It was a pleasant meal of roast duck with savory dressing, beets and carrots, and a fine red wine the captain had purchased in Portugal the previous year.

He raised his glass to toast to the king's health in Petersbourg; then the conversation turned to lighter matters. They discussed theater and the arts in both England and Petersbourg, and only briefly touched upon the war with Napoléon in relation to recent celebrations and the return of the soldiers.

Afterward, the gentlemen remained at the table to smoke cigars with the captain while the ladies stood to return to their cabins.

As soon as the door closed behind them and they found themselves being escorted down the narrow passageway by a steward with a lamp, Rose took hold of Alex's arm. "Alexandra. If I may have a word with you please. In private."

A sudden tension filled the air.

"Of course."

Alex followed her new sister-in-law to her cabin on the port side of the ship. The steward led them inside and hung the lamp on a peg. It swung back and forth with the movement of the ship.

"Will there be anything else, ma'am?" he asked.

"No, that will be all," Rose replied.

As soon as he was gone, Rose faced Alex. "I thought it would be sensible for us to speak openly with each other, since we are now sisters. I would offer you tea, but I'm afraid I am not equipped to entertain. My poor maid has been seasick since we stepped on board."

"I am sorry to hear it. My stepmother does not fare much better."

"You and I are fortunate, then, to have been blessed with good sea legs."

"And strong stomachs," Alexandra agreed.

They stared at each other intensely. It was clearly not an occasion for relaxed and friendly conversation, so Alex steeled her nerves for battle.

Rose gestured for her to sit down on one of two chairs at a small, round table. "I would like to speak plainly if you do not object."

"Speak as plainly as you wish."

Rose hesitated a moment, then removed her gloves and sat down. "My brother has explained the situation to Nicholas and me. We both know who you are, and that you came to London with the sole purpose of winning a proposal of marriage from my brother in order to take back the throne."

Alexandra also removed her gloves and tossed them

onto the table. "That is correct, Rose, for my ancestors occupied the Petersbourg throne for more than three hundred years before yours. Did Rand also explain that I, too, was tricked by his dishonest but clever scheme to switch places with his brother, and that I fell so deeply in love, I was prepared to throw away all my political ambitions in order to elope with him to Scotland?"

Rose sat back in her chair, looking more than a little skeptical. "Yes, he did explain that, and I am not sure if you are aware, but that clever scheme to which you are referring was *my* idea."

Surprised by this information, Alex leaned forward slightly. *"You."*

"Yes," Rose replied. "I knew he would never allow himself to feel any true affection for a woman if he believed she only wanted him for his crown, and I wanted him to find true love."

"But you neglected to consider the feelings of the woman. I did not like being lied to."

"But you fell in love, did you not? Or so you claim." She sighed heavily in defeat. "It was a test in many ways for both of you, and I am disappointed that it did not achieve its purpose. But know this: Nick and I are very loyal to our brother. He is a good man, but when he loves he loves deeply. It is his Achilles' heel. We will not stand by to see him hurt."

"I have no intention of hurting your brother, and I rather wish I had someone looking out for me in such a way, for surely you can see that I am at great risk of being hurt, for Rand does not trust me, and I am about to enter a new country and I have no idea if I will be welcomed or imprisoned upon arrival."

"I don't know either," Rose flatly said, "for the Revolution is still fresh in the hearts and minds of our people." She sat forward. "This is no fairy tale, Alexandra. You will not find it easy. My father, for one, will not be pleased to learn that a Tremaine will again sit on the throne, when he worked so hard to put an end to your father's dictatorship and create a democratic government."

Alexandra drew back in surprise. "First of all, let me assure you that I am not operating under the false impression that this is a fairy tale. I wish only for an opportunity to sit beside your brother, and perhaps in time win back the esteem of the people. I do not intend to change the government. In fact, I believe a constitutional monarchy is the best way to give a voice to the people and yet to maintain a strong sense of tradition and identity at the same time. It is what I have grown up with, after all, as a citizen of England."

Rose's eyes narrowed dubiously. "I am pleased to hear it. I hope you will make your intentions known to my father. If, God willing, he is well enough to hear them when we arrive."

Alexandra tried to envision herself entering King Frederick's bedchamber and curtsying before him, perhaps even kissing the ring on his finger that once belonged to her own father.

How many nights had she lain awake dreaming of the day she would see the former general's body entombed and revel in the fact that she would be the mother of the future king, and her own father's death would be avenged in this way?

Even now, a part of her hoped King Frederick would already be dead when she arrived so that she would not be forced to bow down before him or struggle with conflicting loyalties—for he was her husband's father.

She could not say any of these things to Rose, of course, nor could she voice such thoughts to her husband. She must keep them to herself, for not only were they immoral, they were treasonous.

"I hope your father will be feeling better when we arrive," she said.

Rose nodded. "I say a prayer every night for such a blessing." She was quiet for a moment; then she lifted her chin and regarded Alexandra earnestly. "But that is enough talk of politics and illness. Now that we have laid our cards on the table, let us talk about something else."

They stared at each other questioningly.

"What would you like to talk about?" Alex asked.

Rose drummed her fingers on the table. "Oh, for pity's sake. Tell me about your sisters, so I can plan for their arrival in Petersbourg. When will they join you?"

More than a little surprised by this unexpected turn in the conversation, Alexandra described the looks and temperaments of her three siblings, starting with the youngest, who was uncommonly pretty but enjoyed catching bugs and frogs. . . .

"They will join us next spring."

An hour later Alex walked out of Rose's cabin feeling slightly more relaxed about their encounter, for they did not mention politics or thrones again after they began to discuss other things.

Alex was surprised to learn that Rose was already betrothed to marry an Austrian archduke whom she had met only once. Rose admitted it was an arranged marriage but insisted that the gentleman was extremely handsome and she was overjoyed to do what she must to foster a strong political alliance with Austria.

This from the woman who had concocted a plan for her brothers to switch places in order to find true love . . .

A short while later Alex returned to her own cabin, but was startled to discover another person occupying the space, pacing back and forth impatiently.

She walked in and closed the door behind her.

Chapter
Twenty-two

"Why are you looking at me like that?" Alex asked. "As if I have been colluding with enemies and sharing state secrets."

Her husband's accusing eyes raked down the length of her body. "Where were you?" he asked. "I've been waiting here for a quarter of an hour, and was about to go searching the ship."

"I do beg your pardon," she replied. "I didn't realize we had an appointment."

"You still haven't answered my question. Where were you?"

"If you must know, I was with Rose discussing fabrics and gowns for my sisters for their presentation at court. Does that suffice? If you don't believe me, go and ask her. She will confirm my whereabouts, and you will be able to sleep soundly tonight, knowing I am not plotting a *coup d'état*."

He ripped his jacket off and angrily began to unbutton his waistcoat. "I don't want to sleep. All I want to do is make love to you."

A burst of heat flared through her blood at the sight of her husband's impressive arousal.

"And what if I am offended by your demands?" she

replied as she quickly toed off her slippers, lifted her skirts, and rolled her stockings down her legs. "What if I think you are behaving in a tyrannical fashion?"

"Then I will remind you that you are my wife and you quite enjoy the benefits of my tyrannical demands, since most of them result in you feeling exceptionally well pleasured."

He removed his waistcoat, tossed it onto the floor, untied his cravat, and ripped his shirt off over his head.

She stood before him, desperate for his touch and angry with him at the same time, speechless and short of breath as she admired the smooth contours of his chest and the broad muscles at his shoulders.

"Do you need assistance with your gown?" he asked in a demanding voice that sent her passions into a wild frenzy.

"Yes." She furiously turned her back on him, as if it were his fault the gown fastenings were so complex, and he was quick to take up the task.

Her heart raced feverishly at the sensation of his hands moving slower now, delaying the pleasure she knew awaited her. It was enough to drive her mad with yearning.

When the gown came loose, he slid the delicate satin and crepe fabric off her shoulders and brushed his lips across the sensitive flesh at her nape.

Gooseflesh tingled across her skin, and she sucked in a breath of eager anticipation as the gown fell lightly to the floor and she stepped out of it, while turning slowly to face him.

The waters were calm tonight, she noticed suddenly. The floor was steady beneath her feet.

His gaze dipped to her breasts, crushed tight beneath her corset. She shivered with arousal and glanced down at his breeches.

"You'll need to take those off," she said in an impatient rush of desire.

"Why don't you do that for me," he suggested, "so that I can put my hands to better use."

More than willing to oblige, she reached out to work the fastenings while he untied the laces of her corset. They undressed each other with impressive efficiency and indulgence.

Soon they stood naked in the cabin, saying nothing in the flickering glow of the lamplight.

"All day long, I thought of nothing but bedding you," he irritably confessed. "You have cast some sort of spell on me, and I don't know what to make of it."

"You have cast a similar spell on me," she replied as she laid her open palms on the firm muscles of his chest. "I feel drunk with desire most of the time at the mere sight of you. All I want to do is touch you, and I fear it will be my undoing."

He ran a hand from her bare shoulder down to her breast; then at last he covered her mouth with his own—a deep soul-reaching kiss of uncompromising possession. For a moment she felt as if she were floating, then realized that she was indeed floating—in the middle of the North Sea—but that was something different. It wouldn't matter where she stood. Whenever he put his hands on her body, she was instantly cast adrift into an erotic sea of surrender, and there was no escaping it.

Leading her to the bed, he eased her onto her back, then came down upon her.

"What would you like tonight, Wife?" he asked. "Fast or slow? Rough or gentle?"

"Slow and gentle," she replied. "Let us make it last."

His eyes clouded over with uncertainty. "I must know that you will be faithful to me," he said.

Surprised at this unexpected plea, she nodded. "Of course I will be. If ever you doubt it, think only of that day in your carriage when I believed you had no claim to the throne, yet I wanted you regardless with more passion than I ever dreamed possible. Imagine us escaping to Scotland together. Married by a blacksmith."

He slid into her body then, and she threw her head back in rapture at the intense sensation that flooded through her veins.

They made love twice that night, then slept soundly together in the darkness until dawn, when they woke to the sound of the ship's bell ringing up on deck.

Again they made love and spoke nothing of the future, or what would happen when they reached the coast. It was a subject they chose to avoid.

All that mattered was the passion they shared as they found pleasure in the darkness. Alexandra even began to believe that one day her husband might begin to understand who she truly was, and a mutual trust would eventually find its way into their marriage.

When he stood up to leave her cabin later that morning, she felt surprisingly sated and optimistic about their future and began to wonder if the throne of Petersbourg was not her destiny after all.

Perhaps this *man* was her destiny, and she might very well have been born to be his queen. It was a lovely thought that filled her with inconceivable pleasure.

* * *

Meanwhile, somewhere along the rugged coast of northern England, another ship set sail for Petersbourg but remained a full day behind the *Abigail* so as not to be seen. It was unfortunate that Alexandra knew nothing of the plots that were taking shape on that particular ship, for if she had known, she may have been able to do something about it, or at least she could have warned her husband of the danger that awaited them at the palace.

All she knew, however, was a nightly passion so intense, she was completely blinded by it.

Chapter Twenty-three

The wind blew sure and true for the remainder of the journey, and the Royal Party reached the Petersbourg coast a half day sooner than expected. Standing at the rail, Alexandra laid a gloved hand on top of her bonnet to keep it from flying off in the fierce coastal winds and, with great fascination, took in the awe-inspiring sight of her homeland.

"Is it what you were expecting?" Rose asked as she approached, shouting over the thunderous roar of the sea and the wind in the sails.

Alexandra tried to make sense of what she was feeling. "I am not sure. A part of me is eager to reach the dock and set foot on Petersbourg soil. I want to see the city and the palace that was home to my parents, yet another part of me feels anxious. What if I am not welcome here? What if the people don't want me as their queen?"

Rose laid a gloved hand on top of her arm. "Think no more of that. You will do fine. I am certain you will capture everyone's hearts—especially when they learn about Randolph's clever switch of identities. Nicholas has already composed the announcement for the *Petersbourg Chronicle*. He will present your marriage as a great love match and the stuff of fairy tales. What are the odds, after all, that a secret prince could unwittingly fall in love with a secret princess? And vice versa?"

"It sounds very romantic when you put it that way," Alexandra replied, "but as you know, it has not been entirely without obstacles."

There was compassion in Rose's voice. "Perhaps you will overcome them in time, as long as you are truthful and open from this day forward."

Alexandra wondered how long it would take to earn her husband's trust. "I give you my word that I will never again keep anything from your brother."

Except for her dread about curtsying before his father and her shame at having wished, on countless occasions in the past, for the king's early demise.

She was not proud of those angry and degenerate thoughts.

For that reason, they would follow her to her grave.

* * *

"Look out the window," Randolph said as the coach approached the palace gates. "This was the birthplace of your father, Alexandra, and it will be your home from this day forward."

As the coach and its team of gray thoroughbreds clattered across the cobblestones, Alex leaned closer to the window to see an extraordinary white Baroque palace beyond a flat tree-lined expanse of grass and a rectangular reflecting pool. The building spanned a number of acres and boasted ornamental statues and brass-topped domes. She'd once heard it rivaled the Palace of Versailles in France, and she was inclined to agree.

The coach drove up to the steps, and a flood of liveried servants poured out the front doors.

Rand and Nick exited first and spoke in low tones to the man who came to greet them. A moment later, Rand leaned into the coach and offered his hand. "Come. They say Father has rallied. He is well today."

"Oh, thank heavens for that," Rose replied as she stepped out of the coach.

A few minutes later they entered the great marble hall with four lavish crystal chandeliers overhead. Gilded statues of dancing cupids lined the walls.

With great haste they climbed the grand staircase and began the long trek down a red-carpeted corridor with double-oak doors at the end, safeguarded by two uniformed guards with swords. The instant the guards spotted Randolph, they opened the door for him and bowed with a theatrical flourish.

Alexandra barely had time to prepare herself for this momentous entry into the king's apartments before the doors swung shut behind them and she found herself standing in the reception hall that had once belonged to her parents.

A chill ran down her spine, and she halted on the thick Persian carpet. "I do beg your pardon," she said. "I am not prepared."

Her eyes lifted to the frescoed ceiling above her head—a colorful depiction of Phaëthon and the horses of the Sun, which made her feel small and insignificant and filled her with an unexpected wave of contempt.

She was about to meet the man who had raised an army to invade this palace and seize her father's crown. That man was now lying in her father's bed while her own father was cold and dead in his grave. How in the world could she walk into that room and bow to him?

Randolph turned to her. "You must wait here then," he said. "I will go in first with Rose and Nicholas. We will speak of our visit to England and explain the situation. I must prepare him for the truth in my own way."

"You fear he may not approve?" she asked, fighting against the umbrage she felt deep in her core at the idea that she must seek his approval for something that was hers by hereditary right.

"We'll know soon enough."

"I will wait for you here then," she replied, willing herself to gain the upper hand over her emotions.

Randolph turned to a footman standing in the corner of the reception hall. She had not noticed him there.

"Take Princess Alexandra to the library and send for a light tea." With that, he turned and led his brother and sister to a separate corridor.

The footman approached her and bowed. She regarded him carefully, for he had crafty eyes.

"Your Royal Highness, if you will follow me this way."

She nodded, and he took her in the opposite direction.

* * *

"I don't know what to expect," Rose said as they reached their father's bedchamber door. "Father was fine when we left here not so long ago."

"He was not completely fine," Nicholas reminded them. "He was complaining of headaches and fatigue for weeks. It's why he was so anxious for Rand to take a wife and produce an heir. I believe he may have known that he would not be long for this world."

Rose shot Nicholas a look. "But we were just told he was rallying."

Nicholas glanced uneasily at Rand.

"Let us go in," Rand said, "and see for ourselves."

He opened the door, and they entered the darkened

chamber. The window curtains were drawn and the velvet bed curtains were pulled closed. Three tall floor candelabras blazed at each corner of the room, and a priest in heavy black robes sat beside the bed.

He looked up from the Bible on his lap when he heard them enter and immediately rose to his feet and bowed. "Your Royal Highness. Welcome home."

Rand's heart turned over in his chest, for he had expected to see the palace physician, not the priest.

"Good afternoon, Father Cornwell," he said. "How is he?"

"Better today. His Majesty was lucid for a full hour."

"Only an hour?" Rose stepped forward in shock. "No wonder he's ill. It's dreadfully dark in here. It's like a tomb. Why are all the curtains drawn closed?"

"His Majesty prefers it that way," Father Cornwell explained. "He says he cannot sleep with the light in his eyes, and all he wishes to do, I regret to say, is sleep."

Rand and Nicholas remained at the foot of the bed while Rose hurried to pull open the heavy velvet bed curtains. "Father . . ." She sat down on the edge of the mattress and took his hand.

Rand could barely speak or move. Stains from frequent bloodletting marked their father's nightshirt. His thin hair was damp with sweat. He looked gaunt and frail, as if he had already succumbed to the angels.

"Christ Almighty," Nicholas whispered.

"Is there any hope?" Rand asked the priest.

"Very little, I'm afraid. Though you should speak to Sir William for the particulars."

Sir William was the palace physician—a man of great learning and expertise, one of their father's most trusted servants.

"Where is he? Why is he not here?"

"He has been at the king's bedside for a fortnight, sir.

This morning I implored him to go home to his family and rest."

Rose turned her stricken eyes to Rand. "Is there nothing we can do?"

"I believe it is in God's hands now," he replied.

Just then, their father's eyes flew open and he tried to sit up. "My son, is that you? Have you come home? Speak to me, Randolph."

Rand moved to the edge of the bed. "Yes, I am here, Father. I have returned from England. I have commissioned the ships you wanted."

The king lay back down on the pillows. "I dreamed you were dead."

"No, I am very much alive, and I have good news. I have taken a wife."

"A wife . . ." The king wet his dry lips. "Bring her to me. I wish to meet her."

Rand glanced sharply at Nicholas, who nodded with encouragement.

"She wishes to meet you, too," Rand replied, "and I will fetch her straightaway. But first I must tell you something about her."

He sat down on the edge of the bed and wondered how in all the world he was going to explain this.

* * *

Two footmen—or perhaps they were guards—stood outside the library door chatting idly while Alexandra sat waiting to be summoned to the king's bedside.

She had not been able to eat a single bite of the cakes that had been brought to her, though she did manage to sip a little tea.

She waited a full hour while Randolph attended to his father. She passed the time by examining the impressive collection of leather-bound books on the shelves and the brightly colored upholstery on the chairs—all the while planning what she would say to His Majesty when she finally confronted him. It was not difficult to work out, for she'd been imagining that particular conversation in her mind for six years.

When the door finally swung open and her husband strode into the room, she turned confidently to face him. "Will he see me now?"

Randolph's eyes were stricken, however, and all thoughts of confrontation with that malicious usurping king flew out of her mind.

"Are you all right?" She moved closer. "Was he worse off than you expected?"

Rand glanced at the bookcases along the wall and loosened his neckcloth. "He won't last long. I've never seen him look so frail."

Rand moved to the nearest chair, sat down, rested his elbows on his knees, and buried his forehead into the heels of his hands. "Bloody hell, I always knew this day would come, but it's never as you expect it will be. He's my father, Alex. He was a great man. I never imagined I would see him like this."

The floor seemed to shift beneath Alexandra's feet. It was as if someone had whisked her back to that painful day six years ago when she sat at her adoptive father's bedside and watched him take his last breath. She had not yet known about her true identity, and in her eyes he was still the greatest man who ever lived. She had loved him desperately, and the grief had been debilitating.

Slowly she knelt down before her husband. "I understand. Is there anything I can do?"

He lifted his weary eyes and sat back in the chair. "No."

"Were you able to tell him about our marriage?" she carefully asked.

"Yes, I told him."

"How did he respond?"

Randolph rested his temple on a finger. "He didn't believe it at first. He felt certain you were an impostor, and that I had been tricked."

Alex rose from her kneeling position and stood. "Did you also tell him that you had put on a great performance as well, and that you tricked me into falling in love with *you*?"

His dark eyes glimmered with what appeared, to her surprise, to be admiration. "Yes, Wife. I told him that very thing. Exactly."

"And what did he say to that?"

Rand stood up, and her body grew tense with anxiety.

"He asked to see you with his own eyes, and to speak to you. Alone."

"How very convenient, for that is exactly what I wish for as well." Yet her heart was racing with fear.

"Then let us go now while he is still lucid enough to understand who you are."

Chapter Twenty-four

The door to the king's bedchamber swung shut behind Alexandra before she had a chance to glance over her shoulder at her husband, and all at once she found herself standing in an enormous candlelit room that smelled of spices and incense. Colorful tapestries lined the walls, rich velvet curtains covered the windows, and a massive canopied bed stood elevated upon a dais against the far wall.

Her gaze fell instantly upon the man in that bed, frail and sickly. He was sitting up against the thick feather pillows, though it looked as if someone had propped him up that way. A magnificent fur cape had been draped around his shoulders.

Inexplicably overcome by an inherent sense of duty, she dipped into a deep curtsy, then rose again to meet the king's frowning expression.

"Your Majesty," she said while her heart pounded heavily with trepidation.

He continued to frown at her in the flickering candlelight, then waved her over with a shaky gnarled hand. "Come closer so I can get a look at you."

Taking a few deep breaths, she walked to the foot of the bed and held her head high.

"I did not believe it at first," he said, his eyes sparkling with wetness. "I thought it was another Royalist plot, but you are an exact likeness of your mother, Queen Isabelle. It is quite something to behold."

Alexandra wasn't sure what to make of this response. "Unfortunately, I never had the pleasure of meeting her," she said.

His shoulders beneath the fur cape rose and fell with a deep sigh that appeared to cause him some discomfort in his abdomen. "She was a kind woman who enjoyed dancing and always seemed to be smiling. She was an exceptionally beautiful woman as well. You have her eyes, and your hair color is the same. I cannot get over it."

Taking note of the painful grimace on his face, Alex moved slowly to the side of the bed. "I see that you are suffering, Your Majesty. Is there anything that can be done for you? Should I send for your physician?"

Discreetly she glanced around the room, surprised by the fact that they were completely alone. There were no servants here, no one to bear witness to their conversation. Was there something he wished to say that he did not want others to hear? Not even his own son?

"There is nothing anyone can do for me now," he told her. "I am filled with a cancer, they tell me. It won't be long."

She had come here expecting to confront a tyrant, to demand to know the truth about what had happened to her family twenty years ago. She'd expected to feel hatred and a measure of satisfaction after she spoke her mind. But somehow pity was nudging its way in, especially when she looked at this man and saw something of his son in him—the son who had bewitched her with his charm and convinced her that his heart was true.

"Please, sir, I wish to know what happened to my parents."

The king wet his lips and spoke hoarsely. "Randolph told me you heard rumors that your father was murdered. A moment ago, he asked me if those rumors were true." He paused and winced with pain. "It was the first time he had ever dared to ask such a thing."

"And what did you tell him?"

"The truth, of course. That I did not order your father's death. I may be a military man, and I may have killed more than a few of my enemies in times of war, but I am not an executioner, nor would I ever kill a king. I sent him into exile with a staff of guards and servants."

"Then how did my father die?" she asked. "Why is it so impossible to learn the facts? All I ever hear is conjecture. A brief illness. A fall from a horse. Which was it?"

The king tried to answer but began to cough. "Ack, my mouth tastes like metal. A drink of water, if you would be so kind."

She reached for the goblet on the side table and poured water from a heavy pewter jug. Realizing the king was too weak to hold the goblet, she sat beside him and held it to his lips.

A heavy ache settled into the pit of her stomach as she remembered Randolph's expression when he first entered the library.

This was her husband's father—and he was dying.

At last, he found the strength to continue. "The circumstances of your father's death were kept secret because it was not something I felt the world should know."

"Why?"

He paused again. "I regret to say this, Alexandra, but your father took his own life."

For a moment she was too taken aback to speak. Then

she stood abruptly. "Surely that cannot be true. Do you have proof of this?"

His eyes closed, as if he was drifting off to sleep, but thank God he answered her question first. "There was a letter written in his own hand. It is a sad farewell to your mother."

"Does he mention me at all in this letter?" she asked desperately, reeling with horror, needing to know more. "Does he say anything about the unborn child he was about to leave alone in the world?"

The king opened his eyes and regarded her with melancholy. "No, but I do not believe he knew about you, for you were born eight months after his death. I doubt the queen even knew she was with child when she learned what he had done. Perhaps if he had known, he may not have chosen such a dark path for himself."

Overcome by a sharp, piercing sensation of grief, Alex turned away from the king and fought to control her emotions, but there was nothing she could do to prevent the tears from flooding her eyes and spilling onto her cheeks. Quickly she wiped them away.

"I am deeply sorry," he said in a voice that was somehow peaceful in the hush of the room. "I have always blamed myself. I led the rebellion that resulted in your father's deposition. I now understand that the shame of that defeat was too great a burden for him. If only there was something I could have done differently to prevent him from coming to such a tragic end. I have always believed it was my greatest failure."

Alexandra turned to face her husband's father. "I have lately begun to see that there are certain events in our lives we are not meant to control. We do our best to make the world work the way we want it to, but sometimes God has other plans."

The king laid a hand on his stomach and clenched his jaw against another bout of pain. "As he has a plan for me now."

She returned to his side and took hold of his hand until the pain subsided and the look of agony departed from his face.

"I must rest," he said. "If you could send for my children and Father Cornwell . . ."

"I will do so immediately, sir, but first may I ask one more thing? Does the letter still exist? I feel I must see it for myself."

He nodded. "I expected as much, and I have already told Randolph where to find it. He will take you there."

She bent forward and kissed his hand. "Thank you, Majesty. I will go now and send for the priest."

She turned to leave.

"Alexandra," he said, struggling to sit up.

She stopped and turned.

"I was not aware of your existence until today. I was told the queen died before she could deliver you into the world."

"And I was told she held me in her arms for an hour before she passed."

"Told by whom?" he asked, lying back. "Who knew of your birth?"

"Nigel Carmichael, my father's secretary. He did not believe I would be safe in the wake of the Revolution, so he smuggled me away to England. It was he who arranged for my introduction to your son. Do you remember him?"

"Yes," the king replied. "He and I did not agree on much of anything when it came to ruling this country, but if things were simpler, there would have been no need for a revolution, would there?"

* * *

Outside in the corridor, Randolph rose quickly from his seat on an upholstered bench as soon as Alex appeared. He studied her with curious eyes.

"He wishes to see you, Nicholas, and Rose," she said to him, "and for the priest to return as well."

Randolph made no move to leave just yet. "Did you find the answers you were seeking?" he asked.

"Yes," she replied.

"Then I presume you will wish to see the letter."

She nodded. "I will, but it can wait. You must go to your father's bedside now, Randolph. Have my rooms been prepared?"

He waved a hand at one of the servants, who quickly came to show her to her royal chamber.

* * *

It was past midnight by the time Randolph left his father's chamber and made his way through the palace corridors on a dark errand, then eventually found his way back to his wife's door.

He felt almost sick to his stomach as he raised his hand to knock but steeled himself against the bitter sense of dread, for it was a task he was duty bound to complete.

Alexandra's maid answered the door but quickly disappeared after announcing him. He walked fully into the room to find his wife sitting in her nightgown before a roaring hot fire in the eight-foot stone hearth.

She stood as he approached, and the sight of her ebony hair falling loose upon her shoulders kindled a very different sort of fire deep inside him. All he wanted to do was hold her in his arms and forget the letter in his breast pocket.

"How is your father?" she asked. "Is there any improvement?"

"No, he is the same, but at least he is resting now. He is not in pain."

"That, in itself, is a blessing."

A gust of wind moaned down the chimney while they regarded each other in uneasy silence.

"You have something for me," she said. "I see it in your eyes."

He nodded, reached into his jacket pocket, and handed her the letter.

She took it from him but did not unfold it right away. Instead she held it at her side and stared into the dancing flames.

For a moment he thought she might simply toss it in and watch it burn, but then she turned away from the blaze and crossed to the window, where a single candle was burning on the sill.

He waited while she unfolded the letter and read it. When she finished, she set it down on the sill and lifted her eyes to meet his.

Driven solely by instinct, he strode toward her as quickly as his legs would carry him, gathered her into his arms, and held her while she clutched onto his shoulders and pressed her hand to the nape of his neck.

She did not sob or weep. She merely held him.

When at last they stepped apart, he cupped her cheek in his hand and pushed a lock of hair behind her ear.

"It has not been an easy day for either one of us," he said.

"No, it has not. Will you come and lay with me for a while?"

He needed no further bidding as she moved to the bed and climbed on top of the covers. He removed his jacket and joined her there, sitting up against the pillows with his boots still on, while she curled her body into his and rested her head on his shoulder.

"I am not sure what to do with this letter," she said. "I considered burning it just now, but perhaps that would be a mistake."

"You don't have to decide right away," he said. "Things will seem clearer in the morning."

For a long while they lay without talking, and Randolph wondered how it was possible that he could feel so protective of this woman he did not yet trust. It was inconceivable to him that she could somehow temper the depth of his grief simply by lying beside him.

She lifted her head and looked up at him. "You have not yet asked me about my meeting with your father. Are you not curious what was said?"

"That is between you and him," Rand replied, "but if you wish to tell me . . ."

She laid her cheek on his shoulder again. "I did not say all the things I imagined I would say. I did not call him a usurper or a tyrant. I feel rather ashamed of myself, if you must know, for despite his weakened state, I found myself immensely intimidated by his greatness. And he reminded me of you."

Rand listened without judgment. He merely stroked her shoulder with the pad of his thumb.

"But I did accomplish what I set out to accomplish," she continued. "I made myself known to him, and I learned the truth about what happened to my father."

"And you accepted it?" Rand carefully asked.

She lifted her head and blinked up at him. "Why? Didn't you?"

He paused. "I wasn't sure, so I felt a need to confirm it."

"What do you mean?"

"I compared the penmanship of the letter to other palace documents. It was indeed written in your father's hand. There can be no doubt about it. I can show you tomorrow if you wish, so that there will be no questions in your mind about what my father told you."

"I would be most grateful," she said. "I also wish to learn more of my father's legacy. Are there any portraits here, or other artefacts from his reign?"

Rand sighed heavily. "I regret to say that most of it was destroyed during the Revolution. The mob was not easily subdued. There was thievery and violence."

She sat up. "But it was your father who subdued them, was it not?"

"Yes. He had the benefit of an army at his disposal, and he has a talent for calming heated tempers."

Alexandra met his gaze with a look of strength and determination, and he was unnerved by the intensity of his feelings for her when he wanted to remain guarded. "I wish to learn everything there is to know about my father's reign. I want to know what incited the rebellion. There was so little information in England, and most of it painted your father with a very unflattering brush, for our king was not pleased about what happened here. No king wishes to see another king deposed. And Mr. Carmichael . . . He, too, has led me to believe that my father was greatly wronged by those who were greedy for wealth and power, but I wish to learn the truth for myself, now that I am here."

"That can be arranged," Randolph said, pleased that she was not afraid to face a painful truth—and she would most definitely be forced to face it once she learned more about this country's volatile past.

Lying down again and snuggling close to him, she very quickly fell asleep in his arms. Still wearing his boots and exhausted from the day, he, too, let himself drift into a deep slumber, for he hadn't the heart to wake her, nor did he wish to let her go.

* * *

Shortly before dawn, Rand woke to the sensation of his wife's hand sliding across his pelvis and massaging his erection through the fabric of his breeches.

Instantly aroused and in need of distraction from the grief that weighed so heavily upon him, he turned his head to kiss her. She reached to unfasten his breeches, and his body exploded with desire.

A flashing heartbeat later, he was rolling on top of her and settling himself between her soft, luscious thighs. She was slick and wet down there, and when she thrust her hips upward he slid right in.

"Am I dreaming?" he whispered as he made love to her slowly on the soft bed, gazing down at her in the murky pre-dawn light.

It felt dreamlike. He had no sense of reality. He was floating in a thick haze of eroticism, but he preferred it that way, for life was not easy at the moment.

"No, you are awake. Perhaps I am the one who is dreaming."

He pushed in as deep as possible, repeating each thrust with an equal measure of fortitude until he felt the white-hot flooding of sensation in his groin.

A low groan escaped him. It was a cry of resistance, for he had traveled to England with the noblest intentions of marrying for love yet had discovered he could not give in to it after all, for he had been burned once before, and burned yet again by Alexandra when she did not run away with him to Scotland, and yet again when he discovered her true identity.

His body and mind were waging war against each other. Part of him relished the euphoria he felt in her arms, while another part wrestled violently with such dangerous, trusting vulnerability.

Suddenly the throbbing contractions of her womanhood—so hot and tight around his sex—sent him into a spinning vortex of pleasure, and he poured into her with a hot gush of seed that drained him of all strength and the ability to reason. He collapsed upon her in shock and disbelief, for he had never known such ecstasy.

For a long while he lay there, still inside her, unwilling to withdraw until he feared he might crush her with his weight.

Carefully he rolled off her, and she gazed up at him in rapture, then kissed him on the cheek.

It was a sweet, affectionate gesture that should have touched his heart, but instead it filled him with dread, for he was not ready to feel this way about her. He wanted to, but it wasn't safe, and he had instructed his brother to keep a watchful eye on him for this reason exactly—because he was far too vulnerable. There was too much at risk.

As soon as Alex fell back to sleep, Randolph rose from the bed and took great care not to wake her. He then slipped out of the room and wondered how he was going to manage this strange and complicated marriage that was supposed to be based on politics when all he wanted to do was fall completely, devotedly in love with her.

Chapter
Twenty-five

The following day, the news about Randolph's marriage to Alexandra was printed in the *Petersbourg Chronicle*, but the people barely had a moment to comprehend the information before King Frederick's health deteriorated more quickly than expected. That very night he suffered a series of violent convulsions and slipped into a coma.

Thirty-six hours later, he was dead.

All members of the Privy Council were summoned to the court chamber, and Randolph was proclaimed the new sovereign. He read the Declaration of Accession from the balcony overlooking the Square, where the people of Petersbourg gathered to mourn their beloved king. From there Rand took a sacred oath to fulfill his duty to the country and to preserve all laws governing the rights of the populace.

Days later, the coffin—draped in the crimson and gold silk of the Petersbourg flag—traveled in state procession through the cobblestoned streets of the city in an open black carriage to the Abbey of St. Peter for the official lying in state.

Thousands of Petersbourg citizens flowed through the great marble arch and walked upon the colorful mosaic floor to bid a final farewell to their sovereign.

King Frederick was laid to rest in the royal tomb at the

abbey, and a date was set for the coronation of his elder son and the queen consort, which would take place in three months' time.

Through it all, Alexandra stood by Randolph's side for the official state ceremonies and was keenly aware that she was regarded with suspicious curiosity by many. Certain members of the Privy Council spoke to her with chilly superiority, while the archbishop seemed quite taken with her and was quick to express his happiness at her return to eminence. A devoted Royalist, he was.

How the public felt about her she could not yet be certain, for the king's funeral was a somber affair denoted by bowed heads and silence in the streets. It was not a time for celebration or cheering crowds, nor was it a time for scandal.

She suspected, however, that scandal was nevertheless brewing quietly behind a number of closed doors at the palace, mostly inhabited by ambitious members of the New Regime. It was all she could do to remain calm and patient. And wait for the dust to settle.

* * *

For a full week after the funeral Randolph did not come to Alexandra's bed, and with each passing day she grew increasingly uneasy.

"Why does he not come to me?" she asked Lucille as they strolled past the reflecting pool one afternoon in the palace gardens. "I feel terribly closed off from the world, and I have no notion of what is going on out there in the minds of the people. My ladies-in-waiting tell me nothing. I respect that my husband is in mourning, but I wish he would allow me to share in his grief. When he stays away like this, it makes me wonder if he has come to regret his decision to marry me. Perhaps there are others who are poisoning his mind against me."

Lucille glanced over her shoulder to ensure they were not being followed too closely. "Then you must go to him and remind him of the passion that exists between you. He is in love with you, Alexandra. There is no doubt about that. And what of your courses? Is there any chance you are with child yet?"

Alexandra frowned. "Now is hardly the time to be plotting, Mama. King Frederick has been gone only a week. Besides, it is a private matter between my husband and me."

"It most certainly is *not* a private matter," Lucille replied. "It is the business of the state. You must prove that you are fertile and produce an heir as quickly as possible to secure your position. I assure you it will gain you much popularity, especially since the king's death. The people are crying for good news. They need you now more than ever."

Again they began walking at a relaxed pace that revealed nothing of the mad chaos that was overtaking Alexandra's mind. When she arrived in Petersbourg she had felt like an interloper, yet she had been hopeful. Certainly she had not expected the king to die so soon after their arrival.

Often she was met with silence and lowered gazes. She tried to tell herself that it was proper protocol, for she was a queen now and there were certain rules of etiquette to obey, but she had never felt so alone in her entire life.

Why wouldn't Randolph come to her? All she wanted was to feel the pleasure of his touch and to know that what they had enjoyed together during the North Sea crossing was not a dream.

Just then, Nicholas came striding out of the palace door on a direct path toward them. He reached them not far from a tall cedar hedge and bowed. "Your Majesty, the king has requested your presence in the Privy Council Chamber." He nodded at Lucille. "Good afternoon, Your Grace."

"He wishes to see me now?" Alex inquired.

"Yes, he is waiting for you."

Her belly exploded with apprehension. "May I ask what this is about?"

Nicholas met her gaze directly. "I cannot say."

"Cannot or *will* not?" she pressed him.

He gave no reply as he waited to escort her into the palace.

"Fine," she said as she picked up her skirts and brushed past him to lead the way. "Take me to him, if you please, Nicholas—for I wish to speak to him as well."

Her brother-in-law followed her while Lucille was left behind, standing in the cool shelter of the cedars.

* * *

Alexandra walked into the court chamber and stopped just inside the door. Randolph was pacing back and forth in front of an unlit fireplace, looking handsome and regal in a dark green coat and fawn breeches, an elaborately tied cravat and dark brown boots polished to a fine sheen.

"You summoned me, Majesty."

"Yes," he replied. "There is something we must discuss."

Acutely aware of Nicholas standing just behind her, she turned and said, "Leave us, please."

He did not need to be asked twice. With a courtly bow, he backed out of the room.

"There is no need to be rude," Randolph said without humor as he approached her.

"That was not rude, and I cannot help it if I am irritable.

You have been ignoring me for seven days. Why do you wish to see me now? Have I been remiss in my queenly duties, though I have no notion of what they are, for you have provided me with no guidance whatsoever. I can barely find my way around the palace. Perhaps you wish me simply to perform my marital duties. I am beginning to think that is the only thing required of me."

Randolph regarded her steadily in the hush of the room. "You are displeased with me."

Her blood was already boiling, and she hated the fact that just the sound of his voice could stroke her like a caress.

"Yes," she replied, less hostile now. "I only wish to know why you have been avoiding me. I understand it has been a difficult time, but I would like to be of some comfort to you."

He turned his back on her. "It is not comfort I need from you presently," he said. "It is something else entirely."

She frowned. "And what would that be?"

"Strength." He faced her again.

She shook her head as a dark shadow of apprehension moved over her. "Why? Has something happened?"

"Yes, and you must know every detail. There are some members of the household who are suspicious of the fact that only days after I arrived at the palace—having taken a Tremaine princess as my bride—the king is pronounced dead."

Her stomach clenched tight with panic. "What are you suggesting?"

"I am suggesting that you are being watched very carefully."

She understood this hidden accusation and strode forward. "By whom? And who is responsible for such slander? I demand to know."

"Indeed you should," he quickly replied. "I have traced

the accusation to its source and have removed the offender from his position at the palace and imprisoned him for uttering words of treason."

Surprised by her husband's firm and swift hand at administering justice and defending her honor, she inclined her head curiously. "Who was this offender?"

He pinched the bridge of his nose. "An underbutler."

Her head drew back in surprise. "A servant? How old?"

"Not yet twenty. Perhaps you should sit down."

She sank into a chair at the polished mahogany table and considered this information. "I was expecting it to be the Lord Chamberlain, or someone from the Treasurer's Office, not a servant, so young."

"In my experience the most outspoken rebels are usually the young ones," he told her. "With age and maturity, one learns the importance of discretion."

She watched him pace in front of the stone fireplace. "Your father was already ill when I arrived," she mentioned. "You know I had nothing to do with it."

"Of course I know," he replied, sounding almost angry that she would suggest otherwise. "He was ill before I even decided to travel to England. It is idle gossip, nothing more, but I made an example of the man so others will know better in the future."

"How wonderful," she said. "They will be whipped into thinking and feeling exactly what we wish them to think and feel, or at least learn how to be silent."

He regarded her curiously. "You believe I should have acted differently?"

"No," she replied, gathering her composure and rising from her chair to pace about the room. "I am grateful that you were so steadfast in your defense of my honor. It is important that we present a united front. We told them it was a love match after all, didn't we?"

His blue eyes narrowed with intensity as he stared at her.

She glanced toward the door, wondering if he wished for her to leave now.

"You walked in here with a fire at your heels," he said, changing the subject.

"Yes."

Slowly, he strode closer, and though she tried to resist his allure, the husky timbre of his voice stirred her blood.

"You indicated that you were displeased with me," he said. "Are you displeased with me *now*?"

She could not ignore the passionate fire that sizzled between them. One look from him and desire was everywhere.

"Yes," she replied. "Nothing has changed, and you have not yet answered my question."

"Which question?"

"Why you have not come to my bed."

He backed her up against the table and stood very close—so close she could feel his moist breath against her cheek. "I've had much to do," he told her.

"Ah, yes . . . you are a king now and must fulfill your duties, but may I remind you, sir, that one very important duty for us both is to provide this country with an heir."

His hand slid around her waist, and he pulled her close. "I do not need to be reminded, Wife. I am quite aware of it, every second of the day."

Knowing it was pointless to fight the intensity of her passions, she slid up onto the table, parted her knees, and gracefully lay back.

Her husband gazed down at her for the longest moment; then, with a smooth touch that made her quiver, he ran his hand slowly up her leg, raised her skirts, and began to stroke the tingling flesh between her thighs.

She let out a soft moan of rapture, and just before she reached the pinnacle of her desire he hooked his arms under her knees and tugged her closer to the edge. He then leaned down over her and began to kiss her throat while he unbuttoned his jacket and unfastened his breeches.

Soon their mouths met in a hot kiss of ravenous hunger, and she struggled to push his jacket off over his broad shoulders. He helped to rip it off, then climbed onto the table, came down upon her, and thrust deep inside her aching womanhood.

"I apologize," he said as he made love to her with exquisite control and unimaginable skill, "for not coming to you sooner, but I cannot become too distracted."

"Like you are distracted now?"

He sucked at her neck. "You mock me, darling."

"Yes, and if you want me to behave myself, you must promise to come to me each and every night."

He began to thrust harder and faster. "Maybe I don't want you to behave yourself."

The scorching heat of a climax began to mobilize within her, and she could not hold back. Her body erupted with a thousand tiny bursts of pleasure, and she arched her back on the table, biting back a wanton, impetuous cry.

She had barely recovered her senses when he followed her with an equally violent climax, groaned passionately, and shot his seed into her womb.

Exhausted and spent, he collapsed upon her and whispered in her ear, "I will come to you again tonight."

"Do I have your word?"

"Yes. It will take an army to keep me away."

A short while later they parted at the door, and with flushed cheeks and an untidy knot in her hair Alexandra exited the court chamber.

As she made her way across the great banqueting hall, her shoes clicking noisily over the marble floor, she was keenly aware of Prince Nicholas leaning at his ease against the far wall, idly plucking grapes from a small bunch in his hand and popping them into his mouth. He watched her with dark, hooded eyes.

As she approached, he finished the grapes, pushed away from the wall, and bowed to her, as was required of him, but she felt his dangerous gaze burning into her back until she reached the door in haste and headed back to her private chamber.

* * *

"And what did she have to say about it?" Nicholas asked as he shut the door behind him and strode into the court chamber with a passing glance at the mahogany table.

Randolph poured each of them a glass of brandy. "She thanked me for defending her honor, of course, and denied any involvement."

"Do you believe her?"

"Yes. Father's health was failing long before we set sail for England, and the doctor confirmed it was cancer. To think otherwise is pure conjecture."

Nicholas took a sip of the brandy and regarded Rand shrewdly. "Are you sure you can be objective about her?"

"What are you saying, Nick?"

His brother merely shrugged. "I am only here to remind you of our conversation on the ship. You told me that she prevents you from thinking clearly."

All at once, Rand experienced a flash memory of the sexual frenzy that had exploded in his brain just now when she reclined on the table before him.

He swirled his brandy around a few times before raising it to his lips.

God, he could still smell her intoxicating womanly scent on his fingers. . . .

Nick finished his drink and set it down on the table. "Just be careful. That is all I ask."

"No need for concern," Rand replied. "I've got my wits about me."

He waited for Nick to leave the chamber, then had to fight hard to focus on official palace correspondence.

Chapter Twenty-six

"I am not quite sure what to expect," Alexandra said to Randolph as she stepped up onto the dais and sat down beside him.

Her first lady-in-waiting arranged Alexandra's skirts around the throne—an ornately carved monster of a chair, identical in size and design to her husband's—while the Lord Chamberlain stood inside the door, speaking quietly to Nicholas.

"It may take a few hours," Randolph explained, leaning close over the armrest. "Presently the visitors are assembled in the antechamber, where they will wait until the Lord Chamberlain invites them to enter individually. Each guest will make his reverence to us just inside the door and present a wedding gift. He will then withdraw, and the next guest will be escorted inside."

"I don't require gifts," Alex said. "You gave me everything I wanted last night, and the night before that, and the night before that."

Within moments, the great doors swung open and the Lord Chamberlain announced the American Ambassador, who presented Alex and Randolph with two jewel-encrusted golden goblets. They spoke to him briefly, thanked him for the gift, and awaited the next visitor.

"The Marquess of Cavanaugh," the Lord Chamberlain

announced, "on behalf of his father, the Duke of Kaulbach."

The marquess—a handsome young aristocrat with chestnut-colored hair and a muscular build—bowed deeply. "Your Majesty, allow me to present this gift to you in celebration of your recent nuptials, for which my father sends his most exultant regards."

His servant approached from behind and opened a long, narrow box, which contained a shiny broadsword with a golden hilt and pommel, lying on a bed of crimson velvet.

Randolph immediately rose from his throne to take a closer look. "A Scottish claymore," he said with approval, removing it from the box and testing its weight. "Well done, Leopold."

"His Majesty knows his weapons," the marquess replied with a friendly smile that revealed an obvious familiarity between them. "My father obtained it from the Scottish Duke of Moncrieffe when he visited the Highlands."

Alex watched her husband move closer to the windows, where he swung the blade around. He then set it back in the box and returned to his throne.

"We will see you at the banquet this evening," he said to the marquess. "We will plan our next hunt."

"I shall look forward to it."

"The banquet or the hunt?" Rand asked with a hint of mischief.

Lord Cavanaugh smiled. "Both, Your Majesty, with equal enthusiasm."

After he was gone and before the next visitor was announced, Alexandra leaned close. "He is a friend of yours?"

"Yes. Leopold is a decorated war hero who helped defeat Napoleon. He is a brilliant strategist on the battlefield. His father is Lord President of the Privy Council and Duke of Kaulbach."

"He is away at the moment?"

"Yes, traveling abroad."

Alexandra leaned closer, laid her hand upon Rand's, and stroked his knuckles with the soft pad of her middle finger. "Is the marquess a married man?"

He gave her a dubious glance. "Why do you ask?"

She leaned back in her chair and lifted an eyebrow. "I have three unmarried sisters if you will recall, and he is quite a handsome man."

Her husband smirked. "Are you trying to make me jealous, Wife?"

"That depends. Will it inspire you to put courtly matters aside at an earlier hour this evening, and join me for a different sort of celebration?"

He chuckled softly. "I need no further inspiration than the mere knowledge of your existence. And I thought it was duty, not celebration, that required us to engage in those particular frolics you so enjoy."

"Can it not be both?"

They leaned together for a kiss but drew back when the Lord Chamberlain cleared his throat and announced the next visitor to the throne room.

At that moment, Alexandra caught Nicholas watching from the corner of the room. He swiped a hand at the velvet curtain at the window and walked out the side door.

* * *

Three hundred guests attended the banquet that evening—most of them of noble blood, as well as a few well-favored musicians, poets, and senior bishops.

After a sumptuous four-course dinner that included turtle soup, roast pheasant in brandy sauce, followed by raspberry rum cakes for dessert, the guests moved into the green and gold ballroom for dancing.

Randolph, dressed in his magnificent royal scarlet regalia with tasseled epaulets at his shoulders, led Alexandra onto the floor in the center of the room for the first dance of the evening.

While she waited for the music to begin she looked up at the giant crystal chandelier over her head. It reflected the light from hundreds of flickering candles, and she wondered if she should pinch herself, for her life seemed transformed.

She had never expected any of it to turn out quite like this. Even when she learned the Prince of Petersbourg was traveling to London in search of a wife, she had not known she would succeed in winning his hand, nor had she imagined she could ever be truly happy with him—for she had long been preparing herself for a loveless marriage she would be forced to endure in the name of duty and vengeance.

Yet here she stood, wildly passionate for her husband, who had proven himself to be a magnificent lover and an honorable gentleman.

Perhaps happy endings were possible after all, she thought with a smile as the orchestra began to play and her husband led her through a lively country dance. Afterward, they were rewarded with generous applause and shouts of approval.

"You are glowing tonight," Randolph whispered in her ear as he led her off the floor.

"For once I feel as if I belong."

Then they walked to meet his brother, Nicholas, and that sense of belonging died a quick death.

"Truly a night to remember," Nick said with a chivalrous bow as he turned to Alexandra. "Your Majesty, will you do me the honor of accompanying me onto the floor?"

Her happy mood darkened further, for she had no choice

but to accept. Placing her gloved hand in his, she allowed him to escort her to three couples waiting to perform a quadrille.

As the music began, the head couple moved through the figures, and Alexandra soon followed with Nicholas. As they finished their part he kept his eyes on the others while leaning close to speak to her.

"It seems you have bewitched my brother," he said. "He is completely besotted."

"As am I," she replied. "Should that not always be the case with newlyweds?"

A group of men on the edges of the room burst into a chorus of laughter. Growing increasingly uneasy, Alexandra glanced over her shoulder at them.

"You have certainly kept him preoccupied," Nicholas said.

She shot him a look. "Let us not be cryptic. What are you insinuating?"

They stepped apart and crossed over to the opposite dancers, changed partners, and came around to each other again.

"I am not insinuating anything," he replied.

"I think you are. And if you believe any of what that unfortunate underbutler was gossiping about, I will question your intelligence, sir, for I am in love with the king and I wish only to be a dutiful queen. So I beg of you, do not spoil his happiness, or mine, for that matter, with your unfounded suspicions."

They turned to opposite partners and stepped forward into the center.

"I am only taking care of his best interests," Nicholas replied. "As is my duty."

"Perhaps you should make it your duty to look out for *my* best interests as well," she suggested. They moved around the circle together. "Because I am not unconscious of the fact that I have enemies in this country. I know how my father was despised in the final months of his reign, so do not assume, sir, that I mean to repeat his mistakes. I am your brother's queen and loyal to the end. Take me at my word on that."

The dance came to an end, but they remained in the center of the floor while the other dancers cleared away.

"How can I," he asked, "when you have achieved your position through deceit?"

She scoffed. "Is that not the pot calling the kettle black? If I do recall, the night I met you, you were wearing your brother's clothing."

Other new couples began to crowd onto the floor, so he escorted her back to her stepmother. With a courtly bow, he turned and walked away.

"He doesn't like me," Alex said to Lucille.

The duchess watched him leave with a haughty note of disdain. "Well, I do not like him either," she replied. "He is too confident in his good looks, and seems hell-bent on assuming that anyone new who enters this court is an enemy of the king. You should have heard how he questioned Nigel tonight."

"Mr. Carmichael is here?" Alex asked, surprised.

She blushed. "Yes. Randolph was very generous and extended an invitation to him, and I dearly hope that later this evening we may have an announcement to make."

"What sort of announcement?"

Lucille's eyes glimmered with satisfaction. "The very best sort a woman can hope for, of course."

"You intend to marry him?" Alex had not expected this.

Lucille turned to her with dismay. "Surely you cannot be surprised, nor could you possibly object. You owe him a great debt, Alexandra. If not for him, you would not even be here. We would both still be back in that putrid little cottage in Wales, huddled around the fire while our tapers burned down to nothing."

"Of course I am grateful," she replied, "but I have learned many things since we arrived here, and I am quite certain that much of what Mr. Carmichael told us about the Revolution was not entirely true."

Lucille regarded her with incredulity. "How so?"

"He made me believe that my father was a saint, and that he was removed from power by warmongers—I believe he once used the word 'barbarians'—who wished only to seize my family's wealth and position."

"They were revolutionaries!" Lucille argued in his defense. "Are you forgetting what happened in Paris? The Reign of Terror? Would you wish that on King George, mad though he may be?"

"Of course not," Alex replied. "But I am not certain that the people of Petersbourg were not somewhat justified in their grievances. They wanted change and progress, and my father was . . ."

Still with the same horror-stricken expression, Lucille pushed her to complete the thought: "He was *what*?"

"Stubborn," Alex replied. "Perhaps also blind to what was happening beyond these palace walls—in the streets and in the private parlors of the common man. I can almost understand it. I have felt quite far removed from the world these past few weeks. You cannot deny that it is a fairy tale sort of existence here."

"But I enjoy fairy tales," Lucille argued. "Isn't that what we all want? Is that not why you are so happy tonight?"

Alexandra flicked open her fan and waved it briskly in front of her face. "I do not deny that I feel very blessed, but it has nothing to do with dreams or fairy stories. My feet are planted quite firmly on the ground."

They were interrupted in that moment by the Marquess of Cavanaugh, the handsome young aristocrat who had presented Randolph with a sword earlier in the day. He bowed elegantly to her. "Your Majesty, I trust you are enjoying yourself this evening."

"Yes, my lord. And you?"

"Very much indeed."

They watched the dancing for a moment; then she turned to the marquess. "Thank you for the wedding gift. It was most generous."

"It was an item I knew the king would appreciate, but I fear it is not something for the queen to enjoy."

She chuckled lightly. "One never knows. Perhaps I will have a use for it one day. Nevertheless, it will look very handsome on display in the Privy Council Chamber."

They continued to watch the dancing; then Lucille noticed Mr. Carmichael enter the room and excused herself to go and greet him.

As soon as she was gone, Lord Cavanaugh turned to Alex. "If you will permit me, madam, I would like to offer another gift, again on behalf of my father."

"What is it?" she asked. "And why did you not bring it to the throne room?"

"I did not feel it would be appropriate," he replied, "for it is a portrait of your parents, in happier times."

The air sailed out of her lungs, but she recovered quickly.

"I am not sure what your intentions are, my lord, but I do hope this is not a secret gift, for I cannot keep secrets from my husband."

His blue eyes warmed. "Rest assured that I have already spoken to the king about the portrait and he suggested I handle it with . . ."—he paused—"*discretion*, for there are some who may not approve of such a gift. The country wishes to embrace the future, not the past, and the king is aware of that."

She glanced toward her husband. "I see. Well then, I

must apologize for suggesting otherwise. May I ask how you came into possession of the portrait?"

He led her away from others who might be listening. "My father and your father were close friends since early childhood. The portrait was a gift to my parents on their wedding day, and has been kept safely hidden at my father's country estate all these years. But now that you have come home, we believe its rightful place is with you."

She reached out to touch Lord Cavanaugh's arm. "Thank you, my lord. I will treasure it always."

He bowed to her. "I am pleased to hear it, and have already taken the liberty of having it delivered to your chamber. It will be waiting for you when you retire this evening."

The marquess turned to go, but she stopped him. "Wait. My husband said your father is chief officer of the Privy Council, and has held that position for many years."

Cavanaugh spoke in a hushed tone. "Yes, and it wasn't always easy for him after what happened to your family. But we put all that behind us and placed duty above all. We pledged an oath to King Frederick and are loyal subjects." He glanced over his shoulder. "But know this, madam. Despite appearances, you have many friends here at court, even among the New Regime. In our hearts, a great number of us are celebrating your return."

She nodded at him. "Thank you."

She would endeavor to remember that. Especially when her husband's brother was accusing her of seduction and deceit.

With a great show of respect, Lord Cavanaugh bowed and backed away.

Chapter
Twenty-seven

Alexandra closed her bedchamber door behind her and stared at the gift leaning against the side of her bed—a large package half the size of the mattress and wrapped in fine white linen, tied up in a blue satin ribbon.

Having already dismissed her ladies-in-waiting—for she wished to be alone to unveil the portrait—she moved closer to the bed and took a deep breath. With hands that trembled slightly, she pulled the delicate ribbon free and unfolded the fabric away from the canvas.

The fire crackled and sparked in the hearth while she beheld the handsome couple before her. Her mother was young and vibrant, not much older than Alexandra was to-day. She was seated in a gilded ceremonial chair and wore a heavy brocade gown and powdered wig. On her finger she wore the ruby ring.

Alex's father was a fine-looking man, also in a pow-dered wig. He stood behind the queen and stared dream-ily into space, while the queen kept her eyes fixed on the artist with an expression of bold confidence.

Or perhaps it was a look of warning?

A knock sounded at the door just then. Startled almost out of her wits, Alexandra swung around. "Who is it?"

"It's Randolph."

Glancing back at the portrait, she wondered briefly if

she should drape the linen back over it, but remembered that her husband already knew of the gift and had, according to Lord Cavanaugh, given his blessing.

She crossed to the door and let Rand in, then locked it behind him. "I was not expecting you so soon," she said.

He began to untie his cravat as he strolled closer to the fire. "I couldn't stay away." Naturally, his gaze was drawn to the bed and the portrait that leaned against it.

"The Duke of Kaulbach's gift has arrived," she explained. "Come and see it." She waved him over.

Together they stood before it.

"My father was right," he said. "You bear a striking resemblance to your mother."

"Yes, and look at that." Alex pointed. "She is wearing the ring you gave me."

He nodded and took hold of her hand.

"Is it safe for me to keep it in this room?" she asked. "I would mount it above the mantel."

He glanced at the painting that now occupied that space—a landscape by a local artist of mediocre talent. "This is your personal chamber," he said. "Of course you may hang it wherever you like."

"It won't incite more gossip in the household?"

"If it does, I will deal with it accordingly." The note of confidence in his voice and the cool gleam in his eyes gave her every assurance that he would indeed block any foe. She felt a stirring of arousal at the awesome display of his authority and wondered absently if she would ever be able to look at him and not find him overwhelmingly attractive.

"For now," he added, "let us move it to a safer location . . . over here against the wall where you can see it." He picked it up as if it weighed nothing and carried it across the room. Once he had set it in place, he pulled the protective linen away and tossed the fabric over the back of a chair.

"There now, that's better. It's quite a magnificent piece, isn't it?"

"Yes, absolutely magnificent," she replied in a haze of sensual yearning as she crossed to her husband and began to unbutton his waistcoat.

*   *   *

Later, when the fire was reduced to a few glowing embers in the hearth, Alexandra turned to her husband on the soft feather mattress and rested her cheek on a hand. "May I ask you something?"

He lay quietly on his back, naked and beautiful in the golden light of a single candle at the bedside, blinking up at the silk canopy. "Anything."

"Why does Nicholas hate me so much?"

His blue eyes caught hers in a deep, penetrating gaze. "He does not hate you."

"Yes, I believe he does. He certainly doesn't trust me."

Rand exhaled slowly—which she interpreted as a sign of impatience—then sat up on the edge of the bed. "Must we talk about this now?"

"Why *not* now?" she asked. "It must be dealt with, Randolph, for I do not appreciate being treated as if I were your enemy."

He reached for his trousers and pulled them on. "I will ask him to be more gracious toward you in the future."

"No, do not try to appease me in such a way. It is more than a simple case of poor courtly manners. He appears to find me quite detestable, and for that reason I do not trust *him*."

Randolph turned on the bed to look at her. "Watch your tongue, Alex. I trust *no* one more than my brother."

"No one . . . including me, I suppose."

He quickly stood and fastened his trousers.

The fact that he did not reply caused a wave of anger to rise up and crest within her.

She leaned across the bed. "Tonight he accused me of seduction and deceit. You must talk to him."

Rand pulled his shirt on over his head. "I will, but I cannot put a leash on him, Alex, for I need him to be my eyes and ears here at the palace. It is his duty to be suspicious of everyone."

"Including his queen?"

Rand shrugged into his waistcoat and buttoned it. "Yes."

Her mouth fell open. "What are you saying? Have you instructed him to spy on me? I thought we were past all that."

"No, I am afraid not. You are a Tremaine by blood, and there are those who would see me dead to make you their sole sovereign, and others who would enjoy seeing *your* head roll." He went looking for his neckcloth, which had somehow ended up on the floor under the bed.

"That is not what I heard tonight," she said with a twinge of satisfaction while he was still on his hands and knees.

He rose to his feet. "What exactly did you hear?"

"That I have many friends at the palace, more than I know."

"What sorts of friends?" He inclined his head with concern.

"No one was named specifically, but it was implied that members of your father's government are celebrating my return."

He immediately advanced upon her, leaned over the bed, and took hold of her chin. "What are you suggesting, Alex? That people of this court will divide into two separate factions?" She tried to pull away, but he refused to let go. His eyes burned with fury. "Are you taking pleasure in this? I certainly hope not, for when I proposed to you I did so under the assumption that a union between our two families would unite the country, not tear it apart. You are not encouraging this sort of talk, I hope."

Realizing the implications of her statements, she quickly clarified her meaning. "No, of course not. It is just something that was said to me. That is all. I took it as a compliment and a show of support, nothing more."

He roughly let go of her chin and removed himself from the bed. "Who said this to you?"

"Lord Cavanaugh," she replied.

His head drew back. "Leopold?"

"Yes. He told me that his father and mine were good friends, but that the duke later pledged loyalty to your father, and that he remains ever loyal. I apologize, Randolph. I did not mean to suggest that he is a rebel, nor do I wish to incite conflict."

He reached for his jacket and pulled it on. "I am pleased to hear that, at least."

It was a glib reply. She doubted he believed her.

"Must you leave like this?" she asked as he strode to the door.

"My apologies, but it is very late. Good evening, Alex."

With that, he bowed to her and walked out, and she collapsed onto the bed in frustration.

*   *   *

Randolph shut the door behind him and strode down the long red-carpeted corridor on a direct path to his brother's bedchamber, but stopped along the way to utter a few oaths and pound a fist against the wall.

He had never imagined wearing the crown would be easy, but had not expected matters to become so bloody complicated so soon after his father's death, thanks to a wife who could potentially undo everything he had worked so hard to achieve.

Leaning against the wall, Rand massaged his weary eyes with the heels of his hands and fought to maintain his calm. All along, since the first moment he met Alexandra, his instincts told him that she was destined to be his queen. And dammit, the white-hot desire he felt for her was overpowering. Pray God he had not made a mistake.

And what if Nicholas was right? Rand trusted his brother, perhaps more than he trusted his own mind, for he was inebriated with lust half the time, whenever he thought about bedding his new wife.

For that reason, he simply could not let down his guard. He must remain rational and practical.

Pushing away from the wall and continuing on his way, he headed to Nick's chamber to inform him of Leopold's private conversation with Alexandra, and to talk further about the future.

* * *

When the first light of dawn touched the paned windows of the queen's chamber, Alex woke with a sick feeling in her stomach as she recalled the heated argument she'd had with Randolph the night before. Thoughts of it spun in her head like a hurricane, so she called for her first lady-in-waiting, who quickly came running.

After emptying the contents of her stomach into the washbasin in her dressing room, Alexandra wanted only to go and speak to her husband to resolve their disagreement as quickly as possible, but her first lady pleaded with her to remain in bed.

While Alex waited miserably for the palace physician

to arrive, she wondered if this infirmity was some sort of punishment for her pride and lofty ambitions. Was it not enough that her husband had taken his brother's side against hers and by now probably believed she wanted to rouse a civil war? Was it really necessary to turn her stomach into a torture chamber?

Imagine her surprise when the doctor smiled down at her and congratulated her on a job well done.

"It is my pleasure to inform you, Your Majesty," he said, "that you are with child. Shall I be the one to inform the king, or would you prefer to deliver the happy news yourself?"

She sat up instantly with eyes wide, laughed with astonishment, then heaved forward and vomited again over the side of the bed.

Chapter
Twenty-eight

The king was overjoyed, of course, at the news of his wife's blessed condition, and that night he raised a glass in celebration at dinner.

It was a private affair for members of the royal family only, which included Alexandra, Rose, Nicholas, and Lucille, who arrived late and apologized for keeping everyone waiting.

Nicholas was as polite and warm to Alex as any brother-in-law could be, which did nothing to ease her mind, however, for she recognized a well-scripted performance when she saw one.

After dessert, the men remained at the table to discuss politics and smoke cigars while the ladies retired to the drawing room.

Rose sat down at the pianoforte and invited Alex to help her select a piece of music. While Alex flipped through the pages, Rose watched her intently.

"May I have your permission to speak plainly about something?"

Alex's eyes lifted. "Of course."

"I see you are having some trouble with Nicholas, but don't judge him too harshly. He is protective. That is all."

"But I love your brother," Alex explained as she lowered

the pages to her side. "Why would Nicholas wish to protect him from *that*?"

"Because he remembers what happened the last time Rand gave his heart to an ambitious woman. It did not end well, it took him forever to recover."

Alex glanced over her shoulder at Lucille, who was shuffling a deck of cards, and lowered her voice. "You are referring to his former fiancée—the lady who jilted him?"

"Correct. Rand was devastated when he discovered her infidelity."

"He loved her very much, then."

"Yes, though I am afraid love has turned to hate where she is concerned."

"He has not forgiven her?"

"No, and neither has Nicholas. Nor I, for that matter. We remember all too well how she pretended to be devoted, and how Randolph suffered at the loss of her."

Alexandra handed Rose a piece of music. "Where is she now?"

"She is married to Earl Ainsley, the wretched rake who led her astray. They spend most of their time in the country, for they were both banished from court." Rose set the music on the stand and laid her fingers on the keys. "I sometimes wonder if she regrets her actions. Her family assured Randolph that she could be persuaded to leave the earl and go through with the wedding, but he would have none of that. He couldn't bear to think that a woman would marry him for the sake of duty. He loved her, and he wanted to be loved in return. Is that not what we all want?"

Rose seemed especially melancholy that night, and Alexandra suspected she was lamenting her dutiful engagement to the Austrian archduke.

The gentlemen arrived just as Rose began to play a sorrowful tune, and Alex turned expectantly to face them.

* * *

"I wish to propose a truce," she said privately to Nicholas, who was pouring himself a drink from the brandy tray.

He faced her with curious interest.

"I believe we both have Randolph's best interests at heart," she continued. "I am carrying his child now, and I assure you, all I want is a happy home and a country that is at peace. I am in love with your brother and will never do anything to jeopardize our marriage."

Nicholas swirled his drink around. "I don't doubt your passion," he said, "but what if you are a dangerous addiction?"

"Dangerous?" She frowned. "I think you are confusing me with the woman he almost married but was fortunate enough to have escaped. I understand it was an ugly situation and did not end well, but I promise nothing like that will ever happen to him again."

Nicholas said nothing for a moment. "We shall see."

" 'We shall see'? That is the best you can do?"

He smirked gallingly as he backed away to join Randolph and Lucille at the card table.

"What will it take, then?" Alex demanded to know, stepping forward and loathing the fact that she had to prove herself to this man who thought so little of her.

"Just time," he replied. "That is all. Now if you will excuse me . . ."

Alexandra watched him join Randolph for a game of whist, then wrestled with her umbrage as she went to sit with Rose at the piano.

Chapter Twenty-nine

October 2, 1814

Dressed in a newly made gown of crimson silk trimmed with gold lace, which she wore beneath the green velvet Imperial Robe of State, Alexandra took hold of her husband's hand and stepped out of the coronation coach to a chorus of cheers from thousands of Petersbourg citizens, who had lined the streets along the procession route from the palace to the Abbey of St. Peter.

She and Randolph paused briefly to wave at the people and allow the Master and Mistress of Robes a moment to arrange their heavy velvet trains, trimmed in ermine and woven with national symbols.

When at last they proceeded up the steps to the massive front gate and entered the ancient Gothic abbey, Alexandra glanced up at the high cathedral ceiling, listened to the angelic voices of the choir that led them up the wide center aisle, and could scarcely believe all of this was happening.

Not only had she succeeded in winning the hand of the Prince of Petersbourg; she was now to be crowned queen consort, would pledge her oath to the people, and in her womb she carried an heir, quite possibly the future king.

They reached the altar and climbed the steps to the two

ancient medieval thrones that stood side by side, where they sat and listened to another hymn. Next, the Great Lord Chamberlain of Arms, robed in navy and wearing the heraldic coronet of the Royal Guard, called for the archbishop to come forward and begin the ceremony.

Randolph took the sacred coronation oath and solemnly swore to govern the people of Petersbourg and uphold the sacred laws of the church. A communion ceremony followed, and he was then crowned and presented with the Royal Bible and the Sceptre of the Imperial State.

He stood for the removal of the state robe, which was replaced by the blue velvet Robe Royal, with a mantle of white fur.

The archbishops and peers of the country pledged their loyalty to him; then Alexandra was crowned as queen consort in a shorter, simpler ceremony. She, too, was presented with a Bible. She then stood for the removal of her state robe, which was replaced by the queen's Robe Royal.

While the congregation stood and the choir sang another hymn, she was overcome by an emotion so powerful, it caused her flesh to tingle and her eyes to fill with tears. It was followed by an overwhelming sense of pride and a deeply profound joy that took her breath away.

In that moment, Randolph turned his head and looked at her. They stared at each other as the hymn rose to a crescendo and the congregation sat down.

The ceremony was all but complete, except for one last ancient ritual.

The doors to the abbey swung wide open, and a knight in armor upon an enormous black warhorse with a purple plume at his forelock rode into the basilica. The horse's giant hooves clopped noisily upon the gray stone floor and echoed up into the rafters, then quieted as the knight urged his steed onto the red carpet and trotted up the center aisle.

The horse reared up before Alexandra and Randolph, and the knight lifted the visor of his helmet.

Her heart raced with exhilaration as she beheld her brother-in-law, Prince Nicholas, who had been given the traditional honor of being King's Champion at the coronation.

He drew his sword and looked Alexandra straight in the eye as he shouted, "Let it be known throughout this land—within and beyond its borders—that our Lord Sovereign shall be protected by this Champion! Any enemy who dares challenge his rule must raise a sword against me, as divine Lord of the Royal Guard!"

He held the sword upright before his helmet and eased his mount into a courtly bow. The warhorse dipped down on one knee, lowered his plumed head, then rose again and reared up on his hind legs, clawing at the air in a fine display of courage and valor.

Nicholas shut his visor and wheeled the beast around to gallop back down the aisle and out of the abbey. He was not yet gone before the congregation erupted into a chorus of cheers and applause.

Again Alexandra turned to look at her husband. This time he did not meet her gaze. He was smiling and watching his brother.

* * *

"Why must you go?" Alexandra asked. "It is too soon. The coronation was only a week ago."

Randolph slipped naked into bed beside her and laid a hand on her belly. "All the allied sovereigns will be there," he replied. "I cannot possibly remain at home."

"Then why can't I go with you?"

"Because you are with child," he gently explained with more charm than she cared to observe in that moment, for when he spoke to her like that he had the power to sway and appease her, make her agree to anything. "Quite possibly carrying the future monarch," he continued. "We must take great care with your health, darling."

She narrowed her eyes flirtatiously and set out to challenge him in every possible way. "We could take great care of me in Vienna. Or perhaps I could take great care of *you*."

He leaned over to kiss her. "I will miss you terribly while I am away."

She laid her open palms flat on his chest and pushed him back. "You will write to me?"

"Yes," he replied with a chuckle. "Each night before bed, when I am longing for you like a schoolboy. And I promise to have a dreadful time," he added. "I will enjoy myself not in the least."

She rose up, flipped him onto his back, pinned his wrists to the mattress, and straddled him. "I am sorry to hear it, sir, because I intend to enjoy myself quite tremendously while you are gone. I will host a dozen parties in your honor and create a new holiday. I will call it . . ." She swiveled her hips alluringly. "Randolph's Rising."

He grinned and thrust his pelvis upward, nearly bucking her onto the floor.

"Relax, Your Majesty," she said. "You are not trapped here. I only wish to pleasure you."

She slid up the length of his manhood and dipped her naked breasts low. He lifted his head to taste her, but she playfully drew back, just out of reach.

In short order, his muscular brawn won the day and he rose up and flipped her over again. Suddenly she found herself on her back, sinking into the feather mattress beneath the glorious weight of his virility.

"It is our last night together for at least a month," he said, "possibly longer, so you must permit me to pleasure *you* this evening." He gazed down at her with tenderness.

"And also promise me . . . there will be no tearful good-byes."

His mouth covered hers in an intimate kiss, and she melted into the warmth of his body.

Later he used his mouth to bring her to climax, and she reciprocated with an equal measure of generosity.

Finally, exhausted and well-satisfied, they slept for an hour or two, then woke again to fill their cups for the coming drought when he would leave Petersbourg to attend the Congress of Vienna.

If she were not already with child, it was very likely they would have conceived at least three more that night.

When she woke in the morning, however, Randolph was gone, and she was strangely thankful for her husband's quiet decree: *There will be no tearful good-byes . . .*

She was therefore left only with the memory of his final kiss before dawn, and the rapture to which she would cling in the coming weeks while he was gone.

When her dresser arrived to draw the curtains and welcome in the new day, Alexandra rose from bed to look out at a heavy downpour of rain outside her window, ran her hands slowly over her belly, and said a silent prayer for her husband's safe journey overland and his swift return to her side—with their hearts still entwined and their passions still burning as hot as the sun.

PART IV
Enemies and Allies

Chapter Thirty

To Her Majesty the Queen
Petersbourg Palace
October 20, 1814

My dearest Alexandra,

Nicholas and I arrived in the capital three days ago and are privileged to be occupying suites in the Imperial Court Chancellery of Emperor Francis's palace, Hofburg. The King of Prussia is also here in a separate section of the palace called the Schweizerhof, where the King of Denmark is housed.

The four of us shared a fine bottle of brandy last night while overlooking the Danube, and enjoyed a heated debate about what will happen to all the artistic masterpieces—the sculptures, jewels, and paintings—that were pilfered by Napoléon during the war and packed into the Louvre. Naturally the French don't wish to part with anything, but I am convinced that by the end of this important congress much of it will be returned to its rightful owners.

I wish you could join me here and see the city proper. Everywhere I look, I see white domes and towers and, below that, a spirit of victory and celebration has overtaken the streets. There are elaborate banquets at the palace each night, and the emperor has appointed an official Festivals Committee to keep us all entertained with operas and balls and other such frivolities.

All that is incidental, however, to my true purpose here, for I believe this will be the greatest peacemaking venture in world history, and I feel privileged to be among those who will decide upon the future of Europe. Maps are already being redrawn, and a new balance of power is being decided upon. I shall do my best to keep you informed of our progress here, but my schedule is full, so forgive me if I do not write every day.

Devotedly yours,
Randolph

* * *

My love,

I was elated to receive your letter and devoured every word. Please write as often as you are able and tell me of the operas and balls, and be sure to include the sort of thought-provoking gossip that will keep my ladies-in-waiting adequately entertained, for they seem quite fed up most of the time since you and Nicholas departed. There are so few social events for which to prepare, and you know how they enjoy their gowns and jewels and all those frivolous evenings that last until dawn. They have made no secret of the fact that they long for nothing more than a dull banquet with dry beef, but it seems every person of any stature worth entertaining has left our great city for Vienna.

But that is enough talk of gossip and balls. I am eager to hear of the work you are doing, as I believe you will accomplish great things. Before you left, you mentioned the possible abolition of the slave trade in France. I do hope you will persist in that most noble of objectives. And please continue to keep me abreast of what is happening with the French border, and let me know if Russia will be allowed to keep quite so much of Poland. I long to hear every detail, but of course I understand that much of what is happening must be kept confidential until treaties are signed and the new balance of power is established.

Sincerely,
Alexandra

P.S. Have you spoken to Rose's fiancé, the archduke?

* * *

Dearest Alexandra,

You write to me of borders and treaties and the boredom of your ladies-in-waiting, but you have said nothing of your heart. Do not forget me while I am gone. I think of you constantly, even when I am arguing with that devious French diplomat Talleyrand over the freedom of the seas. I wish you were here to argue with him as well. I have no doubt you would put him in his place.

And yes, I did speak with the archduke. I told him she'd had second thoughts. I believe he was genuinely disappointed.

Devotedly yours,
R.

* * *

Dear Randolph,

Forgive me, Husband, for not writing of my heart, but I did not wish to burden you with words of woe and longing, and heaven forbid someone might intercept my letters and discover that the Queen of Petersbourg is a wanton woman who ignores politics and demands only that her lover return to her bed. I am of course dreaming of you each night.

But there is another more important matter that I must relay to you. Rose has been melancholy since you left. I suspect she is disappointed as well, but I do not believe she is longing for the archduke. Therefore I am of the opinion you did the right thing in ending their engagement. I believe she is in love with someone else, though she refuses to name the gentleman. I will certainly relay the information if I can discover the secrets she keeps hidden in her heart.

Come home soon. I long for your touch.

* * *

Over the next two weeks, Alexandra received no further letters from Randolph, but she did her best not to worry and reminded herself that he was occupied with very important matters of state.

That did not stop her, however, from longing desperately for his return, and her heart ached when she heard reports that the congress was nowhere near completion. Evidently the kings, princes, emperors, and diplomats were all having too much fun.

She rather wished it were not so.

* * *

Another week went by, and still Alexandra received no letters. She sought out the palace post officer personally and asked if there had been any delay in correspondence from Vienna.

He informed her that a few letters had indeed found their way across the border and Prince Nicholas's official reports from Vienna to the Privy Council had been received, but no personal correspondence had come from the king.

He apologized, and she did her best to appear cheerful as she thanked him.

* * *

Three days later, a visitor was announced to the queen's chamber.

Alexandra set down her embroidery and stood to receive the Marquess of Cavanaugh, who bowed deeply upon a gallant entry. "Your Majesty."

"Lord Cavanaugh, what a pleasure to see you." She crossed toward him while making a sincere effort to ignore the anxious little gasps from her three ladies-in-waiting, who rose quickly to curtsy. One nearly knocked over a chair in the process.

It did not take a fool to recognize the fact that they were all foolishly besotted, for the future Duke of Kaulbach was a devastatingly handsome man and one of the most sought-after bachelors in Petersbourg. He would one day inherit an ancient and illustrious dukedom and would be one of the highest-ranking peers in the realm.

"What brings you to the palace?" she asked. "I thought you were in Vienna with everyone else."

"I was, madam," he replied, "but I have come home with an important dispatch." He stepped forward to hand over a stack of letters tied in a red ribbon. "For you, from the king."

Her heart ignited with joy and it took great strength of will for her to resist rushing forward to snatch the letters out of his hands.

"Thank you, my lord," she said as she accepted them. "I am in your debt. Tell me, did he send you home just to deliver these letters?"

"No," the marquess replied. "I had already announced my desire to return home, and His Majesty knew I could be trusted to deliver them to you without risk of loss or tardiness."

She smiled. "Very well, then. You must join me for tea and allow me to thank you—for the second time, it seems. I am still deeply touched by the wedding gift you sent. I have had it mounted in my private chamber, and I cherish it deeply."

"I am pleased to hear it."

Her ladies-in-waiting fell into a hush of giggly whispers, then scurried off in all directions to appear busy.

"Tell me about Vienna," Alex said as she sat down at the fireside table across from the marquess. "How I wish I could attend such an important historic event."

He lounged back in the chair and crossed one leg over the other. "Have you been to Vienna before?"

"No, never. Please describe it to me. I wish to know every detail. Tell me about the architecture, the artists, the food . . ."

"Ah, the food . . ." His eyes sparkled with teasing charm as he told her great tales of the Emperor of Austria's culinary extravagances, the nightly feasts with elaborate menus of soups and hors d'oeuvres, main courses of tender venison, followed by sweet indulgences—rum cakes soaked in sugar sauce, raspberry pies with clotted cream, strong coffee, and sweet dessert wines from Hungary . . .

By the marquess's description, it sounded as if the entire city had been transformed into a veritable festival of romance and pleasure.

But there was also other important news the marquess wished to convey. . . .

For a full hour he held nothing back and revealed all he could about the latest negotiations among all the great and lesser allied powers, most of which were taking place in informal settings—at balls and operas, on boat cruises along the Danube, or across the marble-topped card tables in the clubs.

By the time he was finished describing all of it, Alexandra felt as if she had traveled to Vienna and back and had taken part in the carving and sculpting of a new Europe.

After he left, she sat for a long while with her hands upon her belly, staring at the wall. Then she quickly stood up, moved to a more comfortable chair, and settled in with fervor to read her husband's letters.

Most of them were very brief and left her feeling frustrated. She was glad she had not read them in front of the marquess.

* * *

The following day, newspaper in hand, Alexandra entered Rose's chamber just before luncheon. "I must speak with you in private about something," she said.

Rose frowned. "What is it? You look troubled."

Alexandra was not proud of the whirlwind of her emotions—and perhaps it was the pregnancy that caused such irrational thoughts to spin about in her brain—but she could not possibly keep quiet about what she had just read. Rose was the only person she could confide in about this particular subject. It was not something she wished to share with her stepmother.

"Have you seen the *Chronicle* today?"

"Not yet," Rose said.

Alexandra handed it to her and pointed. "See there, on page one. The piece about the masquerade ball." She waited for Rose to find it and begin reading, paced around the room for a moment or two, then spoke up before Rose had a chance to finish. "It says Randolph and Nicholas have been behaving rakishly during the entire congress, and . . ." She paused. "Well . . . read on. Have you gotten to the worst part yet?"

Rose continued to read until her eyebrows lifted. "Oh! Goodness me."

"Indeed," Alexandra replied as she crossed to the window. "I am not pleased about this, Rose. Not at all."

Rose read it again. "It says he was dancing with a mysterious beauty of unknown identity and at the end of the evening she lifted her bejeweled mask and revealed herself. To a great round of applause!"

Alexandra scoffed bitterly.

"I am sure it was nothing," Rose tried to say.

"How could it be nothing?" Alex turned to face her. "That so-called beauty is his ex-fiancée! And it reports quite clearly that her husband, the earl, did not accompany her to Vienna. Why do you think she is there? Is it possible she wants Randolph back?"

"Oh, what difference does it make?" Rose said, tossing the paper onto the bed. "She cannot have him. He belongs to you now, and you are carrying his child."

Alex faced her and tried to convey a measure of confidence. "Yes, I am quite sure you are right, but why must the paper print something so scandalous? You understand what they are implying—that he is ready to take a mistress, and how wonderfully romantic that he can be reunited with his first love, who jilted him. It makes me want to spit."

Rose joined her at the window. "It doesn't matter what they say. It's pure rubbish. May I remind you that she broke his heart and he *hates* her. With a passion."

Alexandra stared out the window while she considered her sister-in-law's assessment of the situation. "Hatred sounds all very well and good, Rose, but I must confess . . . I would prefer a lackluster indifference."

* * *

With Christmas fast approaching, Alexandra made an effort to keep busy so as not to obsess over her husband's social calendar in Vienna.

She took on many charitable duties, including visits to the poorhouses to deliver loaves of bread and soup prepared by the palace kitchen. She also took it upon herself to arrange a full week of gatherings at the palace for sixty aristocratic ladies, where they were each required to knit a pair of woolen mittens every twenty-four hours. At the end of the week, Alexandra delivered the mittens to the Abbey of St. Paul and met with the bishop to organize a gift giving on Christmas Day to those less fortunate.

Her efforts were recognized in the *Chronicle,* and wherever she went she was greeted by throngs of cheering crowds in the streets.

"*Long live the queen!*" someone shouted on one particular afternoon when she unexpectedly stopped her coach to step out and shake hands with a group of musicians playing for coin outside the shops on Solenski Row.

She invited them to play a private concert for the king upon his return.

On the following day, this flattering headline graced the front page of the paper, and she could not help but smile at the satisfaction it roused in her: "QUEEN ALEXANDRA WINS HEART OF THE NATION."

On page 2, however, a detailed account of the latest society gossip at the Vienna Congress outshined that flattering headline—for a banquet and ball had recently been held at the emperor's palace to celebrate the late arrival of an important diplomat from America.

Among the list of attendees was her husband of course, and the next name listed, directly beside his, was that of the Countess of Ainsley.

The baby kicked especially hard just then, and Alexandra laid a hand on her belly. "I know, dearest, I know. I don't like it either, but we must remain sensible."

She set the newspaper aside and wished she could kick someone, too. The Countess of Ainsley perhaps? Or maybe she could stomp hard on her husband's foot the next time they danced.

If he was not too tired of dancing when he returned, for it sounded as if he was overindulging in that particular pastime.

She threw the paper down and counted slowly to ten.

* * *

She received no letters from Randolph for another unbearable week, and despite her busy schedule and the many pleasing reports of her growing popularity in Petersbourg, she could not seem to keep a secure hold on her emotions.

One minute she was blissfully happy, focused on her sovereign duties, and eagerly anticipating the birth of her first child. She enjoyed the distraction of many visitors, including the Marquess of Cavanaugh, who congratulated her on her success and lent her an instruction pamphlet about knitting, which he thought she might enjoy, for it included playful patterns for children's hats.

He was a good friend when she needed one.

The next minute she was imagining that infamous night

at the masquerade ball in Vienna when the Countess of Ainsley had dramatically lifted her mask to reveal herself.

What exactly had occurred before her unveiling? How many times had she and Randolph danced? Had she flirted with him with her eyes?

And dammit, what had she been wearing? Something shimmery with a scandalously low neckline, no doubt.

When at last a letter arrived from Alexandra's husband, it was to inform her that he would be home in time for Christmas. It was a brief letter lacking in the usual passionate outpourings of love, but it was signed, as always, *Devotedly yours.*

She read that particular correspondence with a tight clenching of her jaw and had just stuffed it into the cedar box with the others and slammed the lid shut when a visitor was announced.

In the wake of her husband's dispassionate letter, she was not in the mood to be sociable. Nevertheless, she reminded herself that she could not wallow in petty jealousies. She had a duty to fulfill. A duty to the people of this country. A duty to her heritage.

The door opened, her ladies-in-waiting scampered quite noticeably from the room and, to her incredible surprise, in walked her husband, the king, looking handsome and virile in a long black greatcoat with cape shoulders and a brand-new pair of polished Hessians.

Obviously the festival of pleasures—and all the dancing he'd done in Vienna—had agreed with him. He had never looked better. She wished she could hate him for it, but all she felt was a mad desire to dash into his arms, rip that coat off his body, and make love to him right there on the floor.

Thankfully, however, more sensible thoughts took over, and she wondered what would happen if she threw a brandy decanter at his head.

Chapter Thirty-one

Struggling to remain composed, Alexandra blinked a few times as Randolph closed the door behind him, set down the large leather portfolio he carried, and began to remove his coat.

"Are you not happy to see me?" he asked, slowly striding closer.

All her senses began to hum. Her heart was beating like an army drum in the tense moments before the forward line was called to fire.

"I am in shock," she replied. "I just read your letter. It arrived barely five minutes ago. Was that a joke? Were you toying with me?"

He laughed, and she wanted to pummel his chest with her fists. "Yes," he replied. "I wanted to surprise you."

"Well, you most certainly did. I am not prepared."

Her hair was a mess. She was dressed in a dowdy gown, but everything felt dowdy when her belly stuck out far enough to knock over a table.

He shrugged out of his coat and tossed it onto a chair, gathered her into his arms, and said, "I didn't want you *prepared*. All I wanted was the real you, without any pomp or ceremony." He stepped back and held both her hands out to the side while he took in her appearance. His gaze slid down the length—and width—of her ever-expanding body.

"Look at you," he said. "Our child is growing well, I see."

"Yes, he's strong as an ox." *And I feel as fat as one.*

Randolph pulled her into his arms again and held her tight. "It's so good to be home, my love. It's damn cold out there, and the only thing that kept me from freezing to death in the coach tonight was the thought of your soft, warm body next to mine. Kiss me, Wife, before I throw you on the bed and behave like an ill-bred savage."

She should have resisted. She should have asked him about the Countess of Ainsley and laid all her insecurities to rest before she responded to his sexual overtures—but heaven help her, passion suppressed reason and all she could do was tear furiously at the buttons on his waistcoat and open her mouth for the pounding onslaught of his kiss.

For she needed to prove that he was still hers. And that she still had the power to bewitch him.

* * *

They did not even make it to the bed. They made love like two young, hotheaded lovers on the sheepskin rug before the fire.

Afterward they lay naked, without modesty, sipping wine and wondering if they should cover themselves in case anyone should walk in.

"I have a Christmas gift for you," Rand said, kissing her lightly on the forehead. "Would you like to see it?"

"Of course."

He stood and moved to the door and withdrew a large framed cross-stitch from the leather portfolio he had brought into the room when he arrived.

"It's *you*," he said, holding it up for her, "reclining on the terrace balustrade on the night we met at the Carlton House ball."

Alex sat up to admire the magnificent artistry and work-
manship in the details of the piece. There were tiny beads
and jewels stitched into the intricate folds and ribbons of
her gown, and a crystal chandelier sparkled gorgeously in
the background. Even her long white gloves were trimmed
in tiny pearls.

"It's beautiful, Randolph. Thank you. I will treasure it
always."

He set it down nearby and returned to lie beside her.
"If only you knew how I missed you, and how I wanted
you at my side. That's why I had this commissioned."

"Did you really miss me?" she asked, working hard to
bury her antagonism and not behave like a shrew but,
rather, a seductive wife who merely aimed to stake a claim
upon her husband's affections.

"Of course," he replied with a curious frown. "Could
there be any doubt?"

She shrugged casually as she propped her chin on his
chest.

"Let me guess," he said. "You read the report in the
paper about that awkward masquerade ball."

"Indeed I did," she tersely replied, "and I wanted to go
straight to Vienna and shake you senseless, then take you
to my bed to remind you of the wife you left behind. Then
I would have pushed you off the bed and onto the cold, hard
floor. Was it marble? I imagined it was when I plotted it in
my head."

He stroked her hair and chuckled softly with amusement.
"I am touched by such a tender sentiment," he said, "but no
reminder was necessary. I want no woman but you."

Alex's eyes turned cold. "What a charmer you are." She
rose to her feet, pulled on her silk robe, and tied it above
the monstrous bulge at her belly.

He sat up on the rug. "It was not my intention to charm
you. I meant only to tell you the truth."

"And I believe you," she dutifully replied. "But you must know that it has not been easy."

"Were you jealous?"

The question gnawed at her, made her want to lash out at him.

It was her pride. Damn her stubborn pride. It was like a mangy terrier.

"Not in the least," she answered nevertheless. "Certainly not of *her.*"

His eyes narrowed. "Liar." He raised a knee on the sheepskin rug and spoke warmly in the firelight. "You are the perfect queen, Alexandra. I know it, and the country knows it. Do they not?"

"You have been reading the papers, too," she replied with no small measure of gratification.

"Indeed I have, and I have never felt more proud. Or intimidated. I fear they might adore you more than me. Did you know they egged me this afternoon?"

She faced him. "What do you mean?"

"The coach was pelted with eggs not long after we crossed the border. Perhaps it was a group of rebellious youths who didn't know it was a royal coach. Or perhaps not."

"Does this concern you?" she asked.

He reached for his glass of wine on the stone hearth. "My father was pelted with eggs once, among other things, during his reign. I have come to accept that it is the price of leadership. Even Napoléon had sour fruit thrown in his face on more than one occasion."

"And look at him now," she mentioned with some unease. "He is defeated and exiled."

He shook his head. "I am not Napoléon. Now come back to the fire and lay with me."

She went to him but sat back on her heels. "Forgive me, Randolph, but I must know everything. You have said very little about the countess. Did you see her often after that first night at the masquerade?"

He paused. "Yes."

A knot tightened in Alex's gut. "When? Where?"

"On a number of separate occasions," he replied, leaning back on an arm. "It could not be helped. She has connections, and was invited to most of the conference events."

"Did you talk to her about anything of a private or personal nature?"

"Yes. She apologized for her actions during our engagement, hoped I could forgive her, and asked if she and the earl could be invited back to court."

Alexandra's blood began to boil. "And what did you say?"

"I said no. To both requests."

Her blood cooled again, and she was thankful for it. "Was she disappointed?

"Naturally."

"Did she flirt with you?"

He looked Alex straight in the eye. "Yes."

Alexandra swallowed over her annoyance. She wanted him to be honest, but she did not like these answers. "Did you flirt with her in return?"

"Of course I did not. I avoided her when I could, and when it was not possible to do so I was as polite as the circumstances required. Are we done with the questions yet, woman? I'd prefer to talk of something else."

He stood up in all his naked glory and picked up his empty wineglass to refill it at the table. Alexandra could not take her eyes off him, for he was a magnificent vision of smooth, sinewy muscle and golden flesh in the firelight.

The countess must have been out of her mind to betray this man.

"Why did she leave you for the earl?" Alex asked. "It makes no sense to me."

"I am pleased to hear that at least," he replied. "From what I understand, they were lovers before she was presented to me as a possible bride. It was her family that pushed for our marriage. They were ambitious, and they did not approve of Ainsley. I can hardly blame them. He is a reckless and irresponsible rake, and he has already gambled away most of his inheritance."

"She was very foolish to let you go."

Randolph offered a hand to assist Alex to her feet and led her to the bed.

"I feel fat," she told him. "Like a big whale." Yet she was only six months into her confinement. There was still a great deal of growing to do.

He chuckled as they slid under the covers. "I love the way you look. Would you like me to prove it to you?"

"If His Majesty wishes it."

She quivered with delight as he slowly, teasingly tugged at the tie on her robe and opened it to admire her gigantic belly, and every other trembling inch of her body.

"I am pleased you are home," she said.

"As am I."

Then he silenced any further talk with a soft, warm kiss of glorious, intimate allure.

* * *

The headline in the newspaper the following day informed the nation that the king had returned from the Vienna Congress to celebrate Christmas with the queen, but there was still much work to be done in Vienna—including the important establishment of future diplomatic policies during wartime—and Randolph was therefore expected to return to Austria in the New Year.

On page 5, it was also reported that the Countess of Ainsley had returned from Vienna to celebrate the holiday season at home in Petersbourg, and that she had commissioned a new wardrobe—for her return to Vienna in the New Year.

"It is subtle, but it connects the two of you," Nicholas mentioned to Randolph over breakfast as he came upon the piece about the countess.

"You don't think it is a coincidence?" Rand replied.

Nick lifted his gaze and reached for his coffee. "I do not believe in coincidences, and I've been looking into her affairs. The earl is stone broke and drowning in debt. I cannot imagine he approved the new wardrobe, unless there is some alternative purpose in which he is involved."

"I have a sense of what that is," Randolph replied, "but it's only a hunch."

"Tell me."

Rand sat back in his chair and tapped a finger on the white tablecloth. "She followed me around like a lovesick puppy since that first night at the ball, and practically begged to be invited back to court. For that reason, I believe it is one of two things. Either she wants me to take her as my mistress and provide her with an income, or she is being paid to seduce me and lure me into a scandalous affair to make mud of my name in the eyes of the nation. For what purpose I cannot be sure. Another Royalist revenge plot perhaps?"

Nicholas set down his coffee. "You don't think your wife could be involved somehow? She entered into this marriage with revenge on her mind, and she has enjoyed a suspiciously good deal of public support since you've been gone. Someone at the newspaper loves her."

"You cannot fault her for doing charity work," Rand said.

"Some people use charity for selfish reasons—to further their own interests."

Randolph shook his head. "Not Alexandra. She has

nothing to do with this. She could not possibly collude with the countess. If put in the same room with her, Alex might shove her whole head into a soup terrine."

"I would like to see that," Nicholas said.

Randolph returned his attention to the paper. "As would I."

A quiet moment passed while they finished their breakfasts.

Nick said, "Did you know the Marquess of Cavanaugh paid three visits to your wife while you were gone?"

Rand looked up. "Three visits? I sent him to deliver my letters. That explains one."

"What of the other two times?" Nick asked. "Did she mention anything to you?"

Rand sat back in his chair and fought not to read too deeply into his brother's insinuations.

Though he was oddly inclined to go fetch that Scottish claymore from the Privy Council Chamber and challenge his old friend Leopold to a friendly game of cards.

"No," he easily replied. "But will you look into that for me? Find out the purpose of the visits. I will ask Alex about it personally, of course, and see what she says."

Nicholas immediately stood up and left to investigate.

* * *

"He brought me a pamphlet about knitting," Alexandra told Randolph while she sipped her tea in the drawing room after dinner that night. "It was not long after the newspaper reported upon my efforts to supply the Abbey of St. Paul with mittens for the unfortunate. Why do you ask?"

"Was there another visit?" he offhandedly inquired.

She thought about it a moment and experienced a stirring of unease. "No, Randolph. He came only twice."

"Twice," he repeated.

"That is correct. Did you hear otherwise?"

Her husband leaned back on the sofa and rested an arm along the back of it, toyed with a loose lock of hair over her ear while he regarded her with those charming blue eyes. "No, darling. I was just curious."

Lucille approached just then to suggest a game of whist. Randolph immediately stood up to join her at the table.

* * *

Christmas at Petersbourg Palace was a quiet affair, for King Frederick's passing was still fresh in the hearts of the people, and the family wished to honor his memory in private.

That is not to say there were no public appearances. On Christmas Day, the Royal Family attended mass at the Abbey of St. Peter, and the following evening they hosted a dinner at the orphanage, where they joined the children's choir to sing Yuletide hymns.

Alexandra felt almost completely at ease in her new role as queen. The people had welcomed her in a way she had never imagined possible, and she constantly found herself basking in the sweet glow of impending motherhood. Whenever she felt the baby kick, it was as if a whole new world was opening up inside her and all the angels in heaven were singing *Hallelujah*.

Rose seemed happier as well. She had decided recently that she could not marry for duty alone. She wanted the kind of love that Rand and Alex had, so before Rand left for Vienna, she had asked him to put an end to her engagement to the Austrian archduke. Randolph had honored her wishes, and Alex suspected they would soon learn of a budding romance closer to home, for Rose had a rather blissful look about her.

It was a happy Christmas full of joy and laughter, and there were days when she felt certain that all her hardships and emotional struggles were behind her. Her husband had come home. She believed him about what had happened with the countess in Vienna, and everything seemed perfectly magical.

* * *

Two days before the New Year began, Rand was seated at the head of the large round table in the Privy Council Chamber, reading over the latest reports from Vienna, when the door opened at the far corner of the room. Expecting to see Nicholas, he lifted his gaze from the papers and found himself staring in shock at the Countess of Ainsley.

She shut the door behind her and came dashing toward him in a flurry of silks and ribbons and tearstained cheeks.

"Forgive me, Your Majesty!" she sobbed, dropping to her knees before him. He rose quickly, scraping the chair legs back across the plank floor.

"What is the meaning of this?" he demanded to know. "*Guard!*" he shouted, but no one entered the chamber.

"Get up, Elsbeth!" he commanded, realizing too late that he had used her given name while he hooked an arm under hers and pulled her roughly to her feet.

She dropped back down to her knees, however, like a limp rag doll, and kissed his boots. "Please, sir, take pity on me! I am desperate, and I have nowhere to turn!"

Looking down at the top of her navy winter bonnet, he was momentarily stunned. "I doubt that is the case," he said, then glanced at the door. "*Nicholas!*"

The countess's shoulders heaved with another outrageous sob. "I was so wrong to have betrayed you!" she cried. "If only I could turn back time and return to our engagement ball! I would do it all again so differently, if only I could, for I am now doomed to an eternity of suffering and torment. Oh, how I wish to end it all! I have no choice but to throw myself into the sea! Or perhaps down the palace well. I passed one on my way to see you and had to hold myself back from that tempting dark oblivion!"

"Good God, get a hold of yourself, woman." Rand pulled her to her feet again, this time more gently, with a small show of compassion, even while he suspected this was a well-rehearsed performance. "What is so terrible that you forget your dignity in such a way?"

Still weeping buckets of tears, she let him guide her to a chair at the table. "My husband has abandoned me. He has locked me out of our home and refuses to give me my pin money. My father paid a handsome dowry to him, but it is all gone now, squandered on card games and mistresses."

Randolph moved to the sideboard to pour her a glass of brandy from the crystal decanter. "Perhaps your father is the one you should speak to about these matters."

"I have tried," she sobbed, "but he is a man without compassion. He still has not forgiven me for what happened between you and me. He says I deserve all my suffering, and he is right. I deserve every bit of this agony for what I did to you."

Randolph handed her the drink. "Think no more of it. It is water under the bridge."

She wiped her eyes and sucked back the brandy in a few greedy gulps. "Your Majesty is very generous."

The glass was then set on the table.

Randolph watched her for a moment while she appeared to recover her nerves.

"What is it that you wish me to do?" he asked.

Her puffy red eyes lifted. "Make me your mistress."

He strove to remain calm over the shock and anger that was rising up within him. "I'm afraid that is not possible."

"But why? I'll be very accommodating, I promise, and very discreet. All I require is a place to live. Nothing extravagant. I will live quietly and be available to you at all hours of the day."

He frowned. "Does your husband know of this? Did he send you here?"

"No, but he is a loyal subject. If it is what the king desires, he will not object."

"Are you forgetting that I have taken a wife, Elsbeth, and that she is your queen, carrying my child? Do you honestly believe I have need of a mistress?"

"But you loved me once, did you not?"

He was quite certain she had taken leave of her senses.

"Have you forgotten all that?" she continued. "There was passion between us. Can you not find it in your heart to take pity on me?"

"Pity is one thing," he replied. "Passion is another. You must leave now."

"Please, Randolph, I beg of you. I need your help."

Her eyes glistened with tears, and he suddenly found that he could not simply turn her out onto the street. For yes, indeed, he had loved her once, and despite everything that occurred in the past, he found he could not be cruel.

"I will send a message to your father and suggest that he forgive you and take you in. But I can do no more than that. I will not pay your husband's debts, nor will I use you in the manner you suggest. Do not sell yourself to any man, Elsbeth. You must have more pride than that."

She wiped away her tears. "It is easy for you to speak of pride. You are a king. I am a woman, and I have nowhere to go."

"Go home to your family," he said. "I will have the palace coach deliver you there. You father will not refuse my authority."

Again she dropped to her knees before him, grabbed

hold of the tails of his jacket, and tugged them as she looked up at him. He nearly lost his balance.

"Thank you, Randolph," she said. "You are the most generous, charitable king. I will be forever yours."

He stared down at her and remembered how she had once brought his world to an end. It was the day he caught her with Ainsley in a dark corner of the palace. Her skirts were hoisted up around her hips, and the earl was pumping into her.

The image made his stomach turn.

Just then the door opened and Alexandra walked in. "You sent for me?"

The countess leaped to her feet and wiped a sleeve across her mouth.

Randolph shot Elsbeth a look of red-hot rage. The next few seconds were a blur as the door slammed shut again and, just like that, his wife was gone.

"*Wait!*" he shouted.

He dashed out of the Privy Council Chamber at a frantic pace and chased her across the banqueting hall.

Chapter Thirty-two

By the time Randolph caught up with his wife, she had reached the other side of the hall and was no longer running but striding purposefully into the south corridor with her skirts whipping back and forth between her legs.

He grabbed hold of her arm to stop her.

"Take your hands off me!" she shouted, shrugging roughly out of his grasp and continuing on. He was muddled and dumbfounded.

"Stop!" he commanded. "You must listen to me! That was not what you think you saw."

She whirled around to face him. "Ha! What a clever excuse. I suppose it is never what the wife thinks it is. I saw what I saw."

"You saw nothing!" he argued. "She was pleading with me to make her my mistress, and I refused. I told her I would send her home in the palace coach, and she was thanking me. That is all."

Alexandra laughed bitterly. "Thanking you? Clearly, she was very generous with her gratitude."

He waved a hand through the air. "Bloody hell, have *all* the women in Petersbourg gone mad today?"

They rounded the corner and nearly collided head-on with Lucille.

"What in the world is going on?" the dowager asked, as if caught in a sudden gale.

"Nothing, Mama," Alexandra replied, not stopping to elaborate.

Randolph stormed past her as well. "Do not say a word about this to anyone," he commanded, pointing a threatening finger at his mother-in-law as he passed.

The dowager immediately dipped into a deep curtsy and bowed her head.

"Stop, Alexandra!" he shouted, following her up the wide staircase to the east wing. "I have told you the truth. There is nothing between us. Lady Ainsley walked into the court chamber without being announced and caught me off guard. I assure you I did not invite her, and I certainly did not welcome her."

Alexandra stopped and faced him. "How can I possibly believe that? You were in love with her once, and she broke your heart. You were gone from my bed for nearly two months, enjoying yourself in another country where celebrations abounded. Your letters were too few and far between. What am I *supposed* to think?"

He fought to keep his voice calm. "You must simply trust me."

She laughed at that. "How about I box your ears instead?"

"Go ahead then. Take your pleasure." He spread his arms wide. "If it will alleviate your anger, I will be happy to oblige."

Without hesitation, she slapped him hard across the face. The force of it rattled his teeth.

He took a moment to wait for the stinging shock of the strike to pass; then he met her gaze directly.

She was covering her mouth with a hand and appeared positively horror-struck. "Oh, God. I cannot believe I just did that."

They said nothing for a moment; then Alex turned to look down the long corridor, as if to make sure they were not being watched. "I don't know what to believe."

"Believe that I have been faithful to you."

Her chest was heaving. "That is not going to be easy. You are returning to Vienna again soon, and they say she will return there as well."

"They, they, they. What will it take to earn your trust? Because I must go back to the congress. I cannot be absent from the negotiations."

Her eyes burned with resolve. "Then forbid the countess from leaving the country. You're the king. Command it."

"Consider it done."

Again they stood in silence, saying nothing while the air between them sizzled with hot sparks of tension.

"I must go back now and see if she is still in the court chamber," he said. "Come with me."

Alex needed no further convincing. "I doubt she'll be there."

Together they returned, both of them unsurprised to find the room empty.

Alex walked to the table and picked up the brandy glass. "Is this hers?" she asked.

"Yes."

Nicholas walked in just then. "Someone said you requested my presence."

Randolph watched his wife stride forward and hand Nick the empty glass. "The king had a visitor," she explained. "But perhaps I will let him convey the scandalous details, for I do not wish to hear about it again."

With that, she walked out, and Randolph waved his brother closer.

* * *

On his next two excursions out of the palace and into the city proper, Randolph was greeted with a less than enthusiastic response from the citizens of Petersbourg.

Normally he was accustomed to crowds cheering and red roses dropping onto the roof of his coach, but as the year drew to a close he grew increasingly mindful of the changing tide of the people's affections.

They called out for the queen as he drove by, and certain anonymous individuals printed humorous caricatures of his recent escapades abroad. The most notable was a depiction of his fainting swoon onto a chaise longue as the beautiful Countess of Ainsley removed her mask at a ball and reminded him of their broken engagement.

False rumors abounded—that he had entered into a clandestine affair with his former fiancée—and nothing seemed to quench the appetites of the gossipmongers. His denials only served to stoke the flames of that fire, while Alexandra enjoyed a great show of sympathy and support from the masses.

"You don't think my wife is using these rumors of my infidelity to gain popularity, do you?" he asked Nicholas one afternoon in the Privy Council Chamber while he paced around the session table. "Good God, forget I said that. I am exhausted and my head is pounding. I am not thinking clearly. Has anyone seen or heard from Lady Ainsley since her visit here?"

"No," Nicholas replied. "She did not go home to her husband, nor did she return to her family. She is still missing."

"Have you checked the bottom of the palace well?" Rand asked with a dark note of concern.

Nick lifted his gaze. "The palace has been thoroughly searched. Repeatedly."

Rand continued to pace. "She is a danger to herself, and quite possibly to the queen. Who knows what she might be capable of? She was not rational, Nicholas. We must find her."

"I understand." Nick gave a polite nod and backed out of the room.

* * *

Later that afternoon, Nicholas returned to the Privy Council Chamber, where Rand was replying to correspondence regarding the Vienna Congress.

"The Dowager Duchess of St. George has requested an audience with you," Nicholas announced.

Rand sat back in his chair. "She is my mother-in-law. She does not need to request an audience. She will see me at dinner."

Nicholas lifted a suspicious brow. "I suspect it is a matter of some confidentiality."

Rand wished there was something he could do about the constant pounding in his skull. A headache had been plaguing him all day. "She didn't tell you what it was about?"

"No, and I did not press the matter. She is family after all."

Rand sighed and massaged his temples. "Send her in."

A moment later, the dowager entered the chamber and curtsied. Randolph set down his quill, rose from the chair, and greeted her warmly. "Good afternoon, Lucille. Tell me, what brings you to the dull offices of the king's chamber on such a pleasant winter day?"

She giggled awkwardly. "It is indeed a lovely day, Your Majesty."

He inclined his head as he approached. "You seem unsettled. Is something weighing upon your mind?"

God help him if she wished to reprimand him for what had happened with Lady Ainsley in this very room or the gossip that had resulted after the fact. If he could do something about it, he would, but he couldn't control the minds or tongues of the masses.

"Under normal circumstances," she said, "it would be the gentleman who would approach you in such a situation, but I am at my wit's end, sir. I wish to be married, you see—to Mr. Carmichael—but he is convinced you will oppose the match, and neither of us wishes to proceed without your permission."

She cleared her throat and chewed on her lower lip.

"Is he afraid to come to me himself?" Rand asked.

An awkward silence ensued. "Well . . . He was a devoted servant to Alexandra's father, and he fears that you have not yet accepted him as a loyal subject. I've tried to tell him that you are a generous monarch and will forgive what has gone before. He does not know I am here. He refuses to pursue the matter with you, but I wish he would. If only you could give him some encouragement."

Rand frowned. "You want me to *encourage* him to propose to you?"

Her eyes squinted into a sheepish, pained grimace. "If it would not be too much of an inconvenience."

Randolph regarded her carefully. "You are in love with him—that is quite clear to me, Lucille—but do you trust him?"

Too much had happened of late. It was still a mystery who had admitted the Countess of Ainsley to the palace and arranged for Alexandra to walk into the room at the exact moment when Elsbeth was on her knees before him.

And he had not forgotten that Lucille had been in the corridor seconds later.

"Yes, sir, I believe so," she replied. "He is very kind to me."

Rand was not sure if the dowager was brilliantly cunning or sadly naïve.

"I will not oppose his suit," Randolph replied, "if he

comes to me himself and asks permission to seek your hand. I would be most pleased to see you happy and settled, Lucille, but he must come to me of his own free will. I will not press him."

With another pained grimace, she curtsied again. "Thank you."

She walked out, and while he absently massaged his aching temples he wondered if the second half of the day would be as surprising as the first.

* * *

That night Alexandra lay in bed and waited impatiently for her husband to come to her. They had not made love since their explosive argument over the Countess of Ainsley. Since that day, he had grown increasingly distracted, stressed, and fatigued, and Alex worried that he no longer found her attractive. Or perhaps he thought her a jealous shrew for slapping him so hard.

When the hour grew late and still he did not knock on her door, not even to say good night, her impatience got the better of her. Rising from bed and donning her dressing gown, she picked up a candelabra to light her way through the palace corridors to his apartments, for surely it was time for a cease-fire. Perhaps she had been too demanding in terms of his affections. Other wives turned a blind eye when their husbands took mistresses. Some said it was the behavior *expected* of a king.

Her heart began to pound heavily as she stood outside his door. There had been so much tension between them lately. She wondered if their lives would ever be free of scandal or mistrust. And what in the world was she going to say to him?

Softly she knocked, but received no reply. Was he even there?

With growing unease, she knocked harder.

Still, no one came to answer, not even a servant.

As she stood in the dark corridor with the candelabra gently flickering, she placed her hand on the brass knob but hesitated, for she had no right to enter her husband's bedchamber if he was not there—especially when she was tempted to pry around.

To search for what? Evidence of an affair?

She had been making every effort during the recent flood of gossip to remain rational, but the chatter was not easy to ignore. Especially when her husband refused to make love to her. He had never complained of fatigue before. What had changed?

Glancing over her shoulder to ensure there were no witnesses, she slowly pushed the door open and tiptoed inside.

The oak-paneled chamber was pitch-black and chilly. There was no fire crackling in the hearth, no sign that her husband had been there, though it was past two in the morning. Where the devil was he? And with whom?

Raising her candles over her head, she squinted through the gloom and spotted the desk. She moved around the foot of the massive canopied bed, which had not been slept in, but halted abruptly when she saw the chair knocked over onto its side.

A sharp pang of fear spiked into her as she swung the light around and saw her husband collapsed on the floor, lying on his stomach, just below the bellpull.

Rushing forward, she set down her candles and rolled him onto his back. "Randolph!"

She searched his body for signs of injury but found nothing. No bruises or blood. Slapping him lightly on the cheeks, she shook him and fought to wake him, but he did not regain consciousness.

With a terrible rush of dread, she scrambled to her feet and tugged on the bellpull. "Help! Someone!" she shouted. "Come quickly! The king is ill!"

Chapter
Thirty-three

Alexandra knelt at Randolph's bedside with her hands clasped together in prayer, willing him to regain consciousness and begging God to deliver him from the deadly illness that had taken his father's life such a short time ago.

The palace physician was suggesting it was a hereditary affliction. He had no name for it but claimed the symptoms were the same.

"It is a cancer that spreads quickly through the humors," the doctor whispered in the melancholy silence of the room.

Alexandra did not believe it. She glanced across at Nicholas and saw a muscle flick at his jaw.

He did not believe it either. She was certain of it. But did he suspect foul play? And if so, would he blame her?

"Nicholas, come with me to the chapel." She rose to her feet. "We must pray together."

He regarded her with suspicious eyes, then bowed in agreement and waited for her to lead the way.

They left Rose to watch over Randolph in his deathlike slumber and walked together, without speaking a word, down the wide carpeted corridor.

They descended the main staircase, ventured outside into the bitter chill of a hazy winter morning, and crossed the courtyard to the small stone chapel with a fountain outside the entrance. Everything was covered in a layer of fresh white snow.

Nicholas opened the door for her, then followed her inside, where she could see her breath on the air.

The door swung shut behind them and slammed hard.

Alexandra walked quickly to the altar.

Nicholas followed her up the center aisle, his boots pounding heavily over the flagstones, echoing up into the rafters.

"Is anyone here?" he shouted as Alex whirled around to face him.

The question was met with silence.

They stared at each other fiercely.

"You think I poisoned him, don't you?" she asked.

"I made no such accusation."

She regarded him discerningly. "Well, *I* think someone poisoned him. I don't know who, but whoever it was probably poisoned your father as well."

Nicholas strode forward and caught her by the wrist. "What do you know?"

"Nothing!" she replied, shaking herself free of his punishing, steely grip. "Except that the palace physician is a bloody fool. I watched him examine Randolph. He did nothing but look at his pupils, listen to his heart, and form his diagnosis."

"You have some knowledge of medicine you wish to convey?"

"No," she explained, "but I am quite certain that an otherwise healthy young man found unconscious in his bedchamber—a man who is a king and has many enemies, and has recently been the victim of malicious gossip and slander—should not be diagnosed so quickly. Are you not also suspicious?"

He stared at her a moment, then turned his eyes toward the stained-glass window beyond the altar. His shoulders rose and fell with a deep intake of breath; then he regarded her with dangerous resolve.

"We are of the same mind," he said.

She let out a sharp breath of relief, then turned toward the altar. "Then pray with me, Nicholas, for I fear for Randolph's life."

He hesitated a moment, then knelt down beside her, bowed his head, and clasped his hands. "I will gladly pray," he said, "but it will take more than prayer to stop the damage from this oncoming storm. I believe we are facing another revolution, madam, but this time, it is being waged with a hidden blade."

She shot him a quick look. "As long as you do not think it is *my* blade."

He closed his eyes in prayer and did not respond to the accusation.

* * *

After leaving the chapel, Alex returned to her husband's bedside.

Thank God, her prayers had been answered. He was sitting up in bed.

"Randolph!" A cry of relief broke from her lips.

She hurried to his side and bent to kiss the back of his hand. "I was so afraid I'd lost you. What happened? Where was your valet? I found you on the floor in your bedchamber. Do you have any recollection of anyone coming into the room? Were you struck down perhaps?"

He was dressed in a white linen nightshirt that was open at the neck, and his hair was damp with perspiration. He shook his head on the pillow and regarded her coolly. "No memory. The doctor tells me I collapsed. He says I suffer from the same affliction that killed my father." His blue eyes met hers with steely skepticism. "I cannot believe it.

Does it not seem odd to you that all this tragedy has befallen my family since the day you set out to become queen?"

Alexandra sat back. Her stomach turned over with sickening dread.

"What are you suggesting?" She glanced over her shoulder, fearful that someone might hear him. He was not making sense.

"Not so long ago, I was adored by the people," he said with bitter rancor. "Now they see me as a villain while you have won their sympathy."

"You are confused, Randolph," she gently said, arranging the covers around him. "I do not wish you ill. I love you, and I want you to get well."

He stared at her as if he had not heard a single word; then his eyes rolled back in his head and his body began to convulse.

She tried to restrain him but could not manage on her own. She shouted to the doctor, who was just outside the room, "*Help us! Please help us!*"

He immediately came running.

* * *

"We are seeking a second opinion," Alexandra said to Randolph, after he had recovered sufficiently from the seizure.

He had no memory of the hurtful words that had passed between them beforehand, and she was grateful for that. Yet their quarrel had injured her deeply, and she shuddered inwardly at the remembrance of it. She felt a terrible wretchedness in her heart. Did he truly believe she wished him ill? Would he ever be able to trust her?

"Nicholas and I have already made arrangements," she

explained, "and he has gone to speak to some young medical men at the university. We believe they may have more current knowledge about diseases such as this, or perhaps they have some experience with the most modern treatments."

"I will welcome a new diagnosis," Randolph replied, "other than what that quack doctor has concluded, for that did not end well for my father." He shut his eyes and wet his lips. "Bloody hell, I am so damn tired. Will you fetch me a drink of something?"

She stood up to pour him a glass of water.

"My mouth tastes like metal," he added.

Alex stopped abruptly and turned. "I beg your pardon?"

He opened his eyes. "I am thirsty."

"You said your mouth tastes like metal," she added. "Are you aware that your father complained of the same symptom? He mentioned it when I visited his bedside. Have you told the doctor about this?"

"Yes. He said it's nothing."

"Hmmph." She poured the water into a glass. "You can be sure I will seek a second opinion about that as well. Drink up, Randolph. You must get your strength back."

All of a sudden, he reached out and cupped her cheek in his hand. "Promise me you will be careful," he said with desperate intensity in his eyes. "You must guard our child."

"Is that all that matters to you?" she asked. "The survival of your heir?"

He relaxed back on the pillows and stared at her for a long moment with eyes that glimmered like jewels. Even when he was weak from a deadly poison, he was still the most attractive man she had ever known, and she couldn't bear to imagine losing him.

"No, that is not all that matters," he replied. Then his eyes fell closed and he winced, as if in pain.

Not wanting to exhaust him further, she helped him sit up and handed him the water.

* * *

Later that day, a team of three young physicians from the university arrived to examine Randolph. While they were there, he succumbed to another fit of convulsions, which lasted only a few moments but left him further weakened.

After much poking and prodding and heated debate, during which time the doctors referred to a number of heavy medical books they carried with them, the young medical men determined that the king had indeed been poisoned. The offending substance was arsenic.

Alexandra thanked them profusely, then climbed onto the bed beside Randolph to hold him tight, while her heart rose up in an overflowing flood of emotion. Thank God they knew what it was!

"Oh, Randolph, I am so relieved. I don't know what I would have done if anything had happened to you. I would die without you."

She felt a wild impulse to kiss him passionately on the mouth, right there in front of everyone, but somehow she managed to control those urges.

He kissed the top of her head and stroked her hair away from her face. "Alex, my darling. Do not fret. I'm not going anywhere."

"We will find out who did this," she said. "I swear it on my life, and when I uncover the truth, I will want blood."

"Be careful what you wish for," he gently said. "We must ascertain all the facts before we call in the executioner."

He glanced across at Nicholas, who nodded at him.

"I, too, am relieved," Nick said. "But if you will excuse

me now, I will accompany the doctors to the kitchen to examine the palace food stores."

With that, he took his leave, and Alexandra snuggled ever closer to her husband.

* * *

Below stairs in the palace kitchen, traces of arsenic were indeed detected in the beef that had been served to King Randolph the previous evening.

An interrogation quickly followed. All members of the household staff were questioned personally by Nicholas and the High Constable. It was also discovered that Randolph's valet had been hit over the head and dragged into the belowstairs pantry.

"It could have been anyone," Nick said that night while he played chess with Alexandra in front of the fire.

Randolph sat beside them, watching their game.

They were all extremely grateful that Rand's condition had not worsened since the disturbing seizures that morning, and the doctors' prognosis was promising. They believed he would enjoy a full recovery as long as he did not ingest any more of the deadly poison. Eventually it would simply leach out of his system.

Randolph pointed at one of Alex's chess pieces to suggest a particular move. "I agree it could have been anyone," he said to Nick. "My popularity has most certainly diminished since my return from Vienna. Someone in the street shouted to me a few days ago. He said I was not worthy of the crown."

"Who said such a thing?" Nicholas demanded to know.

"A faceless stranger in the crowd," he replied. "I am no fool, Nick. I know there are many who would take pleasure in seeing me dethroned. We cannot hang them all."

"That will not happen," Alex said. "You will not be dethroned."

She was uncomfortably aware of Nicholas's dark, brooding eyes watching her every move over the chessboard. She was quite certain he still did not trust her, despite how she had proven herself with the doctors.

For that matter, she was not entirely sure of her husband's feelings either.

Not after what he had said to her before his seizure.

"What about the countess?" she asked. "Has it not occurred to either of you that all of this began after she revealed herself at that masquerade ball? Ever since that moment, you have been skewered from all angles, Randolph, and I assure you I have taken no pleasure in it."

"But you have enjoyed the fact that your popularity has grown," Nicholas suggested.

She boldly met his gaze. "You believe I am pleased about this turn of events?"

He repositioned a knight on the game board and lounged back in his chair to await her next move.

"Stop it, both of you," Randolph said. "We are all on the same side. The countess should indeed be a suspect. She is a woman scorned, is she not?"

Alexandra raised an eyebrow. "I certainly hope so."

Randolph leaned closer. "Are you still jealous, Wife?"

"Not of *her*," she replied. "I would never allow myself to indulge in such a pathetic indignity."

Nicholas chuckled as he watched them. "Perhaps not, but I suspect you would enjoy tossing her into a well."

"I beg your pardon?" Alex replied. "You insult me, sir."

Nicholas laughed again, and she found herself bristling in return.

Randolph raised a hand. "I said simmer down, you two."

Alexandra took a deep breath and let it out. "May I

assume that Nicholas has not been able to locate the countess?"

She raised a triumphant eyebrow in his direction over the chessboard.

"Your assumption is correct," Randolph replied. "She is both disgraced and missing."

"And a danger to herself," Alex added. "With a brand-new wardrobe. It reeks like rotten fish to me."

She continued to study the chessboard, but had no idea where to move next.

* * *

After the newspaper reported the botched attempt on the king's life and a great wave of shock rippled through the nation, a most conspicuous letter arrived at the palace, addressed to Her Majesty the Queen.

Alexandra was about to begin breakfast but set down her fork to pick up the letter from the silver salver that was presented to her by a white-gloved footman.

Curious, she broke the seal.

Your Majesty, I must speak with you. I implore you to meet me in the palace chapel this morning. Alone.

I have the honor to remain Your Majesty's most humble and obedient subject,

The Countess of Ainsley

Good God.

Alexandra wished impulsively that she had a quill and ink to write a brash response and inform the countess that she would not, under any circumstances, meet her alone. If Lady Ainsley wished an audience, she would come to the throne room like everyone else.

But Alex did not have a quill at the breakfast table, nor was there a return address on the letter. Nor did she wish to squander an opportunity to apprehend a possible suspect in the attempt on her husband's life.

After a brief moment's consideration, she sent for Nicholas and prayed to God it was the right thing to do.

A short while later Nicholas walked into the breakfast room and bowed to Alexandra. "Your Majesty."

She knew it was time to break bread with Nicholas, or break out the guns. They had been at each other's throats since her arrival in Petersbourg and she very much wanted it to stop. He was her husband's brother and closest ally, and the last thing she wanted was to drive a wedge into their relationship.

But if she was ever going to earn her husband's complete trust, she was going to have to win this man's support as well.

"I have just received a letter," she told him, "and I don't quite know what to do about it. I am seeking your advice."

He regarded her questioningly, then stepped forward to take hold of the letter she held out to him.

He frowned as he read it, and set it down on the table.

"You cannot possibly go alone," he said. "This woman is not balanced in the head. There is no telling what she might do. Your life is far too valuable to risk it."

Alex rose from her chair. "I agree completely," she replied. "Besides, no one orders me about in such a way, demanding that I do this or that." She paused. "I don't want to tell Randolph about this just yet. He is not well enough and will insist on accompanying me. Therefore I need *you*, Nicholas. Someone I can trust. You must bear witness to whatever she wishes to say, and I will rely upon you for protection and the safeguarding of your brother's unborn child."

Nicholas kept his blue eyes fixed upon hers, and for a

long moment they stared at each other intently. She recalled those first days in England when they had danced together and he had worked so hard to be charming and amiable. Much had changed since then, and they had weathered a great deal of suspicion and conflict.

"Will you stand by me?" she asked, keeping a keen eye on his expression.

He took far too long to answer, but when at last he did, she was overcome by gratitude, for he bowed down on one knee and nodded.

"I am the king's champion," he replied, "and it is my solemn duty to protect him and all that he holds dear. Therefore I am at your service, madam."

Alex let out a breath and smiled, laid a hand on his shoulder, and urged him to rise.

* * *

To Alexandra's surprise, when she walked through the chapel doors—with Nicholas and an armed escort of four palace guards—the countess had not changed her mind about the meeting. Wearing a hooded black cloak, Lady Ainsley was kneeling before the altar in prayer.

The instant she heard the door open, she leaped to her feet. Her face went pale with shock and fear when she saw the five men with weapons at the ready.

Nevertheless, she performed a deep curtsy.

"As you can see, I did not come alone," Alex said, gesturing toward her protectors.

The countess lowered the hood of her cloak, and for the first time Alex was able to clearly see the woman her husband had once loved and nearly married. The woman who could have been queen.

Her hair and eyes were brown. She was petite with freckles, which was not how Alexandra had envisioned her when she read about the scandalous events at the masquerade ball. She'd imagined someone tall and swanlike, with flaxen hair.

"Am I to be arrested?" the countess asked, swallowing uneasily.

Alexandra studied her frantic eyes. "Why do you ask? Have you done something wrong? Do you wish to confess it?"

The woman hesitated. "Your Majesty, may we speak in private?"

"Absolutely not," Alex replied, "for you may be hiding a dagger in your cloak. I will not risk it. Whatever you wish to say you will say in front of Prince Nicholas and my guards."

Lady Ainsley began to back away. "I cannot."

Alex moved to follow. "Why?"

"I am frightened."

"Frightened of what?"

"I am not certain."

Beginning to wonder if the woman truly was half-mad, Alex tried to move up the chapel aisle, but Nicholas barred her with his arm.

"Not without me," he said.

Alex nodded at him, then addressed the countess. "Prince Nicholas and I will approach you together. You can speak privately to the two of us. No one else will hear."

Lady Ainsley agreed, and they gathered, all three of them, at the front pews.

"What do you wish to confess?" Nicholas said. "Did you poison the king?"

"Good heavens, no!" Lady Ainsley replied. "But I believe he may be in grave danger. There are plots against him."

"There are always plots against the king," Nick said. "Be more specific, madam."

She turned her stricken eyes to Alexandra. "Nothing untoward ever happened between us. I give you my word. The king has been faithful to you, despite all my efforts."

"Why are you telling me this?" she demanded to know.

"They said it was to make you jealous, and that they wanted to remove *you,* not Randolph, because you sought revenge on the New Regime. They paid me a handsome sum, but I would never have agreed to any of it if I had known they wanted to harm Randolph, for he is a good man."

"But you were willing to harm *me,*" Alexandra challenged.

The countess lowered her eyes in shame. "I apologize, Majesty. It was wrong."

In a sudden flash of movement Nicholas grabbed Lady Ainsley by the throat. "Who are *they?*"

Four swords scraped out of their scabbards at the rear of the chapel as the palace guards dashed forward to assist, but Alex held them off with a raised hand.

"Let her go," she calmly said to Nicholas. "Can you not see she is frightened?"

He refused to release her, while the tension in the chapel rose to a very high pinnacle. The countess gasped for air.

When at last he loosened his grip she fell to the floor, coughing and choking.

Alexandra dropped to her knees beside her and laid a comforting hand on her shoulder. "I apologize. Please understand that Nicholas is very protective of his brother, but it will not happen again. Please tell us what you know. If you reveal the name of the person who paid you, I promise no harm will come to you."

"He did not tell me his name," she explained, "but he was a handsome older gentleman in a top hat. I believe now that he deceived me in order to smear Randolph's good name, and to cause the people to turn against him. The man is a Royalist; I am certain of it. I believe it with all my heart."

"Would you recognize him if you met him again?" Alex asked.

"Yes. He was very tall."

Nick glared down at Alex with raging ire. "Your blasted benefactor . . ." Then he grabbed *her* by the sleeve and pulled her roughly to her feet. "Do not try to tell me you didn't know about this, Alexandra. Where the devil is he? And I swear when I find him I will drown you both."

He let go of her and stormed out. "Arrest the countess," he said to the guards.

"I didn't know about any of this!" Alex shouted after him. "And we must tell Randolph!" She stood back as the guards seized the countess and escorted her to the door. "Have no fear, Lady Ainsley," she said, following them out. "I will speak to my husband on your behalf. You did the right thing coming to me. It will not be forgotten."

Then she hurried to catch up with Nicholas before he reached her husband first.

Chapter Thirty-four

Alex chased Nicholas across the icy courtyard. "Where are you going?"

"To speak to my brother. Where else?"

"I will go with you," she insisted, catching up with him.

"Why? Do you not trust me to convey all the proper details?"

"Quite frankly, I do not," she replied. "Would you trust *me* to go and speak to Randolph alone? Would you not insist on being present while I told him about Lady Ainsley's confession?"

He did not answer the question. He merely continued at a brisk pace into the palace.

Their boots pounded up the grand staircase, and a few short moments later they were admitted to Randolph's chamber.

He was out of bed and fully dressed. His trusted valet was tying his cravat.

"You're feeling better," Alex said as an almost dizzying swell of happiness bubbled up within her. She laid a hand on her heart and fought back tears. "Thank God."

He stared at her with confidence and affection, and she could have wept with joy.

Nicholas stepped between them.

"What's wrong?" Randolph asked. "You both look as if you just escaped a burning building."

"There is news to report," Nick replied. "The Countess of Ainsley sent a letter to Her Majesty to request a private meeting this morning, which has just taken place."

Randolph dismissed his valet. "Why was I not told of this?"

"It was early," Alexandra explained. "We did not wish to wake you and hinder your recovery, but now I see you look very well." She withdrew the letter from the pocket of her cloak. "Here it is. You must see it for yourself."

She handed it to him, and he read the contents. "You've already spoken to her? What did she say?"

Alex repeated every word of their conversation.

"Someone paid her to follow me to Vienna?" he asked. "Who? Why?"

"She did not know the gentleman's identity," Alex replied, "but she said he was very tall. We believe it may be Mr. Carmichael."

Randolph regarded her with dismay. His eyes seemed to impale her. She could barely keep her heart still.

"Did you know about that?"

"Of course not," she replied. "I am shocked, just as you are."

"But why? Carmichael was a Royalist from the beginning, as you have always been, and do not try to deny it, for you are a Tremaine."

She felt all her muscles clench into tight knots. "That does not mean I wanted to depose you. I've always been clear on that point. I wanted to rule beside you, to unite the country. I am carrying your child now, Randolph, and you know I love you. Why would I wish to destroy all that we have accomplished and enjoyed?"

He glanced uncertainly at Nicholas.

"Where is Carmichael?" Randolph demanded to know.

"We have not yet summoned him," she tried to explain, "but I suspect my stepmother will be able to tell us where to find him."

"I shall summon Her Grace to the Privy Council Chamber," Nicholas said, turning to go.

"No, wait," Randolph replied. "We will go to her now, all three of us, for she must not suspect anything and find a way to send him a warning."

Alex followed her husband out of the room and prayed that everything would not come tumbling down onto her shoulders like a deadly avalanche.

* * *

Alexandra knocked on her stepmother's door, but no one answered. She knocked again, more firmly a second time. "She must be here. She never rises early."

There was a heavy *clunk* on the other side of the door.

"It sounds like she just fell out of bed," Nicholas surmised.

"Knock again," Randolph said with an impatient bark of command.

"Who *is* it?" Lucille asked in a sweet, singsong voice.

"It is Alexandra. I must speak with you immediately."

Lucille opened the door. She was just donning her dressing gown, and when she spotted Randolph and Nicholas standing behind Alex, she covered her mouth with a hand.

"Good heavens, Your Majesty! I am not dressed. I do beg your pardon—"

Randolph brushed by her and entered the room to look around. The bed was in shambles, though the curtains were drawn to let in the morning light.

Lucille spoke shakily. "I am pleased to see you are looking so well, sir."

"He is much improved since yesterday," Alexandra

replied, though it was hardly a time for polite conversation. "That is not why we are here, however. We must know the whereabouts of Mr. Carmichael. When was the last time you saw him?"

Lucille's anxious eyes darted back and forth among all three of them. "I . . . I don't know."

Randolph approached her and laid a hand on her shoulder. "Take your time, Lucille. Please tell me where he spends his days. And nights."

The color drained from her face. "I really do not know. I . . . I have not spoken to him since . . ."

"Since when?" Nicholas asked.

She seemed to lose all capacity to put words together in a coherent fashion, and a tense silence enveloped the room.

Tick, tick, tick, went the clock. Then a hinge creaked alarmingly, like a whining cat.

All eyes turned to the wardrobe.

The door was open a crack. It was quickly pulled shut.

"Mama," Alexandra said. "Are you hiding a man in your room?"

Lucille pursed her lips, as if trying to decide how best to reply. "Um . . . Well, you see . . . Oh, I cannot lie. *Yes!*"

Nicholas pinched the bridge of his nose. "What a bloody circus," he whispered.

"Mr. Carmichael. This is the king speaking," Randolph said. "Come out of there at once."

The door opened a crack, and Alexandra's benefactor, wearing nothing but a loose linen nightshirt, spilled out of the tiny space onto the floor on all fours.

He quickly scrambled to his feet and bowed. "Your Majesty."

Alexandra cleared her throat awkwardly.

"Good morning, sir," Randolph said. "We have some

questions to ask you. Have you any connection to the Countess of Ainsley?"

Mr. Carmichael paused. "I know who she is, but I have never had the pleasure of meeting her."

Alex glanced down at his bare feet and scrawny ankles. This was awkward. Most awkward indeed.

"I suspect otherwise," Randolph replied.

Carmichael's mouth began to twitch. "I assure you, sir, I have never even been in the same room with her."

Randolph approached him. "Have you ever entered into a financial arrangement together? Have you sent her funds in exchange for a particular task? Have you purchased gowns for her, or paid for her travel to Vienna?"

Carmichael shook his head frantically. "No, I have not!"

Randolph's charming blue eyes turned to ice. Without ever breaking eye contact with Mr. Carmichael, he said to his brother, "Nicholas, take this man to the old wine cellar and lock him up."

"Please, Your Majesty!" Lucille pleaded. "He has done nothing wrong!"

"That will be determined by the Royal Court," Randolph replied as he shouldered his way past and took hold of Alexandra's hand to pull her roughly from the room.

* * *

As soon as they were alone in the corridor, Randolph used his body to trap Alexandra up against the wall. "Tell me, Wife, what have you been plotting?"

Both his hands were braced on either side of her head, and his lips were mere inches from hers. She breathed in shallow, rapid gasps.

"Nothing. I have wanted only to discover who is

responsible for the attempt on your life. I had nothing to do with this and you know it."

"How am I to believe anything you say? I know about your private visits with the marquess while I was gone. You were not truthful with me about that."

"Of course I was!" she replied. "I kept nothing from you! I told you he came to see me!"

Her husband released her and backed away. His chest was heaving with anger and hurt. He glanced down at her belly, then back up at her eyes. "God help me. I don't know what to believe."

Nicholas came striding down the corridor just then. "Carmichael is being escorted to the cellar now, and I have just spoken again with the dowager. She is distraught, but assures me the man is innocent. She believes she can convince him to talk. If you will both come with me, we may learn something."

Randolph shot Alexandra a sharp look. "After you."

Bouncing between outright umbrage and a terrible fear of eternal heartbreak, she pushed away from the wall, brushed by him, and followed Nicholas to the wine cellar.

* * *

There was no wine in the old cellar. It had been emptied of bottles and barrels and was now a cold dungeon with stone walls, an arched ceiling, and a heavy oak door with no window.

"Nigel, please tell them what you have told me," Lucille pleaded. "If you do not, you may be charged with treason, and I will not let you accept the blame for something you did not do."

Carmichael sank into the only chair in the room. "I cannot be a turncoat."

"A turncoat against whom?" Lucille asked. "The Royalists? Might I remind you that the throne is now occupied by a Tremaine and you have therefore completed your mission. You have been loyal to that cause. What has now occurred is something else entirely, and I will not permit you to die for it."

He looked up with tired eyes and laid a hand on her cheek. "You are a good woman, Lucille. Too good for me."

"That is pure poppycock," she said. "Tell them what you know and the king may be lenient."

He stood up and kissed her tenderly on the cheek. "I do this for you," he said, "because I could not live if I felt you thought me cowardly or dishonorable." Turning to Randolph, he began, at last, to explain.

"I accepted funds from the Duke of Kaulbach in order to bring Alexandra out into London society. He paid for her gowns and her lodgings, but did not wish to be identified as her true benefactor. I believed he wanted what I wanted—to put the true Tremaine princess back on the throne—but I have since grown suspicious of his goals, for he has been pressing me to sing the praises of his son Lord Cavanaugh in various social situations, and to encourage Cavanaugh's friendship with the queen. I believe now that it was the duke's desire all along to establish Alexandra's popularity, wait for her to secure the throne with an heir, then replace you with his son."

"Replace me . . ." Randolph shook his head in disbelief. "By having me assassinated by an unknown culprit? Then Leopold would marry Alexandra? Was that their plot?"

"This is madness!" Alexandra said, stepping forward. "I assure you I knew nothing of this. The marquess has never suggested anything untoward. He has always behaved as a perfect gentleman, and a friend, I believed."

Randolph stared at her as if she had been infected with the plague.

"None of this was ever spoken aloud to me or communicated in writing," Mr. Carmichael said. "It is merely my own conjecture. I said nothing before because they are serious accusations and if I am wrong . . . Well, he is a duke after all."

Randolph moved to the door. "Thank you, Mr. Carmichael. Please remain here until we decide what shall be done with you."

Lucille rushed to the king. "Please, Your Majesty. He knew nothing of the attempt on your life. He has been quite distracted, in fact. We have been together almost constantly. We are in love, you see."

Randolph held the door open for her. "Yes, we can see that you have both become diverted. Please come with me, Your Grace. You must attend to the queen."

Randolph pushed past all of them and addressed his brother. "Put my wife and the dowager together in the queen's chamber," he said. "Lock them in and post three guards at the door. No one shall come in or go out, and they are to remain there until I discover what is true and what is not." He started walking but stopped to face Alexandra. "Was that your plan all along?" he asked. "To seduce me, then get rid of me?"

A sickening dread twisted around her heart. "Of course not. I wanted to sit on the throne *beside* you. Forever."

He studied her with dark suspicion, then turned and walked away.

* * *

The Duke of Kaulbach was enjoying a fine breakfast of poached eggs and toast when a thunderous invasion at the front door of his town house caused him to rise from the white-clothed table and throw down his napkin.

"What the devil is going on here?"

The liveried footman had no time to respond before an armed troop of palace guards burst into the room. The door flew open and slammed against the inside wall, and four guards aimed pistols at the duke's face.

He raised his hands.

They cocked their weapons while two more brawny sentries took hold of him. He struggled ineffectually.

"You are under arrest for high treason," the commander said with one eye closed as he looked down the barrel of his gun. "This includes the murder of King Frederick and the attempted murder of King Randolph."

The duke gave no further resistance as the guards dragged him roughly from the room.

* * *

At the exact moment the duke was being arrested on the east side of the city, Randolph was walking along the edge of the frozen reflecting pool in the palace courtyard. His heavy claymore—a gift from the duke himself—was buckled securely at his hip.

His old friend Leopold waited for him at the far end of the pool, next to a tall row of cedars.

Randolph approached him and came to a halt. "How long have we been friends, Leo?" he asked.

"Since we were children," the marquess replied.

"And how long have you been coveting my throne?"

Leopold inclined his head curiously. "I don't understand, Randolph. What are you asking?"

It was difficult to resist the temptation to shove Leo into the icy pool, but Rand maintained his focus. "Your father was close friends with King Oswald, was he not?"

"That is correct, but—"

"And he wanted a marriage between you, his eldest son, and the firstborn Tremaine princess. Is that not also correct?"

Leopold bowed his head and gave no reply.

"How unfortunate that my father destroyed Oswald's dynasty before your marriage could take place," Randolph said.

Leopold shook his head, as if he had no explanation.

"I trusted you," Randolph said as he drew his sword—the very sword Leo had presented to him as a wedding gift. "I gave you my letters to deliver, but you tried to seduce my wife."

"I never touched her," Leopold argued, backing away. "I only wished to be a friend while you were away in Vienna. Lord knows she needed one."

"Ah," Randolph snarled. "There we have it. The plot revealed. What a shame I didn't die quicker. Alexandra might have sought solace with you. She may have wanted a father for her unborn child, and to bear more children of course. Is that what you intended?"

Leopold continued to back away until he stumbled over a raised stone and fell to the ground.

Randolph pointed the broadsword at his throat. "Do not lie to me, Leo. Your father has already been arrested. Nigel Carmichael has confessed his part in all of this. Tell me how you got the arsenic into the palace and perhaps I will spare your life."

"I know nothing of any arsenic," Leo insisted.

"I don't believe you. There was a third time you came to the palace, allegedly to visit the queen. I have witnesses to prove it, yet my wife reported no third visit, so clearly you had some other reason to be skulking about."

"There was no third visit," he insisted. "I came only twice."

Randolph glanced up and nodded at Nicholas, who

was waiting with five guards behind the cedars. They trotted over on foot and took Leopold into custody.

"I knew nothing of the attempt on your life!" Leopold shouted. "I give you my word!"

Rand watched in agony and despair as they dragged Leo away in the direction of the palace prison, for he had never expected to be betrayed by someone he considered a friend.

Sadly, this was not new to him. It was something he must learn to accept, for he was king now. There would always be enemies.

Carefully, he resheathed his sword.

"He's lying," Nicholas said as he approached. "I know when a man is hiding something."

Drained of all strength, Randolph dropped to his knees on the icy ground. He was still so bloody weak from the poison. It was a miracle he had not collapsed before now.

Nicholas knelt down beside him. "Are you all right? Do you need a doctor?"

Randolph held up a hand to refuse any help. "I'm fine."

All he needed was a moment to recover.

Placing all five fingers on the ground, he carefully steadied himself and rose to his feet, then turned to face the palace.

For some unknown reason his eyes lifted, and there she was.

His wife. His queen.

Alexandra was watching from her bedchamber window on the second floor. She stood with one palm pressed open against the glass.

He stared at her for a thoughtful moment while his body relaxed in the winter chill and his mind woke up to this new reality.

He had almost died two days ago—just like his father—but he had been given a second chance, all because of Alexandra and her steadfast, unwavering attention.

A flood of sensual memories came streaming through his mind just then as he recalled all the intimacies they'd shared since the first moment they met. She had held nothing back. She had given him all of her heart, and he felt as if he owed her a great debt that would take a lifetime to repay.

All at once his world seemed clear as he watched her in the window.

She was the woman who had captured his soul and saved his life in the process, and he knew, somehow he knew, she was innocent.

Just then, Rose came bursting through the palace doors and ran out onto the terrace. "What is happening?" she shouted, her rapid breaths visible like tiny puffs of smoke on the cold wintry air.

Resting his hand on the hilt of the sword that had been presented to him by an enemy he took for a friend, Rand put one foot in front of the other and walked purposefully toward his sister.

"The marquess has been arrested for high treason and attempted murder." Just speaking the words aloud broke his heart, for he had always trusted Leo.

"No, that cannot be. . . ."

Rose stared after the marquess in shock while Randolph entered the palace to confront his wife.

* * *

"What will happen to us?" Lucille asked. "What if we are accused of treason? What if the duke says you were a conspirator? You received his son on two separate occasions while Randolph was away, did you not?"

"Yes, but I knew nothing of any plot to kill him," she replied. "How could I know of it? I was completely infatuated and blind to anything but the love I felt for him and for the child we created together. It killed me to see him collapse in the courtyard just now. He is still so weak. I cannot lose him."

For the next few minutes they sat in anxious silence with bated breath, waiting for the palace guards to march down the hall and pound heavy fists against the door.

What would happen next?

She—the queen consort—would likely be stripped of her jewels and taken to Briggin's Prison. Or perhaps she would be locked up in that cold damp wine cellar below.

Just thinking about it made her flesh crawl. She began to tremble as frightful images of rats and darkness invaded her mind.

"God help us," she said. "He doesn't trust me. He never has. He thinks I bewitched him."

"As he bewitched you," Lucille said, "when he pretended to be Nicholas."

A key slipped into the lock just then, and the door swung open. . . .

Chapter Thirty-five

In walked Alexandra's husband—King Randolph, the handsome prince who had captured her heart.

Despite the blinding fear that encumbered her, she was at least pleased to see that the frosty chill of the winter air had put some color back into his cheeks. His life was no longer in danger from the arsenic—but whether or not their love could survive all this treachery, she had yet to discover.

"I must speak with you in private," he said.

Nicholas appeared in the doorway. "Your Grace, if you will come with me," he said.

As Lucille crossed to Rand's brother, she glanced uneasily at Alex. "Where will they take me?"

"I don't know, Mama. You must be brave."

"Have no fear, Your Grace," Nicholas charmingly replied. "You will be quite comfortable, I assure you."

Not entirely convinced, Lucille followed him out.

Alex swallowed uneasily while Randolph shut the door behind them and locked it.

"What happened out there?" she asked. "I watched you knock Lord Cavanaugh to the ground and point the sword at his throat. What did he say?"

Pray God he did not spew lies to incriminate her in order to save himself.

If he was guilty. She honestly had no idea.

"I didn't knock him down," Randolph said. "He tripped and fell."

"I see." She paused. "But you *did* hold the sword to his throat."

"Yes, that I did."

She took a deep breath. "In that regard . . . well done, sir."

He gave no reply. He merely blinked at her and swayed slightly as if he were about to topple over, unconscious.

"I think I need to get off my feet," he said.

She rushed forward and cupped his face in her hands, looked carefully into his eyes. "Oh, my darling. You are still not well. You should not have gone out there to confront him, Randolph. Not today. Promise me you will not do anything like that again until you are stronger. Send Nicholas instead. I am quite sure he would be more than happy to swing a sword at the smallest request."

"I am fine," Randolph assured her as he moved to the bed, unbuckled his belt and scabbard, set the sword on the table, and climbed onto the mattress.

After reclining on his back with his head on the pillows, his booted feet crossed at the ankles, he waved her over. "Come here, Wife."

Bewildered and still fearful of what was yet to come, she moved around the bed and supported her belly as she climbed up next to him.

"This is not what I was expecting from you," she said.

He regarded her curiously. "What *were* you expecting?"

Shrugging, she lay down on her side. "I'm not sure. Perhaps to be dragged down to the wine cellar again. To be interrogated like Mr. Carmichael was."

"I do not need to interrogate you," her husband softly replied as he rolled to face her. "I have already interrogated enough people, and I suspect that Lord Cavanaugh's third visit to the palace was to meet the foolish and rebellious young kitchen maid who kept the arsenic under the plank floor beneath her bed. She has now disappeared."

Alexandra sat up. "So it *was* him after all."

"Yes, it is highly likely. One of the other servants has already admitted to seeing the same kitchen maid flirting with a concealed gentleman in the shadows—on the same night Leo paid his third visit. Nicholas has swallowed his pride and admitted that you may not have been plotting against me after all."

She was, of course, relieved. Thank God for Nicholas, but her tenacious pride bucked like a stallion. "But of course I was not plotting! How could you even think it? Not ever! Except in the beginning, when I wanted to marry you."

He, too, sat up. "To marry *me,* or the future king?"

"You *were* the future king."

"But you didn't know that at the time."

She squinted at him. "Fine then. I wanted to marry *you,* king or pauper, and do not ever ask me that question again, Randolph, or I will begin to suspect you do not trust me!"

He stared at her in utter disbelief, then laughed out loud and regained whatever strength he had lost and pressed his mouth to hers in a fierce kiss of unparalleled passion.

Overwhelmed by his roving hands, so strong and sure across her trembling body, she suddenly found herself flipped over onto her back and gazing up at him in the late-morning light.

"I thought you might hate me forever," she said, clinging tightly to him, reveling in the possibility that her future was not doomed after all and all would be well. "When you accused me of colluding with the marquess . . . how could you ever imagine that I was not yours wholeheartedly and devotedly?"

He shook his head, as if he could not possibly explain.

"Have you not felt the love I bear for you?" She continued. "Do you not understand why I was so hurt and angered by the suggestion that you had taken up with your former fiancée? I have nearly gone mad with my love for you, Randolph. I was jealous and irrational, and I could shake you insensible for making me feel that way!"

He kissed her again with ferocious desire while his hand stroked over her belly. "I've always felt it," he told her, "never so much as when we made love . . . but other times, too. I knew it just now when I looked up and saw you in the window."

"How so?"

"I felt you were watching over me, with more love than I ever imagined I would receive in a lifetime. The first moment I saw you on the terrace at Carlton House, something blew into my brain. It was as if I already knew you were destined to be my wife and queen. I could feel it then, as I feel it now. I am sorry for all that has gone between us. I never meant to hurt you, Alex, but I've been betrayed so many times. You deserved so much better."

Her heart warmed at his words. "Yes, you have been betrayed, but not by me. Never by me. Tell me you love me," she said with a smile, "and I will be able to forgive anything. That is all I want from you, till death do us part."

A great wave of emotion flowed through her, and her eyes filled with sparkling tears.

"*I love you,*" he said. "And there is no one in the world I trust more than you. I am so sorry for everything."

He thrust his hips and held her close in a passionate display of devotion, and she clutched at him desperately, never wanting to let go.

Was this real? At last, did he truly understand how much she loved him?

"You have been a most faithful and loving queen, Alexandra, and I am the most fortunate man on earth." His smile touched her lips as he slid his hand up the curve of her leg. "Let me prove that I am not only your king but your husband and lover until the day I draw my last breath." His hand found the tingling center of her desire, and he stroked her with great care and deliberation.

"Now I believe I am the most fortunate woman on earth," she whispered on a breathless sigh of delight.

"Then we shall be fortunate together, for I believe we are truly blessed."

With a devilish grin, he tugged up her skirts. She parted her legs, impatient for the fulfillment he offered. He entered her with elegant grace, and their hearts beat together as their futures entwined, and at last their destiny was sealed.

Read on for an excerpt from
Julianne MacLean's next book

PRINCESS IN LOVE

Coming soon from St. Martin's Paperbacks

Briggin's Prison, Petersbourg, January 1815

She always knew life did not follow a straight or predict-able path—it was riddled with unexpected twists, turns, and steep inclines—but never had Rose Sebastian under-stood that fact as well as she did on the day her world turned upside down and her heart was smashed to pieces.

As the uniformed guard led her down a steep set of spiraling stone steps that seemed to go on forever into a hellishly dark dungeon in the very guts of the earth, Rose wondered if she would ever look back on these events and understand why it all happened the way it did. Would she ever let go of the regret? Would she ever be grateful for the cruel lessons she had been forced to learn?

The guard continued down a long stone corridor with torches blazing in wall sconces. The hay-strewn floor was wet beneath her feet. She had never ventured this deeply into Briggin's Prison before. How medieval it seemed. The air was cold and damp and made her body shiver.

At last they reached the cell at the end of the corridor, and the guard lifted the bar on the heavy oaken door. It creaked open on rusty iron hinges.

"He's in here, madam. Shall I accompany you, or do you wish me to wait outside?"

Rose hesitated. Of course the guard must wait outside, for there were intimate matters to discuss with the prisoner.

The prisoner. Dear God, what if she lost her temper and struck him? Or worse, what if she took one look at him and the desire still burned, despite everything he had done?

"Wait outside, please," she firmly replied, moving toward the threshold. "Shut the door behind me and bar it. I will knock twice to signal when I am through with him."

She handed the guard a ten-pound note—a small price to pay for his silence—then took a deep breath and steeled her nerves as she entered the prison cell.

The door slammed shut behind her, and she jumped at the sound of it—like a judge's gavel—while her gaze fell upon the man she had come here to confront.

He was already standing in the center of the cell, as if he had known it was she outside the door. She, who had once adored him. Trusted him. Desired him.

He wore the same fashionable clothing from a few short hours ago when he was arrested in the palace courtyard and dragged away for high treason and attempted murder.

For he had tried to kill her beloved brother, the king.

Her heart squeezed like a wrathful fist in her chest, and for a moment she couldn't breathe.

They stared at each other. His eyes darkened with fury.

Fury? Was that what she saw?

If so, how dare he? How dare he?

"You seem surprised to see me," Rose said, lifting her chin and resisting any urge to rush forward into Leopold's arms and beg to hear that he was safe and unharmed, for his welfare did not matter. She should not care about that. He deserved to rot down here with the rest of the rats, and she hoped he would.

"Yes," he replied. "And no, because all I've done since

they dragged me here was pray that you would come to me. I could think of nothing else."

Rose scoffed. "There it is again. The flattery and seduction. Did you imagine I would learn of your peril and try to rescue you? Did you think I would drop to my brother's feet and beg him to set you free, because I had fallen in love with you? Even after what you did to my family and how you used me?"

He stepped forward, but she held up a hand. "Stay where you are, sir. I know everything. My brother told me of your plot to replace him on the throne. I know how you came to the palace to win Alexandra's affections. I know that your father has been planning your marriage to her since the day you were born so that you would one day rule this country at her side. You have been deceiving us all, and for that reason I came here to tell you that anything I felt for you in the past is obliterated. Nothing I said remains true any longer for I was misled, and I certainly have no intention of helping you escape your sentence, whatever it may be."

He shook his head in disbelief. "You're lying. If you felt nothing for me, why did you come here? If I did not matter to you, you would simply watch my head roll."

Her ire erupted again, for he was not wrong. She was not indifferent, but damn him for recognizing it. Damn him for pointing it out.

The chill of the prison cell seeped into her bones, and she rubbed at her arms. "I will never forgive you," she said.

He stared at her. "Yes, you will, Rose, because you know I am innocent."

She felt nauseated suddenly. A part of her wanted to weep at the loss of him. Another part of her wanted to strike him and shake him senseless until he confessed that he had treated her wrongly and that he was sorry. That he regretted all the lies and betrayals and this was all just a bad dream.

"I know no such thing," she replied nevertheless. "My brother was poisoned with arsenic just like my father, who is now dead. You of all people know how much I loved my father. Yet you, as a devout Royalist, were behind the plot to kill him."

He made a fist at his side. "No, I knew nothing of that, just as I knew nothing of the attempt on Randolph's life. I love you, Rose. You know that. You know I would never do anything to hurt you."

He tried to move closer again, and what was left of her heart split in two. He was still the most beautiful man she had ever known, and despite all her cool, contemptuous bravado, she could never forget the passion they shared, how his touch had ignited her whole world into a boundless realm of desire.

But she must push those memories aside, for she was devastated by his betrayal and by the total annihilation of her first love.

How could she have been so foolish? How could she not have seen the truth? How would she ever recover from this?

"Please," he said, spreading his arms wide in open surrender. "Tell Randolph I had nothing to do with the arsenic. I confess I was raised as a Royalist, and yes . . . my father wanted to remove your family from the throne and for me to marry Alexandra. But since the day you and I met on that muddy road in England, Rose, I have cared less and less for politics and thrones. I fell in love with you. You know it in your heart." He inhaled deeply. "Speak to Randolph on my behalf. Tell him I am sincere. I knew nothing of the attempt on his life or your father's murder. Treason, yes . . . I suppose I am guilty of that. I was part of the plot to take back the throne, at least in the beginning, but I am no killer."

Her heart was beating so fast she feared she might faint, but it was not like before, when her heart raced simply because Leopold Hunt, the Marquess of Cavanaugh, entered a room. This was different. Everything had changed. She was not the same naïve girl she was six months ago and her infatuation was now shattered. She was jaded now and feared nothing would ever be the same again. The sky would never be quite so blue. The flowers would not smell so sweet.

"It will fall on the court to determine whether or not you are a killer," she told him. "I cannot help you in that regard, for clearly I am incapable of sensible judgments where you are concerned."

"That is not true."

A part of her wanted to believe him, but she clung to the dark shadow of contempt that had taken over her soul.

"Yes, it is," she replied, "for you were the worst mistake of my life."

All the color drained from his face—as if she had thrust a large knife into his belly.

"I pray you will not feel that way forever," he said.

She laughed bitterly. "Why? So that there might be a chance for us? Or perhaps you hope my feelings might change in time to reduce your sentence."

"It has nothing to do with that."

For a flashing instant, her thoughts flew back to that muddy road in England when the world was a different place and she still believed in heroes and fairy tales . . .

Immediately, Rose pounded the life out of that memory and pushed it into a very deep grave.

"If I must repeat myself, I will," she replied. "I don't believe you, Leopold. You have hurt me terribly. I want nothing more to do with you. I want to forget what happened between us and move on with my life. I wish you luck in the trial, but I will not be here to witness it, for I will be leaving Petersbourg as soon as possible. I intend to marry the Archduke of Austria as planned."

"Rose, wait . . ."

Again, he took a step closer, but she swung around, fearful that he might touch her, hold her, weaken her resolve. She rushed to the door and rapped hard against it with a tight fist. "Guard!"

The bar lifted and the door quickly opened. Rose rushed out.

"Is everything all right, madam?" the guard asked, looking more than a little concerned.

"I am fine," she lied.

While she struggled to resist the treacherous urge to change her mind and return to Leopold's side, the door slammed shut behind her.

Then suddenly, to her utter shame and chagrin, she wondered what would happen if she spoke to Randolph on Leopold's behalf. Would he show mercy? Life in prison perhaps, instead of death?

No! She would do nothing of the sort! She was a Sebastian and had a duty to fulfill. Her brother's new monarchy had only just begun. She must remain strong, serve her beloved country, and marry the Archduke of Austria.

She would forget about Leopold Hunt and she would be sensible from this day forward. She would not spend another moment wondering how this unthinkable heartache had come to pass, nor would she wonder what she could have done differently to avoid it.

What was done was done. He was dead to her now.

It was time to forget him, once and for all.